Harrowing Habits:
And Other Queer Horrors

C.C. Cope

Identifiers: LCCN: 2026903292 | ISBN: 9798993413709 (Hardcover) | ISBN: 9798993413716 (Paperback) | ISBN: 9798993413723 (E-Book) |

Printed in the United States of America

First Paperback Edition 2026

This is a work of fiction. The events described here are imaginary: The names, settings, places, and characters are fictitious and not intended to represent specific places or persons, living or dead. Any resemblance to actual events or persons is entirely coincidental.

To the Monster inside all of us

Table of Contents:

Author's Note:

The Following collection is a work of horror that includes graphic, gory violence, disturbing themes & imagery, depictions of prejudices, both historical and modern, graphic sexual content, and discussion of sexual violence.

Please refer to the index at the back of the book for a story-by-story list (which includes spoilers).

Additionally, several of these stories are set in historical periods, and while some artistic liberties have been taken, great effort was made to portray the past with authenticity and respect for those who have come before us.

One short, *The Crossing* uses the pronouns "thou" and 'you' within the specific context of the period ("you" being more formal and "thou" more personal).

6

Harrowing Habits

Part 1: Gospel of Indemnity

Chapter 1

VANESSA didn't raise her hands to her ears. The screeching, burning sound of rubber was nerve-wracking. The buffeting movements, however, kept her hands busy. It was enough for her to grip the stained metal handrail. Outside the bus, along the dusty turn of the old cobbled-together town, was a rickety two-seater that had spun out after being over eager on the decline. Its driver and passenger and the bus's driver and most of its passengers were shouting obscenities and invectives in a rapid symphony of Spanish. Vanessa whispered to herself in French and English interchangeably, inseparably, as she held on to a necklace, a cross strung along a chain—her prayers for her and God alone.

The calamity passed without much resolution, each vehicle going its separate way. There was far less fanfare and shouting upon Vanessa's arrival at her destination. A single nun was waiting outside the nunnery. The convent was nestled inside a rare double monastery, abutting an aging cathedral, each a dusty tan, bordering on yellow. If it weren't for the vibrant flowers—sprouting out of cracks, filling gardens, hanging off the arcades—the small city would be one parched shaded area. This sacred bastion was no exception.

It had been a long journey, the flight terrifying her. The man beside her had invaded her seat with his bulk, pressing her to the window and all that open air. In her vertigo she saw God; oh, how jealous the angels must have been seeing humans soar. The astronauts piercing the cradle God had crafted for humanity reaching out, always reaching out.

Never worthy of the act.

The itinerary hadn't been her choice. Ostensibly it was an act of charity—first London, then the tunnel beneath the channel, and onto France and its many railways, to arrive in Spain. It was a demotion in everything but name. Vanessa saw it for what it was: they wanted to shuffle her along, a nuisance and aggravation was what they saw her as. There were three choices: an abbey, a church, or a cathedral. Each was in a different country. It didn't take her long to decide. She wouldn't be a picky beggar. Even in denouncement and disillusionment, there was potential.

This is why he has given us adversity. Challenge, strife, and woe. This why. This is why. I must only overcome. If I only overcome. She crafted these words into a mantra, a litany as good as any standardized prayer.

Vanessa repeated it in the cheap motels her meager budget could afford. The rest of her budget was given back to the church, God and his works—

poverty was a vow. *Obedience* and *celibacy* were the other two tenets she had vowed, twice temporarily, then at last permanently. These oaths merged and joined with her own personal mantra. She repeated it, prostrate upon the bristled, tattered carpets. She said it when her habit became hazardously warm and oppressive in the stifling summer: those smooth lines, the simple monochromatic bliss. Again she whispered her litany when protests delayed her. Catalans demanding autonomy. Everywhere were signs of that old civil war. The wounds had never healed properly and the scars were hard to hide.

She had done her research well. Aragon, Catalonia, the culture, the politics. The constant Catholic throughline: inquisitions, discriminations against Romani, the current worries over migrants, and a loss of faith. The youth were fleeing, agnostic, or atheistic. New age spiritualism. Where were the Christians? Vanessa's faith, paired with her youth, was seen as an exhalation. Or so she'd been so assured since she was twelve years old. There at her mother's deathbed, with the light leaving her, Vanessa saw someone: a beautiful, miraculous angel to see her mother off.

She was thankful for it, despite herself, for her mother had been the cruel sort, but if God had forgiven her, perhaps so could she. Regardless, Vanessa was freed. More so, she was *saved*. This salvation scared her father. He was of that agnostic sort, the ones who had only seen a figment of God amid the delirium of mushrooms and CBD in the sixties and seventies. Disillusioned by the world, he'd fled to Canada, tired and guilty of being an American. He'd learned French just to court Vanessa's mother. They'd had twenty-two years together before the cancer tore them apart.

Vanessa's mother had faith, one she kept secret, and when her daughter was born, her baptism was performed without her father's knowledge. The priests were ever ready to add to the flock, even through duplicity. After such extreme means were used, one might expect her mother to have instilled the teachings in her daughter. But it was the opposite. With her mother's passing and her vision,

Vanessa had a pressing need to understand what she had never been taught.

This need consumed her and, in many ways, bore her through the turbulent years to follow. First, her father moved them back to America, "It will be better, the city, more children for you to hang out with. Besides, the church over there…" He looked knowingly out the window where the old wooden edifice loomed a mile away. "It's bad karma, what the church did to the indigenous people and everything." He inclined his head toward the steeple. Something unspoken hung in the air. Her mother resided on those grounds for eternity. That was the real reason he wanted to run. He needed to escape his grief, and Vanessa fled to her prayers, to the vocation that called to her as readily as any *dream* might. While the other girls wanted to be famous or creative or any of those other common dreams, Vanessa was called to a higher purpose.

It bore her through her adolescence and young adulthood, from New York and everything that transpired to Boston, a new convent, a new reverend mother, and a set of priests. Her quiet words, her simple phrasings. The unshaken devotion in her. The beginnings of her litany. Then, a month ago, Mother Elizabeth had informed her she'd be transferred across the Atlantic.

So she stood in a dusty courtyard, a spired gothic cathedral worse for wear dominating the view, the squat stone buildings of supple Renaissance-Florentine influence congregated atop older medieval facets. A plateresque facade dominated the outer building and that nave of worship. It was rife with details from effigies down to the little nubby crosses like handholds on a rock climbing gymnasium. Life sprouted and filled in the rest: a few vines, some bearing grapes, the obvious supermarket sort, roses and hydrangeas and lilies. Vanessa was more invested in the human habitations and habiliments, the newly minted shingles upon the sloped roofs, the aged windowpanes that hid any faces that might be watching the new arrival. So different from the many sculpted faces that watched her unabashedly.

Vanessa took the monastery in for twenty seconds and decided she loved it, down to the last chipped brick.

Chapter 2

VANESSA was greeted by a higher-ranking sister, accompanied by another nun who collected the young woman's few possessions. She was led to the office of the presiding mother superior, Francesca Lapointe. A French nun bearing an Italian religious name for her patron. Beyond her native French, she spoke Italian, Latin, English, a little German, and, upon transferring to the monastery, Spanish. She had worked hard, even as a novitiate, to stay close to the bosom of the church, the city, the state, and Christ's vicar, presiding over the new Israelites.

The closest Lapointe had come was to an ancient and deteriorating monastery in the Italian Alps, where the people spoke German, and the lack of air conditioning led to frostbite so severe that she lost several toes. She made a lateral move to the borderlands of Spain and a convent where she might ascend the ranks. She did this through a disciplined constitution and the careful coddling of the then mother superior, who preferred "the old ways." When at last the aging woman had retired, Lapointe had secured her superiorship at the relatively unheard-of age of thirty-eight, five years ago, almost to the day.

"*Bienvenida*, Sister Christina," the mother superior said, addressing her firstly in Spanish and secondly using Vanessa's religious name, the one she had chosen back in Manhattan. "*Vanessa*" was not religious or martyred, but "Christina," in her view, held a nice ring to it, a name she could understand anyone choosing. If she were to use a name that felt false, it might as well be a pretty set of syllables, so surmised *Sister Christina*.

"You come to us from New York?" the mother said, still in Spanish.

Vanessa remained standing, the rickety wicker chair on offer seeming uncomfortable. "Boston. It was New York before that," she stumbled through her Spanish to reply.

Lapointe switched to French. "This isn't the first time you have been shuffled along?"

"There was a need for me in Boston," Vanessa attempted.

The mother superior twisted her nose at Vanessa's Canadian bastardization of French, so she settled on English. "Or a need to be rid of you in New York." The mother superior held her peevishness fast under the cloak of authority and power. It led her impudence to become imperative.

"That was more or less the situation in Boston, Mother Superior," Vanessa added in deference to her enunciation—an explanation, not an excuse.

Such pitiable naivety, Lapointe concluded. "I understand you're a Carmelite devoted to your local charity work. You earned your degree in marketing, the better to spread word of your work and the great work on the whole. This is commendable, but you must know this is a much more monastic establishment—a Franciscan institution, though the Benedictine and Jesuit ideal of study is encouraged, if not the directed missionary and preacher work."

Vanessa nodded. "I believe others should find Christ, and simply by living the life as we do, one of faith and devotion, shall the path be shown. Leading by example. Is that not how we learn and worship? Our quiet ruminations? Schooled emotion and featureless exuberance."

Lapointe studied the young woman. Did this subtle oration hide a threat to her in its vigor? Shining young lights attract moths, pretty new lanterns. Even the faithful, for their charity and poverty, held an aesthetic eye. She had seen enough bright-faced, doe-eyed seers in her lifetime and watched how ignorance could become a liturgy of its own—an easy usurpation of power or, at the least, attention. The faithful need lightning rods. And the extraordinary is the nature of sainthood. Even relying upon psychologists to diagnose would-be saints, as hysterics (or the more politically correct *"mentally ill"*) could only do so much.

"Certainly quiet contemplation, endless prayer—that is our vow and we are betrothed. Never forget that." Lapointe shuffled the papers on her table and typed a few notes into a decade-old Windows computer, trying to hide her perturbation.

Sensing this immediate resentment, Vanessa watched as she filled out the forms. Those in authority, even members of the church, craved clay. A novitiate or juniorate would have been better, a sister who could be shaped into a nun. Undoubtedly, Mother Superior didn't want a fully formed statue.

This is why he's given us adversity. Challenge, strife, and woe. This is why. This is why. I must only overcome. If I only overcome.

Vanessa reverently repeated this to herself while she went to the desk to sign the paperwork. She sank so deep into her litany that when Mother Superior cried out for "Sister Esther!" Vanessa jumped in her skin, the pen fell from her hand, and she remained frozen, bent over the desk.

Sister Esther, the nun now standing in the open doorway, took a moment to take in the scene, which provoked hesitation in her. She was garbed in black and white, that most stereotypical of habiliments; her hair, where a single lock had escaped the wimple, was chestnut brown, dark above, lighter below, though never reaching the straw blond of Vanessa's mane. A slender, almost oval face. Small but never beady hazel eyes, full of a sunlike warmth. There was an understated plainness to Esther, the way she held her tiny mouth. Everything about her screamed *mousy*, yet never in any way that might be considered demeaning.

When Vanessa knelt to collect the pen, her sleeve caught on some papers, creating a new mess and fresh embarrassment. She kept her eyes on the sheets, trying to stifle how shaky she'd become. A long-fingered hand appeared to assist her, and she looked up to find Esther much nearer. She was smiling serenely, compassionately, without pity.

"Let me help you," she said in French. *She listened through the door,* Vanessa realized.

"Thank you, Sister," Vanessa replied, matching the nun's expression.

Lapointe took little note of this exchange, too focused on how stupid and worthless this latest outcast was. *An imbecile—that's why they've sent her to me,* she concluded.

She dismissed them quickly, ordering a tour and an explanation of their liturgy schedule.

"Certainly, Mother Superior." Esther dipped her head, as did Vanessa.

In the open-air corridors and arcades, Vanessa noted the brown of the wood and the dusty tan, how it blended so well with her brown cloth yet made Esther's black stand out like a shadow, cut through by the light of the white.

Vanessa was familiarized with their little ways of life. Days beginning at five. Morning prayer. Breakfast. Chores: cleaning, gardening. Computer or craft-based projects next, then lunch. After the meal came study and reading. Breaks for walks and conversations (always in sets of three or more, as a general rule). Supper. Sewing and other activities. Turndown. Nighttime prayers (the bell rang for *profound silence,* an unbreachable quiet). Sleep. "And we have a variety of services and prayers in the chapel, as well as the cathedral," said Esther before dropping into a secretive whisper. "Sometimes, instead of the usual hymns, we'll perform a few Gregorian chants. It's really something."

"In a cathedral that large, it must fill the space." Venessa returned.

"Oh, it bounces off the stone and glass like… Well, I don't really know; you'll have to experience it yourself." Esther beamed, clearly not very good at hiding her excitement.

As they toured, Vanessa also noted the many alcoves and pieces of statuary placed between the rooms and workshops, kitchen, and mess hall. The recesses were often inhabited by those kneeling to pray, too suddenly overcome to travel farther.

The color of the flowers and other growths had infected the khaki coloring of the various cloister window arches, the sap bleeding green stains, ichor fresh and long dried alike. Behind the structures was a low-hanging wall that met with the hill, the mound shorn to a smooth finish, acting as a continuation of the wall. This courtyard naturally formed a garden, idyllic and tranquil, with several trees. In one corner stood a bulbous oak, huge in diameter, its roots gnarled, its bark bleached by age. It reminded Vansessa of a portly grandmother, ready to hug her grandchildren and offer sweets.

Esther noted her fondness of the garden and showed her where the wall had been converted into a site for grapevines, as well as brown painted wood slats in a crisscross pattern, giving a bracket for the zip ties to latch on to, keeping the vines trapped like limbs in vises. "We make our wine, stomping and leaping. We have uniforms for that. They become as purple as *Barney* when we're done."

"These grapes seem very red, though," Vanessa pointed out.

"Are you squeamish?" Esther teased.

"I…" Vanessa trailed off, her throat caught up.

Gently Esther laid a hand on her shoulder. "We have each been through toil. God has a habit of making his most devoted endure strife. It can seem so cruel, but that's why it is unknowable."

"You speak from experience."

"So do you."

"You don't want to share, and neither do I,".

"If it is between you and God, then so be it. I only deflect for the sake of time," Esther spoke with careful compassion. The hand at Vanessa's shoulder was firm, Esther so calmly solid. A slender companion to that graceful tree. Its leaves painted the nun's face with a mosaic of light and shadow, one eye dark, the other glowing amber.

Vanessa pulled herself away from the sister and looked back toward the building, its arched roofs ending in points, its uneven cobblestone, the open-air corridor that led to a small courtyard (endless courtyards!), and standing there, at one vaulted opening, a man. He was a priest of the cloth, with an ornate cross hanging off his neck. He had a smattering of brown hair untouched by gray. His shoulder held no cope, for he wasn't of sufficient rank. But he did hold power. His watery eyes were fixed on Vanessa, his pudgy lips slightly parted.

"Oh, that's Father Matthew," Esther explained, catching on to the informal event transpiring. "He's also American. The monks reside in the other half, past the rather crude partition, the priests as well, to serve as confessors for us and the monks."

The particular priest in question turned on his heel and disappeared back inside.

Vanessa took a long breath. "I'm Canadian. I've just spent time in America. Too much time."

"Most of your life, no?"

"You read up on me?"

"Mother Superior asked me to give her an overview."

"Too busy to sweat the details herself?"

"Oh, I'm sure she looked it over first. She likes testing our competence."

"And? Are you competent?"

"Don't know. I'll let you be the judge of that." Esther allowed a sly smile and continued the tour before bringing Vanessa to supper. There, she met her new family—dozens of names, all of them brides wearing wedding bands.

After helping clean the tableware, she was escorted by her sister Agnes to her cell. The room was sunken into the ground, three walls were stone, and one was plastered wood. It lacked anything decorative beyond the divine. (And peasant depictions at that.)

Agnes inferred Vanessa was tired from the weary expression pulling at her dour face. "I'll leave you to it. If you have any questions, I'm one door over."

Vanessa unpacked, prayed, and turned in early, though sleep eluded her and she heard Agnes return at curfew, doing her rounds quietly. The noises of her washing herself from a basin and changing into pajamas were noteworthy, seeping into Vanessa's room like fog.

Quiet and careful as could be, Vanessa moved to the wooden wall, finding part of it eaten away by insects. A small aperture through which to peer in on Agnes, a bit like a keyhole.

The sister moved beneath her covers, too eager and used to being neighborless. With one hand, she found herself while her other stopped her mouth, but she couldn't prevent every noise from escaping.

Vanessa counted thirteen moaned exaltations of "Jesus" or "Christ," an intimate prayer. She thought of *The Ecstasy of Saint Teresa.* She had seen the statue when her school had held a lottery to visit Italy and she had won. Her father had gone with her to surprise and humor her. Of every majestic object she saw, that work of Bernini was her favorite, held above, hidden away in plain sight, for what it dared to depict. The rapture of divine ecstasy on her marble face. It was far more preferable to his depiction of Persephone or Daphne.

Vanessa returned to her bed, the sounds still audible across the throw of her cell. She decided there and then that she wouldn't report on Agnes for her ecstatic pleasure. *Sometimes the notion of marrying oneself to Jesus carries blunter interpretations,* Vanessa mused before she rolled over, only repeating her litany three times before she fell asleep.

Vision 1

SILENCE dominated the convent, monastery, and cathedral. The enveloping night was pierced by the flicker of flame and the ghastly inclusion of electric lighting. Even the pale moon felt chaste, touching the cloistered halls.

Irrespective of this shy light, there was work to be done. Sister Josephine had drawn the short end of the stick, so her night would be sleepless. The possibility of burglary had ebbed and flowed over the decades, but with the rise in strife, poverty, and global tumults, paranoia had become cloaked in compassionate worry. Officially, while serving as night sister, Josephine was to ensure curfew was heeded, shut loose doors against the wind and the dust it would bring, ensure no candles risked fire, and check the stores were cleaned. Lastly she was to recommit herself to God and never feel lonely under his gaze.

She fought the urge to delve into the endless portal offered by the smartphone in her hand. A communal device passed from nun to nun, sister to sister. The device was strictly for emergencies or as a flashlight, never for dawdling on social media.

Josephine checked some locks, felt the sturdiness of some crossbeams, and was careful to avoid splinters. (She had bled profusely the last time she was on watch.) To her great dismay, the woodworking shop had been left wide open, pooling darkness emanating from it. Turning to illuminating technology, she split the night and came face-to-face with an anguished face drawn out in suffering.

She shuddered and stepped back before shame found her. It was an effigy of her savior, rendered with all the glory of martyrdom.

As the gentle fright abated, she scoured the room, hating the smell of fresh wood and the sharp pieces surrounding her. With nothing out of place save the dust she'd kicked up, she retreated hastily, righting her uniform and ensuring the binding around her chest was still firmly in place (it never moved, but she always checked it anyway). She needed to change her figure, to flatten her contours and shape; she'd always been warned she was a walking temptation. Even secluded in a neglected convent, she felt this pressure and animosity directed toward her, unrepentant eyes and sanctified eyes alike.

At a courtyard with broad columns and thick pillars, she tucked herself into one corner, her garments billowing as she sat. She was penned in by the low-rising wall from the arcade and the pillar's curvature. With the brightness turned low, she browsed the phone with no worry. She could giggle to her heart's content—stifling herself as the internet's many cats made her long for the feline of her childhood (so many years ago, high school adolescence, and now she was thirty-two and still felt as though she wasn't grown up at all).

Amid her mirth, a discordant harmony joined in, a gurgling, an awful arrhythmia of bassy vibrations. The wet sound that followed gave the intrinsic texture of moisture, and then the moaning began.

Josephine moved quickly before slowing, trying to pinpoint the noise. *Above.* The courtyard was two stories, with few rooms above for prayer and storage. But who would be up there in the middle of the night?

As she craned her neck, a fluid, dark and dim, dripped off the sandstone. Tar or blood? Whatever it was came in an awful sludge, little bits caught in the slurry. Viscera and entrails. Josephine had no time to study them. Someone was hurt. She hurried to the tight spiral stones and took them almost three at a time.

At the landing, she stopped dead in her tracks, for there in the pale moonlight, tucked around the bend of a pillar, was a figure, emaciated, a face caught in a pitiful *O*, shuddering as it breathed—gurgling, the fluid seeping like drool from chapped lips, watery eyes. A soul tortured. Matted hair draped the hunched shoulders, while gnarled, broken nails held a stone, more ichor falling between the long, thin fingers. The repose was held with a careful discipline, the fingers arranged in an unknown gesture, each arm kept to a similar level and balance, prudent and practiced. And then that head, the horrified face, turned, peering with the deadened stare of recrimination.

Josephine couldn't fight the lump in her throat, croaking instead of screaming. She held one distinct fact in her mind: *A woman! But how?*

She hid behind the wall, hyperventilating, hand clamped over her lips. *The monstrous woman didn't see me. She didn't! She didn't!*

She was trapped. Neither flight nor fight but *freeze*. She was rooted in place for several agonizing moments listening to the sound, a soft scraping announcing the moving limbs, tapping nails, and she swore it drew closer…the sounds quieting, disappearing. It was just before her. It had to be. She sucked in a hurried breath, waiting for her end.

One that never arrived. The bowstring of her stress stayed coiled, waiting and waiting for nothing, until she smoothed it down enough. Her hands still trembled as she turned on her flashlight and peered around the bend.

The terrace hallway was empty. No woman, no monsters; she struggled to find even a tiny example of the hideous mucus, as if the entire ordeal had never transpired.

Chapter 3

VANESSA dreamed of a monster set upon her. Clothing ripping, her screams unanswered. She woke in a cold sweat, breathing heavily but otherwise silent in the dim predawn light.

She slipped from her bed and bundled herself tightly despite the temperate morning, then shuffled along the arcades and the cloisters. Windows without glass. She welcomed the breeze that swept through them, conveying the sounds of fallen leaves. It wasn't autumn, yet a flurry of them had collected in the crux of the courtyard. She stepped over the faded mosaic and scooped up a few bright examples, bringing them close to herself, embracing them before their final energies dissipated.

Two careful footsteps disrupted the quiet as Esther joined her. "Did you see them fall?" Vanessa asked her softly, for she didn't know how long the nun had been watching her.

"I did!" Esther replied as loud as she dared. "It was beautiful." Her voice dipped toward a whisper. Luscious and sacred. There was a little offering in it. Something shared.

"It was, wasn't it?" An artless response, Vanessa craved commiseration. "Here," she insisted. "Take a few." She pressed several of the greenest examples into Esther's palms as though they were contraband.

The nun accepted them graciously. "Couldn't sleep?"

"A bad dream. That's all." Vanessa responded, averting her gaze. They weren't meant to be behaving this way, alone without anyone else. She'd been told enough times that Lapointe was strict and old-fashioned; she'd even heard the phrase *particular friend* mentioned twice, and that brought her back to her days as a novitiate, when she was told her love and compassion must be given equally to every sister, never just one.

If Esther was worried about this, she didn't show it. "They seem to be going around."

"Sister Josephine didn't seem to think it was a dream."

"Certainly not," Esther said blandly, not inclined to regurgitate the same gossip that had occupied the convent for the past week. "Regardless," she continued, "I'm sorry you had a nightmare." She was fiddling with the ends of the leaves, pulling at one of them. One smooth tear. She brought the piece to her nostrils, absorbing the freshness that clung to it.

Vanessa opened her mouth and closed it. Lacking words, she hummed out a little sound. "We should go to the others. Morning prayers will start soon," she said at last. As she knelt among the leaves, her mind was caught up in a different manner of worship.

When she rose, a few leaves fell from her skirt. Quickly Esther collected them and tried to press them back into Vanessa's hands. The young woman flinched sharply and recoiled, furrowing in on herself. "I apologize. I was…"

"Caught up in your contemplation?" Esther's eyes were wide with worry.

Vanessa nodded stiffly and left Esther to her leaves.

*   *   *

After prayer and breakfast, the day proceeded. Vanessa had been at the convent for two weeks, yet she still felt like she'd just arrived yesterday. She was slipping into the routines well enough. It was the others she felt removed from. However, she did cling to them, like a leaf's bright juice that sticks to the skin. She garnered a reputation for doing any favor as long as she didn't have to enter the men's side of the encampment.

There were whispers about why this charitable nun didn't meet with her community within the township. The superiors respected her interest in adjusting to the convent and her prayer. Others, younger or of lower rank, made snide comments regarding her poor Spanish. Vanessa couldn't decide which was worse: loud ridicule or hushed sneering

Sister Josephine at least treated her fairly. She had a bright smile, and the sunlight made her warm brown complexion glow. She was six years her senior and had gleaned some wisdom and serenity from life but lost none of her youthful vigor. Vanessa and Josephine were often placed within the same group. The odd arrival and the one who'd spent too much time online and dreamt up a demon…or a corpse—it was still up for debate. Most of the moneyless wagers focused less on veracity and more on what odd subconscious impulses had damned their "deviant" sister.

Vanessa ignored all this, enjoying the friendship and companionship. Josephine liked pottery and was teaching Vanessa the proper ways to use clay and a spinner.

"But you see, the real majesty comes from porcelain, like the Hungarian masters. Feel how smooth it is and look at those colors!" She beamed, handing the object to Vanessa, who weighed it in her hands—not too heavy, a fine vase with a thick handle.

"I see," Vanessa murmured, moving up the curving slope of the pear-shaped piece. Her finger found one flaw, a notch; her finger was able to press into it, hard, at a certain angle. She was becoming dizzy, her mind foggy with recollection.

A figure passed across the window, shadowed, lean, with rounded shoulders and a hunched neck, as if peering. Vanessa's hands slipped, and the vase fell to the floor, shattering into a porcelain spray.

Josephine squeaked, hands fluttering uselessly. The others in the room turned, some expressing their shock. Vanessa remained deathly quiet, too rooted and petrified for any vocalization.

The shape had heard the commotion and stepped into the room, forming into the familiar face of Father Arnold, an elderly priest close to the bishop. Age had made his posture stooped. His bushy white brows were knit together in concern. Trailing behind him was a very agitated, wrathful Lapointe.

"Oh dear, what has happened?" the father said.

"Sister Christina was being clumsy," Sister Agnes said.

"She was frightened," Josephine offered.

"By what? Sister Christina?" He looked at her with baleful kindness.

She only shook her head. "I just… It was silly, that's all—clumsy, as Sister Agnes said."

"She had a poor night's sleep. Our tea isn't very caffeinated for someone used to Starbucks." Esther offered a tiny turn at her lips, hoping to convey her teasing intent.

She succeeded at alleviating some of the mother superior's anger. "Our tea is perfectly suitable, so was that vase—expensive too."

"Ah, what is porcelain but a fragile thing? As are we all," the priest spoke, and there was no further arithmetic to be done beyond the cloying serenity. "These things happen," he explained. "We must be thankful for the time we had that gift. Perhaps one of our younger flock can create a *montage* using the pieces, showing God's inventive use of gravity and physics. Hmm, yes, I quite like that idea." Though not so much as the sound of his voice conveyed.

He nodded a few times as if to agree with himself, then departed. Lapointe lingered for a few moments longer, unwilling to let the man swoop in and brush away what fell within her fiefdom. "The object was the result of much skill and was well-liked. Sister Christina, you shall clean up the shards and bundle every one of them up, and then you shall be on bathroom detail today. *Alone.*"

Josephine and Esther were more annoyed than Vanessa, who quietly resigned herself to the work. She didn't even acknowledge her pain when one shard cut through her skin and dipped the tiny fragment startlingly red.

Chapter 4

VANESSA was so silent that the church mice were left snickering with jealousy. There was only the wash of water or the wet slapping of the mop, intermixed with the scratching *rub-dub* of the sudsy, dirty old sponge. But suppose that thoughts could be given to vibrations, chords, or amplitude; then hers would be screaming and rapid.

Her limbs grew more frantic, working out her anger on the grime. Until a soft rasping arrived at the door; her heart leaped, as did her nerves. She neared the door, ever more cautious. Shoes were visible beneath the door, black leather, which was true of nearly everyone there: sister, nun, or priest. Only the bishop had brown Italian couture. Vanessa had no option except to crack the door and see who it was…Esther, waiting and smiling, fresh supplies slung under her arms. "Care for some reinforcements?" she whispered conspiratorially.

"Not scared of getting punished?" Vanessa asked, still holding the door tightly.

"What is she going to do? Make me clean the bathrooms?"

Vanessa snorted out an approximation of a chuckle, and this, in its groaning way, made Esther giggle.

"All right then, but we'll have to be quiet."

"You'll have to teach me a thing or two about that," Esther whispered as she set down the implements.

"What do you mean?"

"I wondered if you'd blown off your assignment. It was so quiet at the door," she explained.

"You were waiting?"

"Only a few moments," Esther deflected, turning away from Vanessa abruptly. She chose to clean the sinks at the far end of the room.

Inwardly shrugging, Vanessa gave up trying to understand her. Throughout their chores, silence was an easy glove for them to fit: they worked and exchanged glances across the length of the room. The toilets, being far too nasty to handle alone, promoted a closer proximity. Disgusted and snickering, they were propelled by a gagging urgency.

"So many elders. Oof, why does God make us age?" Esther pondered with a sneering little slant to it, begging the joke to be taken seriously.

"Mysterious ways, right? Or perhaps, to God, none of this is bad. Perfect naturalism. Or, in his infinite power, he saw a need for balance. Even when a human gives in to pure creativity, issues arise. Perhaps if we didn't defecate, some other worse thing would have sprung from the multitude of variance…" Vanessa spoke with a wise intonation, not overly inflected gravitas. The persuasive tug of her candor was cemented as she slid her eyes back. "But that doesn't make the smell any easier."

They stifled their laughter and continued at their tasks. Soon they brought the bathroom to a pristine sheen (or what can be expected for a building retrofitted atop its old bones). A problem arose, "If I go back now, they'll know I had help. We worked faster than the Devil, each of us," Vanessa concluded.

Esther nodded, feigning consternation. "Oh well, then I suppose we'll just have to bide our time." In a flurry of cloth, she flopped against the wall, one with a full-length mirror resting on a frame stand. A narrow slice of vanity to ensure their uniforms were clean. The elongated oval offered Vanessa a chance to look back at herself. The beauty upon the surface went ignored by her, and she shoved a loose golden lock back into place under her habit.

Esther, on the other hand, took a vested interest in Vanessa's portrait. The chiseled features, riding up alongside the softened cheeks and generous gray eyes, were so perfectly spaced and inset. Only a slight matter of stern brow, chin, and nose kept her from being traditionally and recognizably gorgeous.

Not that Esther seemed to mind. She settled on some of those faults, like the trio of moles dotting the right side of Vanessa's face, not as humilities but beautiful things, for each was part of the whole.

"Why don't you tell me about yourself, Christina?" It had been two weeks, yet Esther had barely cast her hand over the water's surface. A pool she suspected ran deep.

Vanessa had her considerations to make, a similar summation arriving, the chance she wished to take. "If I'm being honest. I'd prefer you call me Vanessa."

"Really?" Esther didn't hide her concern.

"Yes," Vanessa confirmed. "It ' my baptismal name—the name God wants for me. When I selected Christina, I knew it to be a placeholder, a formality. An angel told me, 'This is okay. We know you are Vanessa.' For a few months, I dreamed of becoming an anointed saint. Then I could be known as Saint Vanessa."

"But you've given up on this hubris?" Esther asked.

"I've given up on most things." Vanessa balled up her hand, forming a fist before letting it go. "People cling to it, *desperation*. It forces you to cherish or to fester."

"I choose the former," Esther replied.

Vanessa nodded as if to agree, unwilling to lie. Her hand balled up again, her nails biting into her skin.

"I know what that can be like. I grew up in so many countries," Esther explained. "I've had to give up on so many relationships, friends, and family. God was the one consistency."

"You traveled Europe?" Vanessa inquired, happy to know more, trying not to appear too eager, too prying.

"Well beyond Europe, my silly Canadian. My father was a diplomat. I'd visit a place like the Big Apple while he was dealing with things in DC or take a cruise along the Rhine while he conducted business in Geneva." Esther fussed with the folds of her habit. "My father was a cynical man. Not very Godly—at least not outwardly—but I knew he prayed; I felt it. That faith was passed down to me. I told myself I'd make him proud." Esther left out her guttural need to surpass him. He who had achieved so much at a constant cost to her. Money but never stability. Prestige but never affection. She likened herself to a plant, given to a good groundskeeper but never truly appreciated. She was his in that she was a furtherance, extending the ego.

"He passed on?"

"Prostate cancer, eight years ago," Esther answered.

"My mother, fourteen years now. I was twelve," Vanessa conferred.

"Did it mark a change in you? I mean"—Esther was growing self-conscious—"is that when faith found you, Vanessa?"

Hearing her name was like a tonic or finding a shallow pool of water she might slip into. Calming. Safe. There was another matter affixed to it, the quickening within her chest.

"It is. It found me and I found them."

"Who?"

"The angels. *My* angel."

Esther shifted her hand, grabbing Vanessa's. "Are they still with you?"

"No, they have abandoned me." Vanessa tore her hand away.

Vision 2

THERE was a storm overhead, a furious sputtering that would turn into a vengeful downpour. The dusty, parched earth was ready to run with muddy streams, at last given to rage. It might destroy a house or two or at least harass the bricks.

Dutifully the convent had placed sandbags and shuttered every window. The watch was many bodies strong, their prayers ceaseless.

This didn't change the logistics or layout of the complex. It was a single, confusing structure, but it had abutted sheds, ancillaries, and other small functions. One such storehouse housed modern amenities, including petrol and generators.

Gennies for Jenny, Sister Catherine thought ruefully, for she had been called "Jenny" before her oaths.

The nun passed from one rumbling motor to the next, tinkering, sometimes tampering. The boys of the choir, despite their manly assurances, didn't understand the machinery. Not the way Catherine did. She tried to teach her sisters; she tried with Josephine in particular, but that woman was more creatively inclined—and with a vivid imagination. Catherine had an imagination of her own when it came to Josephine, but she tried her damnedest to ignore these fantasies. Her skill was what mattered—her ability to serve effectively.

Catherine's pride didn't slow her work, and soon she had them all humming to the same energetic tune. She shut the shed's doors like a farmer closing up the barn on the scared cattle.

The advantage of a habit is that it does, in fact, function as a hood. Even if it does tend to become waterlogged. Catherine stepped into an arcade and breached sanctity to wring out the moisture. She shouldn't have refused a waterproof. Some stagnant stoicism. A hint of her old life. The vestiges of the butch she swore she'd buried. Her short, penitent hair was another one.

Catching her breath, she peered out through the growing deluge. She saw the tree, the streaming hill threatening the wine grapes, and there in the muck a person…or was it a part of the tree?

"Hey? Anyone out there?" she called.

The figure stood still a moment longer, a temperate calm within the storm. Then, all at once, it moved, listing, jittering; its silhouette skeletal, the motions unearthly.

Sister Catherine advanced on the lawn, shouting a few more times. She passed the threshold just as the gabled roof's aged girder gave way with a screech of torn metal like a hawk's cry. She was soaked in an instant; her body was locked in an instinctive crouch, hands over her head. But the metal pipe had missed her.

When she looked up, the figure was gone. She scanned the garden, catching a horrifying glimpse of the woman's darting form. The head was craned back, as was was the torso. Rain fell through the sheer clothing, clinging to a bleeding form, with wet hair hiding the face. This wasn't the same creature Josephine had witnessed. The feminine figure was taller, with a longer neck and shorter fingers, ending in talon-like claws. There was no way for Catherine to know this as she watched the creature disappear into another aperture farther down the building.

Catherine chased the creature through the halls, heading her off. She could hear the jittering movements. The lights flickered all around her as if she were blinking. Then they stayed off. Leaving her surrounded by rain.

She huddled against the wall, waiting, listening to the darkness. When the moment passed her by without harm, she, with her night sense, searched anew, listening for the taunting taps of those sharp fingers.

She kept up her pursuit, wondering whether the creature might be above her or below, perhaps in a storeroom, an easy spot for an ambush. She slowed, recalling her muscle memory, placing herself within the convent, the alcoves, blind corners, and buried secrets.

Along the narrow passageway was an old escape tunnel, perhaps from the Inquisition, a route to lead away the Jews or Roma fleeing the torturers. Sensing the guilt etched into the walls, Catherine waited at the door, hesitating. Right as she touched the metal handle, there arose the high-pitched report of a terrible scratching, nails burrowing and fighting against stone, a sound worse than the chalk that had tormented her ears during her schooling.

Catherine screamed as the cacophony invaded her mind. She turned from the door and fled as fast as her legs could carry her.

Part II: Gospel of Countenance

Chapter 5

PETRICHOR filled the air, moist, sweet, damp. Gashes were torn into the walls, and thin red stains persisted despite the dewy environment. A group of nuns clustered around the latest disturbance in the pale overcast light.

For several hours, Catherine couldn't form coherent words. Chalkboards weren't the extent of the horrid memories stirred up within her, and her scars lay reopened and bleeding. It had taken thirty-four minutes of scouring the entire monastery before the evidence was discovered: claw marks, two finger spans across, nearly half an inch deep, with three lines gouged the curved masonry. A devilish symbology was formed if one tilted one's head just so. The three awful digits were unmistakable

Sister Angelica was the first to spot it and make the sign of the cross, followed by a queue of sorts, as each in turn confirmed her findings and prayed. "The sign of the Devil, so it is marked!"

Vanessa and Esther shared a dark look before a booming voice leaped above the hens. Parting the sea of black and white, Father Matthew reached the engraving. He ran a hand in an artless affectation of investigation, declaring, "I will seek out answers to this. With God's aid, we will have answers. Please pray for a swift conclusion." He took one more look at the wall then disengaged, sending a stern glare toward Vanessa as brief as a millisecond.

Gossip settled like over the convent like a fresh rainstorm. Each meal was filled with the secreted whispering. The higher-ranking nuns tried in vain to quell it while the mother superior was in absentia.

"The Devil has decided we are too faithful. He wants a challenge," Sister Jeane declared.

"No, he attacks the weak, for he is the coward of all cowards," rebuffed

Sister Margaret, her voice rolling along its Irish hues. "There are sinners among us. It is God who wishes to challenge us. We must prove him right and Lucifer wrong."

Vanessa followed the back-and-forth, her Spanish improving by the day, thanks to the *immersion* of the convent.

"I think it's a prank," concluded Sister Agnes. "Our security is nonexistent. The hill offers an easy way in. No locks were tried or broken, so it isn't burglary. We have some young idiots trying to get a kick out of scaring the nuns." When everyone looked at her with baleful antipathy, she hunched her shoulders and grew defensive. "What? We *are* the most superstitious of people; that's our worship, our truth, but they don't see it that way." She dipped her head as if to bury her face in her salad. "They think we're a joke."

No one had a response to that. Placations had to suffice—calls to faith, reassuring vapidity.

Vanessa heard them as if from a great distance. Not so much incurious as cautious. She worried silently, watching as the panic stirred. The tide was rising, fermenting anxiety. Worse when the mother superior strode in, took her seat, and scorned the room with reproval, banishing any further discussion. She had a contagion to contend with. The cloistered women were bored. A life of routine and worship, day in and day out. Beautiful contentment, blessings, and gratitude were easily disrupted at the nearest hint of activity.

An evil to be expunged? That was the sort of desperate discovery even those outside the church would find intriguing. Haunted houses, terrified nuns. It was trite, and if this spread to the township, they would have visitors—each with a camera in their pocket. The convent would *go viral*, reporters, mockery, and *memory*, and she would bear the shame. The Church had had enough of prying eyes and blasphemous bastards condemning them. The priest would head the investigation and take credit for whatever solution he devised. But any failure would be levied upon Lapointe.

Vanessa watched the mother superior as best she could without catching her attention. Drawing out what assumptions she could make, Vanessa pondered the politics. In her three weeks at the convent, a quiet tension lay, dialectics: priests and nuns, man and woman. The oldest schism had fresh life poured into it. Teams were being formed. She already had cast her lot. They all had. *Feature creep*. A modernist, contemporary term. It applied well to institutionalized rot, that festering sore.

Vanessa thought back to the New World, not merely the continent, but the people, the ideas. Vestments of progress, spaces that were so different compared to the convent. Garish, alien, otherworldly. She questioned her nostalgia, rehashing arguments about new and old things alike. Endless little trickeries that were tying themselves into knots. There was a time when she had tried to untangle them all. To know every mystery. To reconcile every incongruity. Old and New in a perfected union. At last.

What she had learned over and over was that no one wanted what she did. The harmony that would uplift her soul was discordant to all others. She felt that isolation just as bitterly as when it first had been presented to her. When she had discovered she was truly alone.

So intense were her contemplations that she didn't notice Esther: her stolen glances, her small mouth opening and closing, eyes darting this way and that. Esther wondered if she was being obvious in front of their sisters, yet she remained infuriatingly subtle. *What thoughts occupy her? Is she as faithful as they say? The Lord, taking the lion's share of her thought*. That conclusion gave Esther a twisting spasm of jealousy. Remorse and shame soon followed.

Vanessa couldn't maintain her looping line of thought forever. *The present is where I need to be.* Food was a sensible necessity and she honed in on it: the simple sandwich, the greens, the lettuce, the tomato. Its juice ran red down her chin.

Esther offered her a napkin, a clean, pristine object, mass manufactured, startling modernity. Vanessa accepted it, staining it irrecoverably red. Esther giggled at the sight, and Vanessa smiled as she finished cleaning herself up.

"It's time for crafts. Sisters Agnes and Esther will clean up the meal," Sister Helena announced. She was the right hand of Francesca Lapointe, and when she spoke, it was with the mother superior's authority.

"I can help," Vanessa offered to Esther. She was indebted to her for helping with the bathrooms.

Esther brushed her off with a slight wave of her hand. "No need. Please enjoy your crafts."

The procession marched out of the cafeteria and into the endless arcaded exterior passageways. The nuns were so uniform, the only differences being shape, skin color, gaits, and strides. Vanessa alone stood apart in her brown habit. She longed to disappear into the brown of the earth, that none might observe her. Esther would hate to see Vanessa wilt in this way. There were no marionette strings to lift her up. Even the icons had betrayed her: gilt murals, effigies, saints, and a bruised stone touched countless times.

I must think ahead to the future. I need only persist. I need only persist.

She had fallen to the back of the queue, which made the oncoming interception that much easier. All Father Matthew had to do was step in front of Vanessa at the intersection of two hallways, and suddenly she had nowhere to go.

He held out an arm, indicating a smaller passageway. She flinched and looked away, not daring to meet his eye, nodding meekly as he led her to a smooth portion of the wall. Vanessa stood before Matthew, rigid, her hands clasped tight as any vise.

"Christina," He said, not bothering with the full honorific.

"Father Matthew," she returned in as flat a voice as she could manage.

The pooling shade of the hall only heightened the hard edges of his features. "As you heard earlier, I'm investigating the cause of these disturbances…." He let his words trail off, waiting for the implication to bear fruit.

"I was there. I heard it," Vanessa stated plainly—basic courtesy, overly concise. "Best of luck with it." Her eyes stayed averted.

He took a step nearer, towering over her. "If I am to succeed, I'll need the full support of the convent. Every nun, every sister." As he explained, he modulated his voice to be intimate, unguarded, softened.

"It's pranksters tormenting us. They think we're a relic," Vannessa replied.

The priest brought a hand to her chin, forcing her to lock eyes with him: those sockets of pallid white, dimmest black, and murky brown. "I know you are too faithful to believe that. You know what it is to see the divine. They never believed you in America, too steeped in their cynicism. But here in the Old Continent? You could be seen for the saint that you are."

Vanessa stayed rooted in place, hands limp at her sides, fighting the redoubling panic inside. She set her jaw and confronted him. "I want what is best for this monastery, this congregation. The institution. My sisters."

"And me?" he countered.

"I want what is best for you as well," she spoke through gritted teeth.

Matthew smiled, smug and satisfied. He moved his hands down to her shoulders and squeezed her there. "Good, good. I was worried at first when you joined us here. But the past is the past." He moved his fingers lightly. "God can forgive any indiscretion. Do not worry, Christina. Your secret is safe with me."

There was no way for her to reply, yet he wouldn't budge, leaving her no choice except to forcibly pull away from him. She did so slowly and carefully, a robot, stilted, with isolated movements and rote protocols. She had to consider every step and action she took.

There was a time when she didn't have to.

* * *

Chapter 6

V̲ANESSA rounded a corner, waiting with perked ears for Father Matthew's footsteps to recede. Only then could she begin to breathe again.

This is why he has given us adversity. Challenge, strife, and woe. This is why. This is why. I must only overcome. If I only overcome.

Her litany wasn't enough to get rid of the clump in her throat. She was about to puke, her belly working itself up into a frenzy, when a thin voice called out, "Vanessa, are you okay?" It was her name, alighted over Esther's dainty lips. Sweet sympathy, a gentle approach, the soft touch, her hand hovering near Vanessa's shoulder. "What's the matter?"

"Just the food and cramps," Vanessa lied.

"Oh, you poor thing." There was no pity in it in Esther's response, only empathetic understanding. "Come. Let's sit down," she insisted lightly

It was a narrow hall, and the bench at the end was cramped, set below an arched window frame. They had to squeeze into a small gap. Shafts of soft silver fought through the glass, the spires of the cathedral creating stark shadows. The result painted a tapestry upon Esther's face—a back-and-forth of light and dark.

Vanessa shuddered, and Esther pulled her in closer till the shaking woman's head was resting at her collarbone. Vanessa's body overcame another violent shudder. "It's okay. It's okay. This shall pass. Like the raindrops, evaporation returns to the sky. God brings us a roller coaster, it's true, but this is only an oh-so-temporary bump in the road."

I wish that were true. God above, how I wish you would make this temporary. Vanessa thought miserably.

"You need only be strong," Esther advised, angling her head to pour out her affection, "I believe you are very strong. Fragile as you might assume yourself to be," she exalted. "I think someone can be both at once."

This was a buttress of stone to cling to, lashing waves and those sharp rocks eager to bring Vanessa to a painful conclusion: she could not give in—she who had endured and pressed on. There was no going back. Not when her course had been set. One foot in front of the next; that was her choice. *This is why he has given us adversity. Challenge, strife, woe. This is why. This is why. I must only overcome. If I only overcome.*

As she lay in Esther's arms, her credo regained its strength. "Thank you, Esther. I don't think you realize how much you…your compassion means to me. You're a blessing."

Esther's oval features lifted, and an aureole of light surrounded her, making her brighter than the sunlight. Vanessa thought she might be witnessing an angel once again. But this time she could touch the angel—a warmth so wonderful that she wanted it to consume her to the bone.

Vision 3

FATHER Matthew stalked the halls, from the perimeter to the cathedral, its nave and terraced balcony, as he had done every night since his investigation had begun.

When he found some school children playing and roughhousing by the little stream that trickled out from one monastery garden, he reprimanded them with a brutal tongue so sharp they dared not mock the American slant that flattened every word he spoke.

That had been relatively early in the night, during his second circuit; now he was on his sixth. He rounded the bend between the convent and the monastery proper, which served as the separation between the men and the women. The decorum changed, and so did the architecture, with fewer plants and fewer courtyards. Narrow corridors and old, sunken hovels for praying.

These were the inner sanctums. Near the edges lay modernity, the motor house, for the manly activities of oil and grease. There was also a computer room, nothing too fancy but enough to perform some programming work-for-hire gigs. The parochial vicar had been against this, but the mother superior had convinced him that ignoring technology might alienate the young faithful. Father Matthew's mentee, the seminarian Kayden, had made a strong case for his generation. The bishop and his deacon agreed, overruling the vicar.

Father Matthew was unlikely to consider such matters, not when his discovery was at hand. It came with a rattling, chalky echo—like chimes: a shimmering, bony transference—then an awful screeching, vehement and angry. Matthew followed the hideous sounds, his flashlight fighting the pooling murkiness. His stride firm and accusatory, he intended to pursue this to the fullest.

Appearing like a wannabe soldier, he checked his corners and peered up through the gaps in the arched concourse, catching a brief glimpse of the thin figure. This time, the feminine shape was gray, dripping ink-black blood that turned rose red under the harsh glare of the LED flashlight.

The creature scaled the side of the building before disappearing onto the roof. The courtyards, loggias, arcades, and other open-air passages and halls made it so easy for it to flit in and out, up and down.

Unable to see the creature, Matthew had to follow by sound alone, the tones becoming deeper as the creature descended into the depths of the monastery's guts.

This part of the bastion grew tighter. One door was opened, and Matthew turned his flashlight on an oblivious monk as they careened into each other. "Shhh," he hissed at the flabbergasted elder without breaking his stride, following the renewed clamor.

He rounded a corner, then another one, sweating despite the dank nature of the cellars he through which he passed. As he charged, the auditory scape changed. This time it was the crack of snapping wood.

Matthew emerged into a cramped room stuffed with barrels, most of which had burst. Wine had spilled and gushed onto the stone.

"The unseen shall be seen. That suffering which flowed like spilled blood, invisibly, sightlessly. No more. No more."

The booming voice, coming from everywhere at once, surrounded Matthew as he stepped through the ichor. The bloodbath stained his robes and his leather boots. He splashed about wildly, trying to find the creature, but damning silence had taken hold. The voice did not repeat, and there was no more rattling.

Drawing a long breath, Matthew stepped into the adjoining room, and the metal gate swung open, the lock broken. Beyond the threshold lay the luxurious donations and gifts the monastery kept concealed.

Matthew moved past a painting held in glass, a sculpted cross of clay and gold flakes, a broken pillar, and a relic from some ancient temple.

The creature leaped at him in a flurry of claws and wiry limbs, deft and dexterous despite the blindfold covering her eyes, blinding justice. Matthew threw a haymaker, but the creature was a blur. His hand ripped through empty air until it struck the wall at a painful angle. A crunch of bones and a groaning howl followed as the priest spun about, his injured hand held to his chest. The flashlight fell to the floor, the white walls reflecting its illumination, revealing…nothing.

There was no creature to be seen among the treasures. Matthew was alone and bleeding, a thin reminder sewn across his cheek, trickling damnation seeping from the wound.

Chapter 7

THERE was but one answer to be gleamed the following morning: the monastery had been attacked. Vandalism and physical harm. Moreover, that cacophonous warning had been recorded by a young seminarian, on the phone he was not meant to be on, and posted online for the whole world to see.

Mother Superior stood beside the bandaged Matthew. Next to him stood the deacon and the parochial vicar. The rest of the ecclesiastical flock had gathered before them in the nave of the cathedral.

The bishop was at the altar, making his address. The stained glass and the clerestory windows, mixed with the bright, arid day; painted a far prettier picture than the one the priest illustrated.

"This failure to contain these matters within this holy congregation now places the entire institution in a state of precarity. God, Jesus our savior, and the Holy Mother task us not only with seeing to ourselves but also to the whole of the faithful and even those ignorant of the Lord's salvation.

"We cannot let our present hardships sour and leech out. This pestilence that has beset us is ours. This strife is a matter of faith; it is a matter of our belief itself. The outside world, the nonbelievers, are quick to denigrate, quicker yet to prescribe conclusions."

He waved an arm, shimmering purple cloth arcing through the air. "This is a test. There is something unholy at play. '*What is Unseen shall be seen.*' What is done in the dark can be ignored like water passing over a hand. But wine *stains.* As does blood. As does *sin.* That is the invisible taint. We must find, and excise, the *sin* that bedevils us, that brings these *daemons* upon us…"

The gathered faithful blinked; Esther's foot tapped out a constant rhythm while Vanessa became a pale statue. *The bishop has ruled out earthly answers. He has made it a spiritual dilemma. Supernatural. But how does one fight such a battle here and now? Modernity is allergic to superstition,* she wondered.

Her answer came presently: "To persecute such evil, we must be as in the olden days, no more modern communication, no internet, no phone, limited contact with the people around us. I have asked the township not to harbor any journalists or would-be thrill seekers. We shall study the old texts. And we shall look inward. The cause of this sin is within our troupe. One sheep has darkened our minds and our souls. God calls us as his warriors and we must root out this sinner. Only that can save us all.'

The man, with self-serious pomp, looked over his spectacles, peering with his watery, naked eyes at an enraptured audience. A tremendous wave of ill sentiments, like a foamed-capped tidal wave, poured out from the altar. The rising panic had become the boiling cauldron dubbed paranoia. It was an inquisitorial spirit, hundreds of years removed from the old barbarism but nonetheless dangerous.

As Vanessa scanned the crowd, she didn't sense a mob of pitchforks and torches but rather the insidious start of a chain of gossip that offered death by a thousand paper cuts to whomever it chose as its victim.

Before the address, there had been debate over the veracity of the attack. Vanessa found Esther with Josephine and Agnes, hunched over a mobile phone, rewatching the video. Who exactly had posted it remained a mystery, as it had been shared to a church-affiliated account, deleted, but then picked up by the endless archiving of internet denizens. A Tik-Tok reupload had garnered a few million views, the audio becoming a trending sound—the terrible booming voice of feminine anguish both sibilant and bassy at once.

"It has to be an elaborate ruse," Agnes insisted. "Audio engineering, a few voices layered over each other."

"But with what speaker system?" Josephine argued. "You haven't experienced one of these...*things, the she-demons.*"

"In the echoing tunnels, one small speaker would be enough," Agnes argued.

"But to sound this all-encompassing? This video was taken near the other end of the tunnels—Mathhew said it surrounded him," Esther pointed out. "And Brother Jeremiah said he heard it at the other end as well. Reverberation or no, that's too many speakers."

Vanessa studied her reaction, realizing a moment too late that everyone was waiting for her two cents. "It's an iPhone video," she deflected. "The microphones on them are terrible, and eye-witnesses aren't always reliable. Speaking purely pragmatically, there isn't enough information."

This pleased no one, Agnes most of all. By the time the nuns exited the pews following the bishop's address, Agnes's skepticism had melted away. "Who might it be? What awful deed? What could bring this upon us?" she whispered to Josephine.

"Death, the wine. Blood unseen," Josephine replied.

"But I thought it was a matter of it *being bloodless* and thus invisible," Esther murmured into Vanessa's ear, raising the short hairs on her neck.

"What if you're right?" returned Vanessa.

They proceeded along in their penguin rows, save the one brown sheep. The plaza was blindingly bright and dry as though the heavens sought to bleach them, to demand a burning purification. Father Matthew hurried out of the cathedral, scanning the procession up and down, raising his bandaged hand against the sun to differentiate russet from obsidian.

"Stay close. Block his view," Vanessa pleaded, in a voice only for Esther.

"What? Why?" as she spoke, she angled her body as requested.

"Later," Vanessa assured her, her gaze preoccupied with tracking Matthew's feeble attempts to root her out.

They passed under the arches and made for the kitchen and cafeteria. At the fork in the road that divided the two rooms stood the superioress, surveying each of her subordinates as they passed her by, her confessor Sister Agatha flanking her. Lapointe kept the sharpness out of her eyes; a woman was meant to be congenial and kind, the nurturing sort. Something she'd never known. The aunt who'd raised her led by neglect, an abuse worse than any fist in Francesca's view. She wouldn't repeat that evil. If one of her nuns were the source of this *sin*, she would see to it, excise the paranoia. If she didn't do so quickly, the self-cannibalization would reign. The spectacle had consumed the bishop. Spirit and soul. He would not heed reason and she doubted he cared about collateral damage.

Mother Superior Francesca Lapointe knew better. If someone were to point the rod of suspicion and bring down perilous speculation, it must be her. Even if a soft, feminine voice, Sister Cecilia's voice, whispered inside her mind in bright tones about the nature of compassion and forgiveness. Deep down, she feared there wasn't enough time to find an adequate example. She'd need to buy herself breathing room. She required an easy target.

Vanessa followed her sisters toward the kitchen, and as she passed, the mother superior's gaze lingered on her, veiled and uncertain, which only added to Vanessa's growing unease.

While lunch passed without any gossiping infection, the same could not be said for study and crafts. The superioress and her coterie of picked allies couldn't preside over every activity; thus, the dissemination of rumors began. First was Josephine, but nothing stuck. Subsequently the crosshairs moved onto Catherine. She was so terrified that she locked herself in the privy, expecting everyone to turn on her, just as her childhood bullies had when they'd deemed her too masculine. By the time she chanced a look through the bathroom door, the choir of condemnation had turned toward an elder, Sister Mary, whose years afforded decades worth of slights to be excavated. The most prominent was the allegation of what had happened during the Balkan wars. The younger sisters were adamant that Mary's version of "charity" rivaled Mother Theresa's in terms of damage. The cloister was so confident that the road to hell was paved with good intentions. This surely was the *sin*, not malice but foolhardy, outdated modes of faith.

This lasted until supper, when the mother superior silenced the rumors by proxy. Sister Timothy, ninety years and all the more gnarled and frayed for it, began a drawn-out speech commemorating Sister Mary for all her years of service. She ended her plea by personally asking Mary to accompany her in prayer, seeking guidance on how to root out evil.

"I guarantee you. Over in the men's quarters, the seminarians and priests are pointing their fingers at each other. But how long till they look to us?" Sister Agnes stated, tucked into a corner after the meal had been cleared away. Her eyes probed about for eavesdroppers. "That's what we're doing, assuming it must be us—that we, daughters of Eve, must bear a further punishment. We need to consider what those men have been up to."

"How about their bi-monthly *tours* of the township. They claim to use the donation money for a few drinks and charity," Josephine whispered.

"Yes, and patronage of prostitutes certainly counts as charity, doesn't it?" Agnes sniped.

"Surely not? They are men of the cloth," Esther rebuked, desperate to be naive.

Agnes acted haughty. "Oh, you sweet thing. At least we know it isn't you who's to blame."

It was a schoolgirl's clawing barbs, and it still hurt. Esther brimmed with a scandalous look. Vanessa watched her, thinking of a knocked arrow, barely restrained.

"I think we should wait," Vanessa said, eager to defuse. "The creatures spoke. They have a point to prosecute. Surely they will point the way toward who they think is responsible."

"As if we can trust devilry and demons," Josephine whined, gravitas and immaturity forming a noxious cocktail.

"They're the only reason we're speaking about this at all," Agnes admitted. Her mind was working, its gears stuttering along to no avail.

Vanessa felt a light tugging on her sleeve, the fingers narrow, the articulations startlingly *known* to her. "Conspiring so bluntly will make us look…well, conspiratorial," Esther bemoaned.

"Is that not what we all will be doing?" Agnes shot back.

"Well, I, for one, have little interest in what feels like a reality show segment," Vanessa snapped, finally becoming irate. "Has someone set up a camera in the confessional? Should I complain, whine, and rat out each of you? Are we cats wishing to hiss? Or brides of Christ?!"

With this, she turned away in a heated flurry, storming away in no particular direction. Esther sent Josephine and Agnes a scathing, wordless rebuke, then chased after the fleeing sister.

She caught up to her at one of the innumerable courtyards and spun her around. "Vanessa, are you—" She found Venessa grinning, beaming and… cocky.

"I wanted an excuse to get away from them, and I couldn't think of a better way. "

Esther let out a sharp breath, not annoyed or frustrated but instead *amazed*, so thoroughly invigorated it left her body humming. She grabbed Vanessa by the hand and yanked her along. "Come on."

Carefully the pair wended their way through the convent. Lord knows everyone was watching one another like hawks, but that wouldn't stop Esther, not when she felt so *sure*.

They slunk into the garden and behind that tree, "Here, I'll give you a boost up."

"What?" Vanessa chortled, unsure how to respond.

Esther knelt, those wide hazel eyes forming the picture of innocence. She tapped her habit then held her hands in a bowl shape above it. "You're aiming for the lip of the hill. There's a stone. Grab that."

"Okay," Vanessa managed as she put her hands on Esther's shoulders and her boot in the woman's hand. With one fluid motion, Esther launched upward, and Vanessa lunged, her hands scrambling for purchase. She found it and hoisted herself up, squinting against the last dregs of tiger-orange daylight.

She spun about and went prone, reaching to help her fellow nun, hands clasped at the other's wrist. A few huffing and panting moments later, they were both sprawled out, dusty, and more winded than either would like to admit.

"Come on before someone spots us," Esther encouraged.

Vanessa fell into a crouch, racing behind Esther, sliding down into a natural trench past the far side of the hill. Her heart hammered in her chest from the exertion, the heat, and the thrilling giddiness that mischief alone can conjure.

"You good?" Esther asked.

"Yes, yes. You?"

"Terrific. This way."

She led her past little hills, divots, a road, and finally a natural burrow, like a shallow canyon. A natural staircase formed a few steep steps up, leading into a bone-pallid alcove, private and cozy. Beyond was a view that made Vanessa's eyes water. Dusty plains stretched out as far as the eye could see. A recessed decline snaked toward another township before the horizon became dominated by mountains. The effect was the same as her southwest road trips, when her father and she would drive across the continent as a way to reconnect, first right before she entered religious life; the second time as a desperate measure, a final resort in her father's attempts to reach her as her life crashed around her in pieces.

Here, a world away, there were sparse growths, little tufts of green Vanessa found courageous, a difference in light and mood as the sterling blue evening took over, softening out every rough edge. There was no hurry, no anxiety. And Esther was sitting so near.

She'd wrapped her spindly arms around her knees and put her chin in the crook formed by the intersection, her eyes looking over her joints, drowsily taking in Vanessa's enjoyment.

"It's beautiful." Vanessa was awestruck.

"Yes." Esther wasn't talking about the vista.

"Thank you, Esther," Vanessa spoke as softly as the wind rolled the dust. "I didn't realize how much I needed this." She ran her hands over her clothes, wiping off some of the dust. Her head found the rock, and it cradled her spine.

Vanessa sensed Esther was studying each articulation. There was no ignoring how intent the focus had become. "Why was Matthew trying to single you out?" Esther asked.

Vanessa turned, incredibly exposed, yet Esther wasn't prying. Her astute observation held no gossip in it, only that intractable urge to understand.

Could Vanessa obfuscate or downplay those things she'd held on to so tightly for so long? It felt like holding her breath underwater. Any capitulation would surely drown her. What if there was a hand to rescue her from the deep? If only she had a little faith. What could this moment be if not His Majesty? How much more did she require before she registered His message?

"We knew each other back in New York," Vanessa began.

It had been a large congregation. In a city of ten million, with its history of immigration and centuries-old churches, the struggle of Protestants and Catholics still raged, though this time bloodlessly.

"I was young. I was pretty. You must know how it is."

Esther bowed her head in deference, trying to ignore the warmth that flooded her cheeks.

Vanessa continued, lost to her storytelling. "What stood out more was my faith; they called me effervescent, seraphic. I witnessed angels. Some considered me a deranged liability, others, a miracle maker."

"Or the miracle yourself," Esther noted, conjuring memories for Vanessa, the looks, the awestruck bliss. The way people must have moved around her, spoken past her, their words for the divine, their adoration as well.

"Nothing but a go-between," Vanessa agreed. "My reputation preceded me, and my fame grew in small intersecting segments, peer-to-peer word of mouth. I was being sought out. That's when the whispers of sainthood began."

"So soon as that? But it makes sense," Esther commented.

"You think so?"

Esther dipped her head. "I think so, having met you." Vanessa didn't know how to interpret this. The hand she'd used to annotate her speech gently fell still. Esther recognized the apprehension but not its root cause. "I also think it's hard to keep the faith in this wild modern world. People need something to latch on to."

Vanessa nodded, unsure of this deflection. It was reassuring that Esther wasn't placing her on a pedestal. Simultaneously she yearned for special attention from the woman. Putting a name to this longing, however, appeared horribly dangerous.

Esther broke the silence that followed with a ponderous expression, forming into a quiet sympathy. "What went wrong? How'd you wind up shipped out here to a dusty old cathedral for the disabused and denigrated?"

"Well, if we're all misfits, why are you here?" Vanessa rebuffed.

"We aren't all misfits. Maybe I'm not one of you."

Vanessa rounded on her. "No, no, you can't pretend you aren't in a kindred plight."

"Kindred plight? You speak like a saint, sanctified words." Esther giggled.

"Are you complaining?"

"No." Esther was striking.

"Why are you here?" Vanessa repeated.

"I asked you first."

"But you'll answer first."

"*Sin*, what else?" Esther shrugged and dipped her eyes toward her legs, tracing the dirt, the soil, and the earth itself.

Vanessa needed to know the whole story surrounding that small, weighty word, but she wouldn't force the matter.

"Your turn," Esther reminded her.

Vanessa took a long breath, the soft skin surrounding her eyes furrowing. "Father Matthew and others became more and more certain of me. There was scheming and cynicism. Ambition affixed to the specter of fame held within my 'frail frame.'" She shook her head more violently this time. "I was young, innocent, cherishable, passionate, opinionated… I wasn't as thoroughly docile or obedient as they wanted me to be, bothers welcomed this: my fellow nuns. Veneration toward God as active participants."

"Not just brides or wives or mothers," Esther surmised.

"Precisely. But that was certainly the minority opinion. Most wanted a mouthpiece, a pretty face. The picture of charity, of empathy… No, they wanted pity, aggrandizement. A role model to our fellow women and girls." Her soft cheeks and delicate features fell further into remorse, the painful reverse of nostalgia's grace. "I played to their tune: led events, charity drives, and activities for the other nuns. I was doing *good.* Even if it did come at a personal cost."

"What happened?"

"The price became too great. And it became clear there was to be no sainthood for me," Vanessa replied cryptically.

"How?" Esther pressed, her torso leaning forward.

"*Sin*, what else?" Vanessa said, using Esther's deflection. "No more luster. No more grace. Those stares turned to ash. I felt prosecuted every moment… and I…" She shook her head.

"It's okay. As you now know, I have also erred."

Except I wasn't the one who erred! I wasn't the sinner! Vanessa almost screamed. She wanted to stomp on the rocks and shout till her throat bled. But it would be a step too far; she couldn't give in, not after she had held on for so long.

Then she felt something soft and warm, like the whisper of taffeta, down by her hand, the sensation of skin upon skin. Glancing down, she confirmed three of Esther's fingers, by the lightest interaction, were connecting with her, a hovering silken affection.

"Vanessa…" Esther's voice tumbled to a lower register, as she leaned in, eyelids drooping, her weight upon her arm, mouth inching ever closer. Vanessa put up a hand, a tiny sound like a squeak escaping her lips. Esther's eyes widened and she halted. "I wanted to kiss you." The husky slope of her words was exchanged for bright, pleading panic. "I'm sorry, I'm sorry. Forgive me."

Vanessa shook a little, her eyes blinking, "Yes…" she gulped, her chest ready to burst, her stomach in knots. "Yes." There was panic in her as if she were already out of breath.

Esther found these nerves adorable and wanted to smooth out every last crease. "Yes?"

"Yes," Vanessa repeated, a little more clearly, clawing to regain her composure. "Yes." she said again, her rapturous gray irises holding no doubt.

Reassured, Esther completed the movement. Her lips found Vanessa's, and everything collapsed into soft sensuality, pressed-up flesh, and sweet flavors. Vanessa fell into the kiss as if she were floating without weight. Every moment they stayed connected, she lost a portion of her tension; her spine was unknotted, her tendons unlacing.

With her free hand, Esther cupped her cheek, stroking under her ear. Venessa shuddered in the woman's arms, a soundless exaltation, an inaudible moan of release, of relief, and her lover pulled her in tighter, hugging her as much as kissing her.

It remained beautiful and chaste, the second and third time as well, Vanessa deepening the connection and reciprocating by small increments, her hand at Esther's wrists, her legs lining up with Esther's—small steps, guarded attempts.

Esther was left greedy. In the dwindling light, she felt alight, desire like a flame boiling out of that affectionate kiln. Her hand descended to Vanessa's chest, and she cupped one breast and let out a moan.

Suddenly Vanessa's hand found Esther's forearm and pulled her away. The other woman's eyes shot open wide and worried. Vanessa couldn't face this, her shame, and averted herself, first her head then her body. Esther let her go as Vanessa curled in, guarded and armored, tighter than ever.

This time, when Esther bent forward, it was to check in. "What is it? Do you think this is…"

"Wrong?" Vanessa finished for her. "No. The farthest thing from it." A pronounced sigh buffeted her frame. "It's not you, it's not us, I just…*I can't.*"

"Is it about virginity?"

"No," she whispered.

"Our vows…celibacy?"

Vanessa shook her head mutely.

"Can you tell me what it is then?"

"No." Vanessa was fighting to keep her balance on a listing ship at sea. Then she turned her head and let her weight fall toward Esther, her dainty chin finding her shoulder. "I just need time. That's all. I'm sorry, but if this is going to *happen*, it'll have to be slow."

Misery bloomed in her eyes, some great bravery stipulating this boundary. These were Vanessa's fenceposts, and Esther would honor her. Damn her eternally if she did not. "I can be patient," she insisted. "I can be whatever you need me to be. Just as long as this…" She grabbed Vanessa's palm and laced their fingers together. "…is something you want. Today, tomorrow, or months from now." Her eyelids dropped once again, her warm depths posing the question.

Vanessa trembled through a laugh. "Can I answer that with a kiss?"

"Certainly," Esther breathed.

Their lips met once more, and Esther had the answer she wanted.

Vision 4

THE PARANOIA that had beset the monastery left many with sleepless nights. Men in their cramped quarters and simple beds, tossing and turning. One example was Kayden, Father Matthew's seminarian and protégé. He had become so restless by the sixth night of speculation that he took to the halls, tired of waiting in bed for something to occur.

Or perhaps it was ego, the drive to prove himself to his mentor. Or even usurp him. There was also the possibility of morbid curiosity. When one has the privilege of only fearing the most outrageous perils, a terror might seem like a grand adventure, the blood pulsing with adrenaline.

He proceeded to the computer room, peeking in on the wood furnishings—not every annex of the consecrated estate was stonewalled or dusty. These cleaned-up, more modern (if nineteenth-century stylings are to be considered *modern*) rooms were more frequent among the men's compound than the women's.

Often Kayden could be found bragging about the differences between one side of the compound and the next, and not just the furniture. He always laid out these "facts," as he referred to them, with a distinctly masculine form of presumption. He talked down to people and seemed to enjoy it immensely.

How had he landed on becoming a seminarian, charting a course toward the priesthood? A cynic might observe the keen nature in which he wormed his way out of routine and shirked so many of his duties. The life of a priest can be one without directed paid labor—service to the Lord and one's congregation. A clever but non-enterprising young man might even get it in his head that it would be a more leisurely ride. It might be a mundane life without ornament, but it provided food and housing in an ever-cratering economic landscape.

As he walked the halls, he smiled, smug and self-assured, with a round face; average, homely features; and eyes that were a radiant set of blue pearls, as if a rusted ring had been inset with sapphires.

His stomach gurgled, an obnoxious breach of the summer stillness. He broke the peace further. "Hey, if any of you demons are out there, you probably heard that. Ha-ha…" HE chortled, moving on from the computer room.

If he'd been paying attention to the shadows, he could have answered his question: the moonlight caught in a ruby-red pair of irises, filled with judgment. His judgment.

The seminarian crept along the outer wall of the monastery and, with a light step, crossed over to one of the two-story warehouses: more heavy masonry, more tiled roofs. The open floor plan, with the second floor being more of a balcony, was a relic of olden times. Times had changed, at least when it came to the wood crates being traded out for cardboard boxes. Some were filled with grain and flour, while others held Bibles and other goods for the outreach programs.

Kaydan found a half ladder, half staircase made of red-painted metal and headed up to inspect the higher level. Here were smaller goods, mostly spare tools or bits and bobs for construction or restorative purposes. A few workbenches lined the walls to let these craftsmen's tools be filed away.

Between a stack of spare light bulbs in clear containers and a plastic milk crate full of extension cables was a tucked-away shopping bag, rolled up to insulate its contents.

Eager as a child, Kayden unwound it and pulled out the little luxuries hidden inside: imported candies, Japanese in origin, and a few ubiquitous American invaders. He gorged himself, seated at the workbench like a beggar at a feast. He was lost in the sugar rush, and he didn't hear the groaning breath nearing him—a gurgling, moist refrain, weighty and resounding.

When a solid hand thumped the far end of the workbench, he leaped back, candy clutched in his hands. His azure gaze drew wide as he stared at the beady red malevolence before him, a larger stature than her kin, thicker in the torso, heavy cloth hanging off her wide frame. She was wreathed in shadow, her head protruding out of the inky surroundings. Her face was cut through by ritualistic scars and motifs, a taunting vocalization erupting as red fluid dripped from her bared teeth.

"Hey, hey, I'm sorry about the stomach joke, and…ah, this too." He threw the little packet of gummies toward the creature as if this were repentance. "I mean, come on, I haven't…. The other guys go on their stag outings. Even some of the priests, I can tell you which ones! The parochial. The deacon! He—he likes the men, likes them a lot…" The creature kept advancing, and Kayden backpedaled, stammering. "The nuns! I think Catherine's a dyke; Josephine definitely isn't a virgin."

Like a tug-of-war, they kept up their dance, nearing the edge of the balcony with every step. The boy's words spilled out faster than wine from a barrel, slurred and sloshed as if he were drunk. "Fine! Fine! Matthew likes to sleep around. He says it's why he was shuffled off here. He told me to be careful. You can never trust a woman…but I'm not like him—"

A yelp, a short-lived scream, and a quick fall. Kayden walked right off the rail-less balcony, landing poorly upon a stack of crates, his right leg caught in the gap between two boxes, twisting and snapping. He ended up on the floor in a heap.

He was silent for a moment, stunned, his drool moistening the perpetual dust coating the stone floor, his ragged breath disrupting the tiny particles. He rolled over onto his back and pried his leg free and saw how far his limb was bent.

Kayden howled and screamed and began to weep.

Chapter 8

* * *

In the blistering hot days that followed Kayden's fall, the paranoid infection had metastasized into shouting matches and openly aired accusations. Petty sins, gluttony, the vanity of too much time staring at one's reflection, slight insubordinations (complaining about chores), the foibles growing smaller and smaller from there. A physical altercation had to be broken up, but not before nails and spit had entered the fray.

Lapointe wished to be stern, yet her closest confidantes counseled caution. Discipline would only make things worse.

"How could that possibly be the case?" she asked.

"Because then the sisters will begin to administer the punishments themselves," Sister Helena explained.

"It's a witch hunt and…" Sister Laura trailed off.

"And?" Mother Superior snapped viciously.

"And it would appear sin surrounds us," she answered timidly, her wide, rounded-off features downcast.

Narrow-faced Helena took up the baton next. "News of the fight is sure to reach our male counterparts. They'd love nothing more than to distract from their recent misfortune."

"So should we point a finger toward them?" Helena offered.

"No, they'll see that as petty and gendered. Tribal and territorial," Lapointe rebuked, sitting back in her wicker seat.

"Isn't that what they're doing?" Helena countered.

"It is except for the fact that they're men. They lead and we obey. And they have sympathy for the injured boy," Laura noted with a bone-dry cynicism.

Compassion, care, and an open heart, the little voice called Cecilia whispered to Lapointe. The mother superior sighed. "We must do something. This has gotten out of hand. If the outside world learns of the boy's injury, their interest will be piqued… We must find a tangible sin, not these small grievances."

She looked down her sharp nose and scowled. She wasn't concerned with the creatures or catering to their vigilante whims. She hadn't yet decided what she made of them. The only thing that mattered to her was results. Right now the result was a threat to her cloister and her role as its leader.

Surpassing another ponderous exhalation, she looked out at the township sprawling out below her. More than ever before, it was a world away.

As she turned toward the window, Vanessa and Esther ducked, barely avoiding discovery.

Vanessa and Esther shared a knowing glance and a twin conclusion, one that brought a quivering terror. The harmonious joy they'd unearthed, if discovered, would be labeled as sin. Their higher-ups would be hard-pressed to find a better scapegoat.

Pulling Esther into a small solitary courtyard, Vanessa assured her it wouldn't happen. She squeezed Esther's upper arm—so soft, shaped as if for her hand alone.

"But if they did find out." Esther's features, from the decline of her cheekbone to her button nose, were morphed by fear. Its vividity made Vanessa want her even more.

"We'd weather it. For we have God on our side."

"Do we?" Esther croaked.

The roles had reversed. Esther's affection, the haze of the gentle pursuit, had propelled her past her worries, and the joy of reciprocation had lent itself a thorough bliss. Now the sun had set, and the reality of nightfall was setting in. The guilt, the shame—oh, to weather such contradictory dogmas. Truth versus truth. One must falter and fail, for these edicts and emotions couldn't coexist. *They can't,* Esther whispered within her mind.

Vanessa, however, refused to accept this. These truths weren't mutually exclusive; one only needed to modify one's understanding to allow both to live and breathe together. She just had to prove that to Esther.

"Come on. Let me show you something." Vanessa pulled her along toward a storage closet set in the wall near the entrance to the woodworking shop. After opening it up carefully, Vanessa crouched, uncovering a little box resting on a shelf. The wood was smoothly varnished, the bleeding heart of the savior—a personal sigil of Vanessa's—adorning the lid.

"It's yours? Why keep it here?" Esther asked as she took the box gingerly from Vanessa.

"Because some things are too personal to be kept with personal effects. Especially now of all times."

With a slender hand, Esther lifted the lid. Her eyes widened, then narrowed in hunger. Inside was sacrilege, a wooden effigy of a woman in ecstasy. It was three times the size of her palm as she picked it up. Her eyes searched its every detail, her fingers finding its every secret.

"Why does it feel so precious? It's lewd, but it isn't." She found Vanessa taking in her reaction.

"It's about trying to fight my way back," Vanessa whispered, a tremor coursing through her. She placed her hand under Esther, cupping the figure from the other side, grounding herself.

"Toward what?"

"Sainthood."

The shuffle and clip of shoes broke their connection. The two nuns retreated into a more decent display. The little figure was stored up in Esther's sleeve.

After the sisters had passed, Esther leaned in. "I'll find you later," she said, then slipped away before Vanessa could take back the figure.

Left alone, suddenly exhausted and fragile, Vanessa crumpled into the little storeroom, pulling the door mostly shut. She held herself close, her chest and belly articulating in faster cycles: lungs full, lungs emptied. She knew Esther wasn't reassured. She was doubting them. *Why does it have to be this way?* Not when Vanessa at last had a chance. A hope. She had never thought this could happen again. It felt surreal to her, while everything before had felt all too real.

Her life crashed in around her. She thought of her hands. She remembered them over and over. She remembered the way they had clung; she remembered the pain… She didn't want to. She was tired of remembering. *But what wonders they have hewn. Esther was so happy with the figure. "Look at what I created!" and she did, and she loved it…* Vanessa chose this feeling.

It felt powerful.

*   *   *

For the rest of the day, she oscillated between joy and worry. The weather became similarly at odds with itself. Clouds dappled the bright blue wavelengths, sometimes threatening rain, then clearing completely the next. One courtyard might retain heat, while the next might suffer cold wind whistling through the windows.

As the day began to wane, Vanessa couldn't shake the ill omens pulling at her seams. Mostly she kept waiting for when she might see Esther again.

She moved her toes inside her shoes as she knelt in quiet reverence with her sisters. She prayed and she prayed. Salvation and hope. Wishes and justice. She asked for Jesus's blessing to continue with Esther. She asked for his guidance, his aid.

I might love her or still be falling for her. I think I want to as much as anyone can choose in such matters. I can no longer be sure. If only I could know myself again. I have tried. You who have helped me along this path with your righteous truth. Please. Please help me again. I beg you, if you are my husband, if I am your bride, and if this is true, might you understand? So much is wrong in this world. Not me. This is a good thing. Thank you, God—you who have blessed me.

She rose, contented at last. That's when a tap arrived on her shoulders. She whirled about, finding Esther in the candlelight, her face fanned out in an apologetic expression. She flicked her eyes toward the doorway, and Vanessa understood.

In the moonlit hallway, Esther made her apology official. "Sorry. I meant to surprise you. Not scare you. You're jumpy."

"It's okay, I—" Vanessa attempted.

"I should be considerate of it." Esther insisted.

"It would mean a lot."

"Done. Understood. Now I'll have to say *adieu* for a moment."

"Why?" Vanessa probed.

Esther became sly, and she mixed her postures, swaying back and forth with an uncontrollable breeze. "Because walking you to my room might be noticeable."

"But Sister Agatha—"

"She's always late to check curfew, paying penance."

"For what?"

"Being a daughter of Eve."

"Don't we get punished enough each month?"

Esther shrugged. "Circle around the long way, okay?" She turned to go but was halted by Vanessa's pawing hand.

"Esther, I don't want to… I can't…" Her mouth was open, trying but failing to find the words.

"You don't want to risk it?"

"I'm not ready to share your bed." Vanessa's quiet voice became an urgent hiss, as her eyes wilted, the frame of her body slumping.

"Really? Because all I wanted to do was cuddle," Esther's voice became sing-song. "Can't I offer warmth to my sister on this chilly summer's night?"

"Just cuddling?"

"Just cuddling."

Vanessa blushed. "Okay. I'll be there in five minutes, maybe seven if Sister Margret finds me."

"I won't get annoyed till the tenth minute then." Esther grinned.

They split—one went left and the other went right, like when young Vanessa would play around with figure skates, moving in a straight line but arcing her feet closer and farther away. The cuts in the ice were like a waveform or a figure eight. She thought of the top-down view of the monastery, the squares, the lines, the two nuns moving in and out, in and out. Soon the skates would meet. She felt an exhilarating chill, as if she were out on the ice again, free and happy.

As she rounded the final bend, Vanessa heard footsteps, too many footsteps. She slid into an alcove and waited in the pooling shadow of a saint. She was invisible, but she saw much in the amber light: two sisters hushed and conversing.

"I think we have let in too many of our sisters from farther afield. Don't you?" Sister Elizabeth said with all due conspiracy. She was Spanish, almost thirty, her features sharp, her hair dark. Anywhere else, she'd be considered exotic, but in Spain she was painfully normal.

"Yes, exactly, the 'New World' isn't new. We don't have to be so desperate about everyone getting along…and they have such sin ingrained in them," Sister Bernadette chirped as if it were the lightest of epithets. She was British-Spanish, stocky, and culled into submission by a self-inflicted verdict—ugly.

"They think fighting the protestants or their endless breeding makes them worthy." Elizabeth loved to dance across her words; it was her great egotism. "And when their sisters inevitably—and inventively fail—we get stuck with them."

The two women paused right in front of Vanessa, unbeknownst to them.

Elizabeth continued, "There was a time when this monastery would be the vessel of knowledge. Now everyone carries the world's truths in their pockets and ignores them. Ignores God. It's pathetic."

"Even we faithful can err," Bernadette chirped.

"And we're being collectively punished for it. But God shall make it right. All we have to do is wait and not soil our skirts." Elizabeth walked on with a fitting haughty stride.

Bernadette rushed to follow in more ways than one.

Clear at last, Vanessa wasted no more time, darting across the empty hall. The door to Esther's cell gave way easily, transporting her into a den of scent and perfume, perhaps a little lavishly diffused—flowery, with the thinnest hint of spice, cinnamon, all a breach of those unspoken norms.

The rest of the space was uniformly drab: plaster, wood beams and floor, and a bed with simple sheets and a hard mattress. Vanessa sensed a masochistic quality in this, for in this age, a decent bed could be bought and a few posters of cloth prints could be hung. Godly depictions, church-approved displays. Yet the cloister had fallen on these old habits. *At what point is it suffering for suffering's sake? At what point does God grow annoyed that we choose artificial pain and ignore the gifts he gives? Why do those most gifted choose misery and distract from those who have faced true hardship?*

This train of remuneration led her perfectly to the woman awaiting her, sitting up at the edge of her bed, patting it eagerly.

This is why he has given us adversity. Challenge, strife, and woe. This is why. This is why. I must only overcome. If I only overcome. The litany stormed back through the burrows of her mind, hesitation clawing at her. Jesus had laid a heavy burden on her shoulders. A duty. Was her blossoming romance an abdication of her responsibility?

Esther stifled her own urgent inclinations. Much as she might wish her to leap to action, to press Vanessa into the hard mattress and exert her will, she knew that side of Vanessa was still slumbering beneath the surface. Letting Vanessa admire her might awaken this need.

Esther favored one shoulder, tilting her head, a worldless tease, slender and careful, consecrated with a tiny pout.

Three paces, bending knees, stretching elbows, and the gap between them disappeared. Esther's eyelids fluttered shut as she discovered resoluteness. *I will be here for her. No matter how long I wait, she* determined.

At the same time, Vansessa admired her, just as Esther hoped she would. *Look at the way she squirms, Vanessa thought, the way her needs are piercing her. She wants me. She listens to me. She cares about me. How can I refuse this?*

Vanessa kissed her and then Esther kissed Vanessa. They fell onto the counterpane, their bodies resting against the other's, hands clasped. It was tender with haloing hues—small touches and diminutive details. Vanessa placed her hand over the thrumming heartbeat at the confluence of Esther's chest, her nails sliding along the black cloth, her nostrils filled with the mixture of perfume congealing with their sweat. The tiny droplets arced along the frame of Esther's face. She liked this better than any perfumed scent. Esther's truth, the earthy strike, followed by the gentle rise toward sweetness, all pulled downward by the overpowering musk of her arousal. She became a dark wine, and Vanessa wanted to get drunk off her. She cupped Esther's face, holding her warm, reddened cheek.

Esther was desperate, seeking validation, perhaps even vindication. She was caught trying to unwind the web of dogma's noose. She tucked in closer to Vanessa; her nearness, the sensuality of their bodies pressed together, Vanessa's breasts against hers was too much. A heat was pooling inside Esther, a kiln, producing such a sword that shame couldn't temper it. This was no temptress; this was purified, virtuous, majestic. Her needs overrode her apprehension; the proximity to Vanessa all but guaranteed it.

She began with a slow, tremulous articulation, reaching down to the skirt of her wedding dress. "May I? Would it be too much if I enjoyed myself in your company… You just have an effect on me…" She giggled. "Oh, what you do to me."

Vanessa was performing weighty calculations, the sort devoid of numbers or logic; this was the intrepid, constant stream of emotion. At length, she decided. "Go on, Esther, I'd like to see your enjoyment."

Esther flushed at these words, at Vanessa's permission. She took her time as if to tease herself. Vanessa, feeling the moment, wishing to have a little more for herself, guided her hand beneath Esther's white veil, running her fingers through a few brunette locks before rifling the habit down so she might touch the scalp and pull her hands freely through each strand.

Deft and sweet as this might have been, those few interactions of nails and tugging caused audible responses from Esther, who could no longer hold back.

Vanessa smiled to herself. Esther couldn't see, for her eyes were clamped shut, letting Vanessa have privacy, her lids drooping as she supped upon the sight, sounds, and smells. *Her ecstasy. It's divine.*

Part III: Gospel of Renumeration

Vision 5

"MOTHER SUPERIOR" was a title that made Francesca Lapointe invariably think of Mother Mary, the queen of all saints. That fearless woman who had birthed a demigod. She was the foundation of the Church and brought heaven tangibly into this world. July, Lapointe knew, was the true date of Christ's birth, and she quietly celebrated this every summer. Just as she had with Sister Cecilia those many years before.

The matter of monsters at the monastery had ruined her private festivities. To pray in her reverential way, she had to stay up till the light of dawn materialized, lifting her from the darkness.

Today, not even that was enough as a knock arrived on her door. "Yes, what is it?" she called.

Matthew opened the door, his shoulders hunched. She couldn't calculate whether this was out of deference or pride. It may have been simple logistics.

"I wish to speak with you about recent events." He shut the door behind him.

"Here I thought you had a pressing question about the Biblical text." Her sarcasm was lost on him. "Speak." She refused to curtail her authority over him.

His posture grew rigid. "As I'm the one charged with seeking out these creatures, any knowledge you might have on *unseen sins* should be relayed to me. I need context."

"You want me to tell you which of my charges is the most likely suspect? Or..." She raised a brow. "...do seek confirmation for whom you're suspecting? The open-ended question might offer a blind test, hm? I give the name of whom you seek. Then it seems unbiased. Especially coming from her own mother superior."

Matthew inclined his head, admitting to this. "That was my plan. Clearly I can be more blunt." He glowed as he aired out his accusation. "Has there been any trouble with Sister Christina?"

"Christina?" The mother superior couldn't her confusion. "Whatever would I look at her for?"

"She was sent here for a reason," he prompted.

"A trifling thing." Lapointe rejected this with a wave of her hand.

"So you were told." he replied vaguely, piquing her interest.

Lapointe allowed him this victory as she fell into her seat. "What should I be aware of?"

"In my time with her stateside, I observed certain tendencies. Self-aggrandizement. Pride. Sin was soon to follow. *Coquetry.*"

"Are you accusing her of promiscuity?"

"I would keep an eye on her. I think it's only a matter of time before she falls back into old habits."

"Do you have proof?"

"No, but her words will bring it once she plays the saint or the martyr, once *she* begins accusing. Then you will see."

The nun rubbed her eyelid, weary of his irksome noncommittal wordplay. "It's hard to take such apprehensive slander seriously if you refuse to be specific."

"That would cast a bad light on all those involved. The best thing is to ensure it doesn't happen again."

"You don't want to dredge up another American scandal? It's all the same with you, isn't it? Always causing trouble. Fine. I shall—"

A sound cut her off, wet mass and breaking bone, loud enough to be unmissable. Like alerted animals, each raised their hackles and stood at attention, listening and watching uselessly through the walls. The moist, scraped slide along stone, traveled farther down the passageway, a course away from them, not closer.

The priest and nun exchanged a hasty glance before surging out of the office. Mother Superior, despite her arthritis, kept up as they hurried in parallel.

The racket proceeded into the cathedral, rising, onward and upward till the nave made a resounding reverberation:

"Head, and listen, sup on thine sins! The unheard shall be spoken, and the voiceless will sing! Listen and weep. Feel their shaking torment in your soul. Damned and lost are you!"

Mother Superior gestured toward a spiral stair inlaid with a turret. As they ascended, the voice simultaneously fell behind them and charged ahead of them.

"Fools and the foolish. Ignorance, no bliss, nothing but pitiless excuses. No recusals!"

Matthew slowed, but the mother superior, goaded, pressed on, radiant and glowing. Stepping out onto the landing, she found it awash with an odd light, the clerestory windows painting a mural of shadow and green-tinged light as if the moon had been dipped in pestilence. She waded through this miasma and plague, shielding her eyes against the disquieting patterns. There in the putrid shadows, one of them! Surely that was it, there, at the end of the balcony row. Which one? Which one? This one was large, with ruby eyes, Kayden's assailant surely…and what was it doing, hunched at the rail?

An arc of the light shone in her eyes, making them water. Another creature, mobile, lithe, and blindfolded, darted across the window. Terror rippled through Lapointe like ice water. Just as she wheeled about, she caught a glimpse of another creature clad in gray. *I'm surrounded! I'm surrounded! There's the third, but where is the—*

Her thought was cut off as the final creature leaped out from behind a chiseled column, a face of anguish roaring and screaming, glowering emerald eyes, blood spraying out of her mouth.

The ichor coated Mother Superior's face and stained her habit. She didn't scream or shout; instead everything closed in, and like a curtain, her world went black.

Chapter 9

"Go on, my child," Father Jonathan whispered in the tone he always used when he was behind the grated divider.

"Forgive me, Father, for I have sinned," Vanessa began, before confessing simple sins of gluttony and avarice, taking an extra serving at supper, feeling put out when Sister Elizabeth was praised for a custard that had been Vanessa's idea…and then wrath: "I felt such fury when Catherine was accused and Josephine…When they weren't believed. "But now it's happened to the mother superior… Father, when is it okay to feel such anger? Is it ever permissible?"

"Ah…" He sighed from the other side of the confessional. "You must place your faith in God to decide that. Deuteronomy thirty-three, twenty-seven tells us exactly this. 'The eternal God is your refuge, and underneath are the everlasting arms. He will drive out your enemy before you, saying, "Destroy him!"'"

Vanessa bowed her head, hands caught up in the skirts of her brown bridal gown, God's words, like a brand, searing her skin in the most desirous way, the fire rekindled deep within her. The rage, the righteous wrath, she clung to them.

"Thank you, Father, and God bless you."

*   *   *

* * *

The mother superior wouldn't speak about what had happened to her and demanded Matthew's silence. Too ashamed and angry with herself. At the first sign of danger, a dire threat to her new flock of dependents, she had crumpled like a fickle Victorian heroine. She was strong and durable. Not the sort to faint, she was reliable and dependable. A parent for her five siblings when her parents were too poor and drug-addled (pain-killers for the father, injured as a construction worker, cocaine for the mother who refused to treat her depression) to care for them. Their lives and safety fell to Francesca. She'd done right by them, then checked out from all worldly affairs, fleeing into the bliss of a religious life and permanent vows.

"Matthew, this is the second time you have seen them."

"No, I didn't see them this time. Only you did," he explained. "And they made noise right outside your door," he added dryly, gesturing with one thumb toward that wood frame.

"Only once you showed up." She was gazing at the rocky bluffs surrounding the township, haloed by the morning light, just pure yellowed light —like an old light bulb, the filament burning and beautiful.

"Are you making some sort of accusation?"

She turned her narrowed eyes on him, hoping he'd squirm. "Testy, aren't we?" Her accent made the inference smooth, and she loved nothing more than to figure out the inflections of a native speaker. English was no French to her, and even Spanish was a better tongue, but English could have its uses, slang, and inferences. Americans had clever ones, less pretentious than the Brits.

The bluntness worked a spell, and Matthew became defensive. "I thought I heard something beneath your tone. I must have misread it."

How blithe. Rather *gauche.* That's what he was. The man clung to the pomp of his station. Yet he was here in a backwater town. He was never the first choice for confessionals and was disliked by most of his peers. No sermons, rarely a part of any community outreach. Except for his sycophantic little squire Kayden, he had nothing here. *Why did he end up here?*

"This parish isn't the first choice for anyone. Explain to me how you came to join us here." She wouldn't let go of her matter-of-fact attitude. There was no need to—she was still his better. It reminded her of an old dilemma she'd read about: American colonial troops, during the days of the British colony, had an issue where every American officer was deemed lower than *any* British officer. She wondered if he would try to pull such a stunt here and claim that any priest at all was better than even the highest-ranking member of the cloister.

When he squirmed a little, making this same calculation, she knew she had won. "There was an issue. One I was punished for," he admitted at length.

"Just the one issue then? Wrapped up nice and tidy."

"We are all sinners. Born of it. None are clean." An easy theological excuse, a blasé universalism.

"Clearly, these creatures are concerned with more than the nominal white noise of human fault," she contended.

"Which is why I will unearth what sins are bedeviling us," Matthew insisted.

Mother Superior narrowed her eyes again before relaxing her approach, disarmed by the genuine passion on display—that gleam in the eye that warned: *zealotry.*

She shooed him off. "Then go and find it… But Matthew…" Her words caused him to halt. "Don't think you can investigate my sisters without my involvement. Any hints, any suspicions—you keep me in the loop."

"You make it sound like a spy movie."

"Don't pretend like the clandestine and ecclesiastical don't have overlap. Intrigue, endless intrigue. Don't let your curiosity tread upon my loyalty. Then you'll understand a much older instinct."

A little smirk appeared on the priest's lips, but the mother superior wouldn't give him the satisfaction of being overly self-aware. She meant her words, and she'd stand by them.

With the door shut, Esther and Vanessa snuck away from the window, conspiratorial glances shared in silence until as they retreated to the garden and its tree, offering such sweet shade. Esther pulled at her habit, the heat getting to her. Vanessa enjoyed the flustered sight. She was no longer disturbed by mundanities like perspiration. *Sweat is but sweet nature. It isn't strife.*

"He's hiding something. Do you know what it is?" Esther asked, craning her neck to look at the woman standing above her.

Vanessa leaned into the tree, averting her expression from Esther's view, her fingers fiddling with a tiny branch. "As I told you, Matthew thought I would be a saint. His devotion runs deep. Too often, people think that means they're above reproach. In my experience, it's the opposite."

"How so?" Esther soothed.

"Faith and its precepts, tenets ,and vows are restrictive. We call it temptation. Sometimes I wonder if faith is the temptress. I don't mean that as blasphemy. I think it ' a miracle that we choose our faith, invisible intangibility, to live by and ignore such worldly considerations in service to this ideal…" She snapped the branch and tossed it aside. "Hunger is cumulative, starvation all-encompassing. You eat more ravenously the longer you have gone without." She turned over an empty palm, studying it, tracing the contours. "If the most faithful are the most deprived, they can become the most depraved…in theory."

"In practice. We both know what the Church tries so desperately to ignore," Esther said.

Vanessa sighed and tapped her boot heel against one thick root. "How much has gone ignored? Been covered up, Esther?" She narrowed her eyes, tracking over the monastery's glowing bright facades, the metal cross above the cathedral burning like a star. "Look at how much is being dug up because of these creatures. Who among us doesn't have a skeleton in the closet?"

Esther had grown quiet, and Vanessa found fresh tears wetting her cheek. Vanessa fell onto her in an instant, a thumb to one salty tract, murmuring and cooing. Asking what was wrong.

"Am I starved?" Esther moaned.

Vanessa's mouth opened in an *O*, her face falling as she realized where she had erred.

"Is this not depravity? Is it wrong?" A small, shaking sob held Esther's throat like a vise. "You've heard it your whole life, just as I have. Romans, Leviticus, all the rest."

"No, no, no, no…" Vanessa's words became noises without syllables. She embraced Esther and held her, the other woman lightly sobbing into her. "You're not and we're not. It's different."

"How?"

"Because it is. How can I explain such purity? Such grace we share?" Vanessa had grown wild, beaming with such unbridled surety. "God likes to work in mysterious ways—that's what we always say—and what if sometimes the blind see better than the seeing? What if, in this instance, the secular world, the nonbelievers have it right? We must observe God's plan, even if it manifests in vessels not bearing his cross."

"We made vows and oaths to Jesus. We are his brides. He is our husband. Meant to satisfy such urges. Is this not adultery?"

Vanessa was initially obsessed with the idea of marrying Jesus because, to her, he seemed like the only decent man—the one to purge sin, not wallow in it. Only in her later teens, as she came into her sexuality, did she understand this was *compulsive heterosexuality—comp het*. Once she recognized Jesus as the ideal of a perfect man, she realized her mistake. Whether or not it was blasphemy, she found in him a guide and a figure to follow—her version of being his bride.

"You might view it as polygamy since we've married the same man. Or, in his gentle protections, a modern lavender wedding." Venessa faltered, fighting for genuine sincerity. To believe her own words, for in his way, in his role, Jesus had failed her—an impossible fact she couldn't surmise one way or another.

Esther was left unconvinced. "Gentle things, soft things, but I speak of the full sin. The desolation of worship."

"Sex can be worship," Vanessa admitted, blushing a little, smiling despite herself. "I can worship you and him. There is enough love in my heart for both."

"I know there is." With one fist, Esther wiped the sorrow from her eyes. "I'm sorry to put you through this."

"When I have a hard day, you'll be there for me."

"Absolutely," Esther spoke with clear, precise conviction.

"Good. But you must go. I know you promised to help Sister Mary today."

"I can't complain. She won't be as lucky as I'll be. In my old age, I'll have you to lean upon." The nun smiled and disengaged. She then strode toward the convent, bowing her head to wipe away the last of the moisture stinging her skin.

At the tree, Vanessa was left breathless. *Growing old together. When was the last time I thought of the future? I can't even comprehend that winter will come along with a new year.*

Yet Esther had offered her a splendid continuation, the dream of decades.

She shook her head, dissolving the spell. *This is why he has given us adversity. Challenge, strife, woe. This is why. This is why. I must only overcome. If I only overcome.* She stomped her boots with every line, her hands curled into fists, like an athlete performing a ritual before a match. With her mantra reiterated, she surged into action. Along the hill was a small divot formed by the erosion of two rocks. With gritted teeth and scrambling nails, she ascended the hill, leaving a tuft of dust in her wake. Weary of the noon sun, she moved low.

Her brown bridal gown wasn't any sort of camouflage.

No one was eager to be out in the heat, and the five men at the loading area focused on their work. Careful not to displace any rocks, Vanessa lowered herself and was now deep within the men's side of the monastery; the cathedral looming large, a black monolith.

She skirted the perimeter, slowly looping inward, a bigger risk with every passing hallway, each so bright and tan with nowhere to hide. At last, a vestibule opened wide to her, an open-air stairwell really. The thing was sturdy and solid despite its age. On that second floor, opposite the stairs' landing and parallel to the staircase, were a row of office windows. A thin ledge that ran along the wall was being used to hang plants. Vanessa prayed the thin lip could support her weight; she was dead-set on trying. After balancing on the staircase railing, she hoisted herself onto the thin lip and pressed her back into the scratchy plaster wall.

Taking a fortifying breath, she gingerly stepped over the dangling strings of pearls, petunias, begonias, and some Calibrachoa that stood upright in pots. Her foot caught on one string of green beads, and she almost lost her balance and went down to a hard landing. Her heart hammering in her throat, she imagined the violence of what would occur to her body: head burst, limbs contorted. The fear made her grit her teeth and forge on.

Most of the windows were cracked open to let in the breeze. This included Father Matthew's. Vanessa's heart beat like an anvil as she peeked into his room, finding an empty wood-walled office. *This won't take too long*, she assuaged then clambered through the small opening. Her petite size was finally of some use.

A laptop sat on the desk. It would be password-protected, and besides, Matthew wasn't the sort to leave a trail of digital incrimination. She headed to the filing cabinet, the shelf, and the desk itself. She rifled through every ledger, document, and curio she could find. Matthew had spoken to her about places he used to live and serve the church, but there were gaps.

She found her answers: in 2015 he became a priest at the Cathedral of Our Lady of the Angels in downtown Los Angeles. In 2020, at the onset of the pandemic, he was shuffled to New Orleans. The year 2026 saw him placed in New York. Then he moved again, this time to Cleveland, until late 2027. That winter they shipped him off to Europe.

Footsteps thundered down the hall, rapid and unwavering. Vanessa dashed across the room and hurtled over the sill. Every hair on her neck stood on end as she wobbled upon the narrow edge, battling the adrenaline, like a fire, pouring through her.

 Matthew opened his door and sank into his chair with a great heave of crackling leather. "Fuck," he whispered to himself, then set to work on his computer. His irritation was made manifest as he viciously cleared his desk of paperwork with one broad stroke of his hand.

Vanessa issued a relieved sigh, for in his anger, Matthew had brushed aside any chance of noticing the intrusion.

Like a church mouse, she crept back along the sill and through the halls, edging back out toward the outer edges of the building. Here, she was rewarded again as the computer room of the men's dormitory lay abandoned. The ban on internet use was proving effective.

Settling in at the most enclosed station, she waited impatiently with a tapping foot and drumming fingers. Finally the machine hummed to life. The monitor, however, didn't yield. She had to cup her hand under it, her knuckles crooked to place a finger upon the control nub. She blushed, thinking of Esther in a blasphemous way. A moment later, the screen was alive

Her first step was to download a fresh web browser; mercifully, the internet was half decent, and within minutes she was at work. She searched for news articles first. The stories referenced a scandal-laden Church, offering few specifics. She waded through a seemingly endless cavalcade of corrupt clergy, from those committing the acts to those covering them up. Even Pope Leo was mentioned, as during his time in Chiago he was accused of downplaying reports from several nuns against a priest in his parish and offering zero support to the survivors. The priest supposedly confessed to his crimes; however, the following civil case failed due to the statute of limitations running out. Then there were the matters of the pedophilic priest he'd elected to house half a block from an elementary school. A decision Cardinal Blase Cupich deemed "inappropriate."

New Orleans in 2020 bore the second most news articles and headlines, with five hundred claims by three hundred priests in the area. In May of that year, the archdiocese had filed for bankruptcy. Vanessa lingered, reading about how the court had prolonged the bankruptcy hearings and legal framework, making the entire process hopelessly complicated for survivors seeking their due. But that was utterly dwarfed by the scale of the LA disaster. In 2024 the Los Angeles parish was held liable to the tune of one point five billion dollars in a case that featured fifteen hundred class-action plaintiffs, the court proceedings alone lasting some twenty years. The Church was desperate to avoid paying for what it had done.

Ohio had a similar pattern of abusive activity and courtroom issues, and like the others, the timeframes and accused individuals didn't include Father Matthew. She dug deeper, first on Twitter, BlueSky, and Reddit, the right places to locate those alluding to what had occurred. She found few whispers trailing after each diocese.

Next came forums, more direct inferences, references to a "bad priest" or sentences such as, "Does anyone here know what it's like?" or "What I should do when someone in the Church is hurting me?"

This typically fell on poor sympathies. People demanded evidence, proclaiming "innocent until proven guilty." Many derided the discourse as being a part of cancel culture with adamant zeal: "Our priests are human and they make mistakes. If someone isn't a pedophile, we should give him grace. Think of the lives destroyed by this. One false accusation and someone's entire life of service is over."

The pattern repeated, and Vanessa saw the original posters shouted down, slinking back into their quiet corners, too sacred to mention specifics until she happened upon one person replying cryptically. "In my bio I have a link to a Discord server. It's safer there." That account had been deleted, but through some clever archival sleuthing, Vanessa found that link and, using her own login, located the server. Fortunately one of its moderators responded quickly to her and granted her access.

Here, people were more open about things. Far more open. She found details and corroborating accounts. Firsthand testimonies paired with amateur detective work. There were so many that Vanessa was left reeling, unsure how deep the well of sorrow descended. She kept going and going until a name appeared at the bottom of the screen, and she scrolled down until it sat dead center, staring at her, taunting her.

With a shudder, Vanessa wiped away the tears she hadn't realized were falling. She couldn't stop, not now. The residents of the server had become increasingly disillusioned over time, their spirits breaking.

"All this work for nothing. I contacted the police. Newspapers. No one cares. Unless it's ginormous, we aren't worth the risk. The Church is still too scary."

"I can't afford the legal costs of a lawsuit, and the lawyer I talked to said it would probably wind up like it did in New Orleans."

"Even if it's just one individual?"

"I suspect more people would come out of the woodwork. I mean, could you imagine what would happen to the church if we began a #MeToo moment?"

"Will never happen."

"Yeah, I agree."

Unlike these intrepid, burnt-out investigators, Vanessa held to her emphatic goal. She printed several key pieces of evidence before covering her tracks. She cleared the cache, deleted the web browser, and used the machine's backups to revert the desktop to two weeks prior.

Lastly she folded up her incriminating documents and slid them up each sleeve. They were weighty, like two spears waiting to be hurled. She would have to be patient, await the perfect moment. All she had to do was wait.

Chapter 10

In the following days, no opportunity presented itself. The cloud of unease hung over the double monastery with Esther listening to each rumor, snatching at the trailing lines of gossip as though her life depended on it. In a very real sense, it did: her faith and her affection hung on a tightrope. Esther knew Vanessa suspected Matthew, though she had yet to share her discoveries. This left her to worry, and her anxiety festered. She feared every new suspicion would carry the names *Esther and Christina.*

They were on the way to Sunday Mass when Esther could no longer contain it. She grabbed her lover's arm, if only briefly, and broke away from the group, citing a stomachache. A show so genuine, no one questioned her or Vanessa for rushing to assist her.

"Let me know if you need anything. We'll make your excuses." Josephine assured her sister.

Vanessa flashed a smile of gratitude and hurried along. Rounding the next corner, she found Esther standing in the courtyard. The site of the falling leaves was where her romance with Esther had truly begun.

It was for this exact reason that Esther had stopped there. Its calming green hues and vines coiling memories, bleached by the high sun. Everyone else was at the cathedral, affording privacy for their rendezvous.

As soon as Vanessa joined her upon the cracked tiles, Esther kissed her—desperate and deep. Vanessa felt the tension in her partner contrasting with the ardor of affection. Each emotion redoubled until Esther was left shaking, buffeted by enough love and hatred to unwind the most solidly crafted person.

Vanessa squeezed her fingers around Esther's, then loosened, her eyes becoming intense. She had learned her tells and was still learning. That was her favorite part of loving someone. The endless discovery, the constant mastery. She wanted to know Esther as well as she knew herself—the trust and the respect and softness therein.

"I haven't told you yet about Sister Bridget, have I? Back in New York."

Perplexed, Esther tried to recall such a name. "No, I don't think you have."

"That makes sense. It's a careful subject. She's transgender," Vanessa explained.

"Really?" Esther replied, eyes widening a little.

"She isn't allowed into ecclesial life. And she has never… 'stolen valor' by wearing the habit erroneously. But I've never witnessed a deeper faith. Not even from you or me."

"Yet she lives a life of sin," Esther noted without inflection.

"So it is decreed by the Church, but never by God's word. Even at the most extreme perspective, one must accept that Jesus welcomed eunuchs."

Esther was curious, her expression subtly animating. "God created us and we cannot falsify his image. Francis said such things might break the natural order and the unique dignity of conception is being threatened."

"Sister Agnes wears glasses, as does Mother Superior."

"But if I were to become a man, cut off my breasts and the rest of it, that would be quite different from glasses," Esther countered.

"Agnes wants Lasik eye surgery so she no longer has to. Mother Superior has had an operation done to align her feet, and Sister Mary had a mastectomy." Vanessa paused, finding a different route. "Think of it this way, do you feel compelled to change yourself, to become a man?"

"Well, no."

"Then God doesn't will it."

"But the Devil can tempt."

"If you saw these trans people's lives before and after as I have, you would know which end the Devil has plied. The euphoric joy, their wholeness after they can be themselves. That is holy. A sacred dignity if ever there was one."

Esther let out a smiling breath, rolling her ankles; these glimpses of the old Vanessa, the powerful, persuasive *Saint Vanessa*, made her shy and giddy all at once. "Okay, I see your point… Then again, I've always been predisposed toward our community. Us…queers," she whispered as if that word were the narrowest of confidences. She stroked Vanessa's cheek, glancing about to make sure they were still alone. She tilted her head, her mouth caught open. "There are groups for us. LGBT Catholics, here in Spain."

"CVX, Cursillos de Cristianidad, Ichthys Sevilla… I know them… I've sought aid from the Rainbow Catholics before," Vanessa demurred.

Esther raised Venessa's hand to her chest, rescuing her from her memories. "There's one that meets within the township. We should visit sometime. They might help ease our worries."

Your worries, Vanessa corrected in her mind. *No, no, I have them as well.*

Esther felt the little percolations of sweat on Vanessa's hands, but before she could rescind the offer, Vanessa threw herself at the idea. "Yes, yes, let's go on Monday. The others are going on some outings."

"Perfect," Esther agreed.

"Perfect," Vanessa repeated, wishing she could share Esther's hope. Wishing she could air her every worry and grievance without shattering this beautiful, fragile secret they shared.

* * *

*　　　　　*　　　　　*

Despite every night bringing a hushed fear to the church and its silenced choir, Monday arrived quickly. Esther awoke excited; she wanted to call out to Vanessa's cell like an over-excited schoolgirl. Instead, she opted for a gentle knock. Their plan involved taking food from the pantry to an orphanage down one lane, a cul-de-sac, upon a hill, that abutted a modern community center. Connecting the two was a little idyllic parkway with sharp, steep concrete steps; it would be very romantic, or so Esther hoped, envisaging it as a date of sorts.

There were endless ways for nuns to get distracted and return late to the nest. Stopping to play football with children or leading the locals in prayer.

This time, everyone will be securitized due to recent events. This was a necessary risk, for as much as Esther listened to her soothing guidance, Vanessa feared there would come a point where Esther would presume a lover's bias. *If only I could show her salvation.*

The nuns gathered at the entrance of the monastery, lined up in neat rows, listening as Sister Mary gave them their marching orders. She was so close to being a stereotypical drill sergeant that the sisters wanted to snicker. A few rebels did; fortunately Mary was distracted.

"You are, as women, to comport yourselves to the highest standards of obedience and humility. Make no mention of our plight. Do the Lord's work. We won't be prevented from performing our duties to Christ."

With that, she shooed off the flock, who didn't so much waddle as they did frolic and leap, like gazelles or hyenas. They were uncaged, dispersing down the narrow cobbled streets. A few broke off for a quick treat at an ice cream truck. Or, in Sister Josephine's case, a falafel place tucked into a wall.

Esther and Vanessa were adamant about staying on track. The smells of a bakery, however, were temptation incarnate, the allure of churros too great, and

Esther insisted on using up some of her budget.

Fried cinnamon dough sticks in hand, they slowed, eating as they walked, smiling and laughing. *This is what it feels like to be on a date, isn't it? Vanessa thought.* The breezy afternoon fluffed up clouds above. She saw grace everywhere: the castle walls, the drying clothes on their lines. Oh, to live and love. She could almost ignore the demons and the intrigues. *Almost.*

As they walked past locals and tourists alike, one of those travelers, an American, bulky and blond, grinning and brandishing a small camera, intercepted them, his voice jarringly loud. "Hey, come on. Tell us what's happening! Chat wants to know! Are you nuns really possessed? Stalked by monsters with ten-inch claws?"

Esther rolled her eyes while Vanessa found herself staring into the camera's dimly reflective lens.

"The people want to know! A haunted cathedral, a publicity stunt. You can tell me—is it a cover for orgies?"

"What?" Vanessa stammered.

The man's eyes lolled back and he rolled his head about. "Okay, not orgies, but like, let's be real, you nuns get frisky, right? You're hot, and I mean, I support it; lesbians and nuns are tight. Uh, pun intended!" He directed this last comment to his camera.

"Dude, what's your fucking problem?" Esther snapped, then waved a hand halfway to her mouth, realizing her curse.

"A swearing nun. Clip that shit! But seriously, dude, just chill. I was only joking." The man's expression changed as his mind switched gears. "Look, you got some fucking churros! Where did you get those?"

"Uh, right down the street." Vanessa gulped.

"Bros, should I get some churros?" He looked at his phone, showing him the livestream's chat log. "Yeah, yeah—hell, yeah—churro time, baby!" The man, just like that, was gone, a miracle that his attention span rivaled that of a goldfish. Vanessa and Esther hurried along the lane before he could change his mind again.

Each performed her duties at the orphanage with as much haste as they could afford to. None of the parishioners they met with brought up the troubles at the convent. No suspicions arose. They were too young, pure, and pretty, but not *too* pretty. Their modesty, the lack of makeup, and the bags under Vanessa's eyes helped with this. That day, only one teenage boy ogled her openly. The adults were a little more subtle, at least around their wives.

Vanessa was happy to be rid of her work and those men. She almost leaped from her skin when one man's hand brushed hers to help her with a box. He had been young and suave in a dim, magnanimous way, with curled thick hair, a beaming smile, and an ostentatious goatee. Perfectly nice, perfectly friendly. The most dangerous sort. He could be a monster and no one would believe it. How could they? With his charms and that gold cross on his neck, he was helping the starving find their supper after all.

Esther noticed the interaction, and as they walked to the community center, Vanessa felt the jealousy rolling off her fellow sister in arid currents, a heat to rival the blistering sun.

Vanessa's chest contracted and she made a judgment call, taking a risk. Fighting back her fear, she slipped her hand into Esther's, and suddenly all that envy melted away.

After slipping through a back door, the pair continued along a linoleum-floored hallway, likely from the fifties. Vanessa wondered how long after the Civil War it had been built. The whole town had been a battlefield, with socialists sacrificing their lives to stave off the fascists. The thought rang dismally prescient in Vanessa's mind. Although she was a woman of faith, not politics, she knew her history. The way the church had abandoned Spain, siding with the fascists, was abhorrent. Too often those in positions of authority clung to that authority, to power, and not the Holy Word. She would rather the atheistic socialists win. any day. At least they knew how to argue with one another. She longed for a Church that might argue—a little disobedience to serve the higher obedience.

Around a bend and up two flights of stairs was a small community room, cramped if it weren't for the tall ceilings—bright, in a boxed-in way, with the windows being narrow and set high up. The walls were light gray, and an odd rubbery faux wood squirmed beneath Vanessa's feet, sterile and plush. The people's smiles, however, were genuine, as was their curiosity. The man nearest, gray bearded and sweet in complexion, tilted his head. "Hello. How can we help you, sisters?"

Vanessa glanced at Esther, unsure what to say, and after a moment, Esther replied, "We want to join the meeting. Is this the right spot?"

A portly woman unfolding a pride flag on a little snack table gestured to the rainbow. "If this seems correct, then yes."

Esther turned her lips up tentatively. "Yes, yes!"

Vanessa joined in, finding some enthusiasm. "We're not late, I assume? We could help set things up?"

"Yes, uh, certainly. We just have a few chairs to put out. The younger members tend to be late. You know how it can be…or maybe not. I've heard the mother superior is quite strict," the man said. The half dozen other people in the room, between thirty and sixty, were staring at the nuns, the same question held in their stares.

"We enjoy helping. Are those the chairs over there?" Esther asked, ignoring them.

As they set up, they learned the man's name was Alejandro and the woman was Isabella. They led the group. The man was gay, though his partner of thirty years had kicked him to the curb a year prior. "With the male equivalent of *a floozy*," the man said, borrowing some derogatory English.

"And you?" Vanessa asked.

"Lover of everyone, bi or *pan*, same difference to me," Isabella said.

The group, once settled in the circle, was thirteen strong, the younger ones being from seventeen to twenty-seven. First was Lara, a lesbian; a bisexual man named Javiar; and then Minsk, a nonbinary dyke, as they called themselves, their studded jacket conveying a fifties flavor. The last was Abigail, who was eighteen and accompanied by her parents, who were asked to leave at the door. This space was one for queer participants only. "But we'll bring you some refreshments while you wait," Isabella had assured them.

"*Sí, gracias,*" the pot-bellied father said while his wife kept staring at the two sisters, each turned away to cloak their faces, though Vanessa's distinctive brown uniform presented a terrifying individuality.

Once the parents had vacated, the session began. Abigail went first; she was at the questioning stage, perhaps a she/they, bi, or a lesbian. "I've liked maybe two boys, the rest…girls." She blushed at the mere thought of women.

After reassuring words, things proceeded in an anticlockwise rotation. Esther and Venessa tried to settle in by offering more general advice with a few bits of worship sprinkled in. Their sage input was appreciated, and that calming sensation of belonging washed over Venessa, starting at her feet, as though she were stepping into a cool stream.

The circle reached her, and hesitation overcame her, a stammering tremor vibrating her throat. She attempted an introduction and choked on her name. Too much was rising to the surface. Thought in bleeding colors. A mocking voice invading her mind, like the creatures in the video, crackling with white noise: *What do you think you're doing? What good could they do? They can't know. No one can know!* She squirmed. "*Not even Esther can know. What would she think? What would she say?*

Vanessa shook her head forcibly. *This is why he has given us adversity. Challenge, strife, and woe. This is why. This is why. I must only overcome. If I only overcome.* The clawing memories would not arrest her. She availed herself of them and plowed on ahead.

"My name is Sister Christina, though I still enjoy using my Christian name, Vanessa."

"Hello, Vanessa," the group repeated, Esther, smiling as she did so, her hands clasped in her lap.

"I have far too much to say and not enough time. Some of it, most of it…" She felt a light ringing in her ears, the soul's version of tinnitus, a headache biting at her skull, making her drowsy. "I shall be simple and say …I am a nun. I am faithful. I love my Lord Jesus Christ. He alone is the only man I could ever love…but I also love women. More than as family or friends."

A chorus of sympathetic nods followed. Vanessa scrounged up the courage to weather on. "And I'm here with my Sister Esther to… Well, she and I are here together…"

"We're here because we're in love," Esther spoke, and reached over to grip Vanessa's hand, desperate to assuage her widened eyes and ashen pallor.

That's when they noticed the reactions around them, squirming, unmoored, hard stares. "You're nuns? Cloistered nuns?" Alejandro asked.

"Yes, we are," Esther replied. "Or well, cloistered to a degree. We obviously do enter town and...um…" she trailed off, noting the dry reception.

"So you swore the vows?" Isabella said.

"We did," Esther answered.

"You broke them," concluded Jacob, an American expat.

"Well, no, not really… It's complicated…" Esther stammered.

"But you did, didn't you? That's how it works?" Abigail addressed this as much to the others as she did to either nun.

"Look, we…I came here to ask advice."

"Advice? You know your order's rules better than any of us could. And you know this is wrong."

"Wrong? But we… You're, but…" Esther looked at Vanessa, a heart-wrenching plea caught in her warm gaze, but Vanessa was staring at her lap.

"We aren't mad at you for being lesbians in love," Minsk, cut in. "But if you want to be together, wouldn't it be better to leave the convent?"

"Leave the…what?"

"If you can't fulfill your promise as nuns, there are other ways of living a religious life. Serving God," Alejandro consoled.

Esther pressed her eyes shut and arched her head upward. "That's not fair, though. I love God and Jesus, I'm his bride, but also—"

"Not a very loyal bride," scoffed Javiar.

Everything was closing in on her: shame, guilt, and that churning schism when no one will listen because no one wants to hear. No empathy, only being right, thinking oneself virtuous by way of feeling correct and morally sound,

"This was a mistake," Vanessa declared in a hiss. Her chair screeched as she rose and grabbed at Esther before pulling her away from the circle.

As much as Esther wanted to struggle, she found herself retreating, if only to escape the cruelty of those stares as she wept. Allies, kin, community, each so dragged down by dogma! *Why? Do they think we aren't earnest? Why won't they just listen?!*

Vanessa pushed her out into the hall before turning on the others, stewing in an awkward shock. "You said everything we say here stays here. If you're so obsessed with promises and vows, I trust none of this will reach the monastery." Her blazing gray eyes and bowed posture left little room for negotiation.

"We won't say a word. But please consider ours," Alejandro said, attempting to be the voice of reason.

Vanessa shut the door on his words and joined her love in the hallway. "Come, come. We'll find an alleyway."

Back in the heat once more, tucked between a dirty concrete wall and the flowered hillside, Vanessa held Esther while she sobbed. "It's impossible! The Church is our family. We can't abandon them. It's my life, Vanessa…and so are you."

"I know, I know," Vanessa whispered, for she didn't know what else to say, her confidence and surety cracked open anew. She was so tired of doubting herself, of being laid low. God on high wouldn't let her rise, but again and again she tried. She was weary in her bones, her chest was heavy, and she pressed her eyes tightly against her grief and despair. She would try again—no matter how many times it took, she'd rise.

After the weeping rains subsided, they headed back up the hill. Fearing discovery, Vanessa led them to the loading area where a cracked gouge in the wall was just wide enough for them to pass through.

On the other side, Vanessa suddenly embraced Esther, a ferocity coiling within her limbs. "I don't need any support group. I have you." She held those slender cheeks in her hands and dropped her voice to a whisper. "Esther, you make me feel safe."

"Oh," Esther cooed. "Hearing that makes my heart soar. It's cheesy, but it does." She gulped, her voice falling even lower. "Is it okay if I love you?"

Life had become thin ice, a perilous span of before and after, each woman so fragile, cracked, ready to shatter.

"May I?" she repeated.

"Only if it means I can love you in return," Vanessa replied.

Part IV: Gospel of Vendetta

Vision 6

DESPITE the late hour of their return, no one batted an eye, for the cloister was in a frenzy. At noon a woman had arrived bearing a grievance on her thin shoulders. She claimed her daughter, still a teenager, had been seduced by a priest from the cathedral. He had visited her under the guise of performing his anointed duties. Only by dumb luck did their gardener catch him kissing her. The woman explained to Sister Mary that her daughter "didn't know any better. He wasn't honest with her."

To make matters worse, Sister Mary's office had notoriously thin walls.

By supper, fact and rumor were being shared as one and the same. A wildfire no one could douse. The exact kindling Lapointe had feared.

"She's lucky they didn't go further," Sister Elizabeth declared with her typical haughty delight.

"How do we know they didn't?" Sister Bernadette countered.

"They checked her hymen," Josephine explained, shivering at how draconian things had become.

"I guess she's never gotten unlucky with a tampon," Elizabeth sniped. An elderly nun passed by, causing them to fall into a hush.

Once she was out of earshot, the conversation continued. Josephine leaned in, making a meal out of it. "The question is…what else *did* he do? The Spanish girl was an attempt at seduction. Sounds like she's been punished for the coquetry. But Matthew? There has to be more."

"Matthew?" Vanessa blurted out, her eyes alert, the rest of her freezing up.

"You didn't know? They're trying to keep it anonymous. The superioress ordered our silence, but I was there with Agnes and Catherine, listening in. It was Matthew, I swear." Josephine had been at the center of this since the very first encounter; she wouldn't allow herself to be blamed any further.

"We believe you," Esther assured her.

For the rest of the meal, Vanessa sat staring at the table, doleful and demure. When Esther asked her if she was okay after their evening prayer, she said she was simply tired. Esther didn't trust this. She had watched her in prostration, the tears streaming down her face; she took it as a sign their outing had been a mistake, and she blamed herself for it. *Why can it not be easy for us? Why does God have to challenge us? If not our love, then it's the demons. What test of faith am I meant to endure? Where is the lesson? Am I being led astray?*

Esther brushed aside her concerns, saving them for her pillow. With a tender slowness, she touched Vanessa's forearm and tried her most sibilant voice. "Please get some sleep. Tomorrow is another day."

That night, however, Vansessa's brief patches of sleep were nightmarish; the monster back again, his appearances so sporadic and impossible to judge. She'd had weeks of sublimated thoughts and the mercy of deep slumber, being so exhausted that she didn't have any reveries. This night then was a vengeance, twisting and vicious. When the monster retreated, as was his pattern, she heard those voices again. The devilry. She tried to shout at them: *Protect me!* But they did not. All they did was goad her.

"Little devil."

"Did you think you could do anything?"

"What do a few papers matter?"

"In the hands of one so weak?"

She awoke, blinking and covered in a thin coat of perspiration. Past the thin wall, she heard Sister Angus riffling through her wardrobe. Vanessa checked her watch and saw it was early, too early. She blinked away her confusion and raised her head...

A chorus of voices beamed through the convent, invading every cell.

"Listen! Listen! Fear, rejoice. Cower and revel. Ye who hold such little faith, prostrate thyself and weep!" arrived one commanding voice.

Then another, higher pitched, feigning a more pronounced femininity, saccharine, sibilant, ear bleeding, *"Listen and heed the warnings. Let us show you. Let us guide you on the journey of discovery."*

The next was seduction itself. *"Give in to your intrigue. Satiate your desire for the discovery. Feed your hunger. Cherish your cravings."*

Vanessa stood perfectly still while, through the hole in the wall, she glimpsed Agnes shaking in abject terror upon her counterpane, muttering hysterically to herself in prayer.

Then came the final voice, solid and stern: *"Steel yourself. Find your courage and face your fears. Heed our call, and do not demure. Face it! You reap what you sow."*

"You reap what you sow," the others echoed.

"Come and see. You want to... Yes, you do..." came the placation.

"This way," said the high-pitched voice.

"Be obedient and serve," the first voice reiterated.

The voices then chanted a hymn, an archaic abstraction of Latin. The discordant singing receding down the halls, coaxing, summoning.

Vanessa burst into the hall, and Agnes, despite her fear, joined her, gripping Vanessa's shoulders, an old technique her parents had instilled in her to temper her fear of crowds. It reminded her of piggyback rides; Vanessa was too preoccupied with tracking the song's origin point to care one way or another.

More of their kin bled into the passageways. Esther and Josephine, with Catherine not far behind, made their gaggle into a vanguard four abreast, each with their ears piqued to the ceiling. The sounds rounded off, floating, and curving, the acoustics of the stone making specificity a nightmarish task. Volume alone guided them: a game of *hot and cold*.

Traveling deeper, the triangulation narrowed until they came face-to-face with the male contingent encamped at one of the larger, two-tiered courtyards. The voices boomed from above, their abrasive chants unifying back into words.

"No forgiveness."

"No forgiveness"

"No forgiveness.

"No forgiveness."

"No excuses. No reprieves"

"No forgiveness. No forgiveness."

"Justice. Sweet justice. Sweet lamentation of His smiting will. Weep, weep. Weep! We shall know of ye who fear and those who celebrate. Weep and rejoice, for at last justice comes."

"No forgiveness, no forgiveness."

Displayed upon the back wall of the stone balcony terrace for all to see in the gray dawn was a mural, signage painted in crimson, with a scented drought of fermentation. Wine, dried, and solidified into a message.

Matthew 2015, Matthew 2020, Matthew 2022, Matthew 2024, Matthew 2026???

Below that was a biblical extraction, ***"And when the sun was up, they were scorched; and because they had no root, they withered away…"***

Vanessa paled, her hand clutching at her breast, eyes scanning the text repeatedly as if to sup upon every detail, to reconfirm the facts of its existence. She sucked in a sharp breath, noticed only by Esther.

"Vanessa, what is it?" she whispered.

Vanessa shook her head, bewildered, gulping, "Those years I… After the incident with the mother superior, I snuck into Father Matthew's room and his documents… I saw the different parishes where he was posted. The years when he was shuffled to a new city… Those years…" she said, gesturing to the lurid denouement.

"Oh, my God," Esther exhaled in a sharp hiss.

The voices returned, rejoiced, and exalted. *"The sinner is found! The sinner is found. The sinner is found!"*

All eyes fell on Matthew, who was blinking, hands clenched into fists, staring at the spectacle of his incrimination as any man might stare down the barrel of a gun.

He stammered, he tried to smile, some desperate recusal or protraction, before surging forward, his body jittering and lost. "We cannot believe this! The work of devilry. Or….or…" His eyes raked the crowd, desperate for alms. Not even his maimed seminarian would come to his aid. "We can't believe this. We shouldn't! This is…" His eyes found Vanessa's, and he fell still, bowing his posture. "I have nothing to confess to these creatures. The will of Satan has been exerted against me. That alone proves my righteousness. This is a test for all of us. Baseless accusations cannot lead to unfettered responses. We cannot give in. We shall not!"

He made this declaration and promptly fled the scene. Forcing his way through the throng of his fellows.

The bishop's eyes were groggy and blank as he fiddled with his pajamas. "Perhaps he has a point. God's messages are usually sweet. Jesus's grace and spirit…" The bishop waffled.

Lapointe scowled at his back, the rest of her flock joining her in this.

Chapter 11

NEVER one to let something go, Esther insisted again, "You must speak with the mother superior. The bishop—"

"Yes, the bishop, his word is final!"

"You have evidence," Esther whined.

They stood in a small recess near the outer perimeter, in an open-air hallway, its ceiling more like the gapped slats of a garden arch. The dismally overcast day ruined any majesty the design might radiate.

Arms crossed, Vanessa placed her head against a stone column. "I have suspicions. I can confirm the demonic message on the wall…but that information… The bishop already has access to it. We're all outcasts and strays; that's why we wind up here. He has known and done nothing about it. Now look where we are: haunted and hunted, swept up in a calamity."

Esther shook her head and inched closer, hazel eyes wide, full of fear and faith alike. "We must believe. Belief is how we differentiate what is good from what isn't—that is, the idea that we *can* do good for more than just selfish results. But from the activity itself…"

"Theology?"

"Practicality. If you can stomach it, Matthew has committed many wrongs. The power of our prayer, of us as a united front, can make those prayers a reality."

"What do you mean by *us*?" Vanessa countered.

"The cloister. If every nun demands it, Matthew will have to answer for this!" Esther's expression was like a blooming flower. Her naivety and clarity so beautiful it hurt.

It made Vanessa's heart bleed. "Esther, sweet Esther. If they rally behind him, it won't matter. The Church fears any scandal. They'll shuffle him along, cover it up. That won't be justice."

Esther took Vanessa's hands and brought them to her cheek, nuzzling her soft skin and peach fuzz against Vanessa's coarse fingers. "We must believe. We must try. Please speak to Lapointe. Do it for me."

Vanessa bowed her head, closing her eyes, a thousand thoughts racing and feelings bursting as a river overflowing, flooding and destroying everything in its broken path. Carefully she dammed up the shores and fought back the invasive tide. She reopened herself to the world. "For you," she murmured.

In one smooth motion, Esther lowered her arms and pulled Vanessa toward the superioress. A rising expectation urged them along two different streams: optimism and fatalism.

Mother Superior was behind her desk, rubbing her forehead. Was this the price of power? A queen sat on the throne, listening to the plights of her people. One after the other, the knocks had struck her door. Although she thought it might fall off its haggard hinges, it held fast. So did she. Even as an email hung suspended on her monitor, someone reaching out from beyond *the community*, reaching across the *years*, to ask if she was doing all right, considering everything being put out online regarding the odd little monastery beset by demons.

She still heard the echoing chant: "No forgiveness." The voices, the din they made, the silent echoing of that sentiment she gleaned in the eyes of her cloister. A migraine slammed against her skull; three Tylenols had yet to yield results.

The bishop should have held his tongue! she lamented. *If only the old codger had thought to wait!*

The sisterhood had but two options: side with the bishop and consider due process, whatever that might entail. Or trust the creatures. Which seemed more authoritative? What seemed to offer power and resolutions? What would Sister Cecilia advise?

Obeisance is a virtue, a blessing, and our charge. Yet the men make it so that it renders us invisible. Silent. Her frown deepened as she realized she was beginning to repeat the creatures' words in her mind. The unseen and unheard at last receiving their due. This angry, riotous voice had replaced the soft caresses of Cecilia's humming voice.

She cleared her computer screen, emptied her mind, and placed a hand upon her wrist's pressure point, seeking some inner peace.

Her door rattled with an anxious and urgent request.

"Please return in thirty minutes," Lapointe commanded. It sounded too close to a plea for her liking. "I have important work that cannot be put off." A truth, as she'd attempted to pen a letter imploring the bishop to take matters seriously instead of spurious dismissal before *that* email notification had distracted her.

"Please! You must hear this! You must!" Esther bleated through the door. "Please…"

Lapointe had heard many different entreaties and supplications. Angry or sacred. This carried a different tenor. "Enter, Sister Esther." She gave the permission begrudgingly but no less reverently. For all her pride, Francesca still knew why she had chosen the sisterhood. The service she provided. The women she wanted to protect.

In contrast to the banging, the door opened meekly, Esther dipping her head in greeting while Vanessa shuffled in, hands clasped at her waist.

Lapointe narrowed her eyes, "Sister Christina. I should have been expecting you."

The young woman grew fearful, her slate gray eyes flashing, her oval lips parting slightly. "Why's that?"

"You knew Matthew in New York. A large congregation. Here at the cloister, we're all intimately acquainted with how gossip functions."

"I have more than gossip, Venerable Mother," Vanessa corrected with a meek touch.

"Explain." Lapointe held her firmly in her stern gaze. She wouldn't worm away from this again. Things had gone too far for this young sister to cower any longer.

"The creature's mural lines up with when Father Matthew was reassigned."

"I already know this." She had spent the morning combing over such records. Finding little. Conspicuously little, considering everyone at the double monastery had some misadventure staining their past.

"Do you have anything beyond that?" Vanessa spoke with a more confrontational edge.

Francesca did not care for this attitude but found it odd how little hubris was held in it…only pain.

"Then elucidate me. Please." Lapointe's voice softened. She'd coax this information out. Vanessa was prone to fright, like a reed. No, a petite daisy whipped this way and that by the slightest wind.

"Online, I have seen accusations, the sort that nuns—women have difficulties making more publicly."

"Accusations?"

"In New Orleans, Father Matthew made inappropriate advances with local women, potentially breaking his vows. It was worse elsewhere, in Cleveland, in Los Angeles." She took a breath before continuing. "He forced himself onto nuns."

Esther's eyes widened. Now she understood Vanessa's hesitancy.

"And in New York?" The mother superior prodded.

Vanessa nodded. "I saw similar stories posted."

"You lived there. I want your personal opinion. Anecdotal or biased as it may be, tell me, Sister Christina." She knew gentleness would be an open door, so she employed a direct intonation.

This left Vanessa stammering, fighting back tears, and her lips quivering. "My opinion is he did the same things in New York. Based upon…Yes, we were all very scared of him."

"You were scared of him?"

"Yes."

"Even as he advocated for your sainthood?"

Vanessa visibly cringed. "I became venerated, gained notoriety, and was noteworthy. A good reputation…"

"I am aware, and that didn't last forever. Skittish, lazy, unable to complete your basic duties. You thought fame might make your life easy. Everyone wrapped around your thumb. Matthew thought you a miracle, yet you claim he was a terror upon the sisterhood."

Vanessa bowed her head, eyes closed. Esther could do nothing for her. Regardless, Lapointe flashed Esther a warning glare before returning to Vanessa.

"Yes, Mother Superior," the shivering woman admitted in a whisper.

Esther's heart sank. She imagined the boisterous, attention-seeking version of Sister Christina, full of solipsism and selfishness. She must have been radiant. Now she was penitent. *How can Mother Superior miss her earnestness? The sincerity?*

Lapointe continued her interrogation. "So you knew of him by rumor and did nothing?"

Vanessa shuddered: a sob, a fright, or a nervous tic—Lapointe couldn't tell. "There was ample worry he was breaking his vows. Was a threat to your sisters, yet you and your fellows did nothing?"

"There was nothing to do. No one would listen," Vanessa pleaded, unable to look up.

"Evidently someone did."

Here, Vanessa raised her head, eyes burning and red. "And all that came of it was that he was shuffled along to another parish! Where it all repeated! Every time they did nothing!"

"Who?"

"The priesthood. The bishops. Whoever was in charge!" Vanessa shouted before quieting herself, eyes averting again, the firestorm doused as quickly as it had arisen. "My apologies."

The wicker seat creaked beneath Lapointe as she leaned back. She was simmering, her expression conveying the ghost of a smile, eyes aglow and satisfied. "Do you believe the creatures are here because of him? These sins you have reported?"

Vanessa locked eyes with the superioress. "Yes. These sins and more, I'm sure. There's no doubt in my mind."

Lapointe processed this without expression before letting her eyelids fall low, her exhaustion reaching its peak. Now it was necessary to make a mutinous climb. Did she have the strength to do it?

"So you shall report him? Take this to the bishop?" Esther bleated out

Lapointe pulled her glasses off, gripping them tightly between her fingers. "I will do as I think is best for this convent." Then she softened, her grip relaxing. "I'll discuss these matters with him." Both nuns stood waiting expectantly. "You are dismissed," Lapointe ordered before adding, "It goes without saying that everything we discussed here stays in this office."

Vanessa's hand twitched as she nodded nimbly. "Yes, Mother Superior."

Esther gave only a passing confirmation before she rushed after Vanessa. The other woman was walking rapidly, nearly at a run. Esther had to hurry to keep up.

Vanessa didn't stop until she reached the tree, where she crumpled. She didn't sob; she merely sat—legs splayed, knees up, elbows resting on her kneecaps. She stared at an ordinary patch of dirt and that was it.

Esther wanted to weep for her. Even so, she knew that would be worse than useless, so she knelt and carefully touched the woman's shoulder, rubbing her thumb along the bone that became her collar. "Vanessa, things will be okay. Mother Superior will get the bishop to see reason."

Vanessa looked up at her with a vacant expression. "I wish I could have your faith."

Chapter 12

* * *

The next morning, Sister Mary and the other elders went to each nun and brought them the news. The pronouncements were the same for each nun. Esther sat on a bed while Mary occupied the chair.

"My dear sister, our mother superior has tasked me with providing an update on recent events. Regarding the worrying display referencing our own Father Matthew…" Esther sat forward with bated breath. "After a close conference with the bishop and his closest advisors, and with wisdom conveyed from the highest echelons of our Church, it has been conveyed that the proclamation of ill-intended impudent entities will not rattle the faith or the faithful." Esther couldn't register what she was hearing.

"Accusations and terror spread by such unholy creatures, even if with overtures of justice, cannot dethrone wisdom from on high or the tangible evidence of human intelligence. Father Matthew is a cherished part of our community. We won't denigrate or punish such a faithful servant of our Lord without due reason. We expect every member of this convent to heed these words and join us in prayer for Matthew and for God to cast aside these demons. He will reward us for our diligence and loyalty."

Sister Mary sat still, pondering if she had recited this speech accurately; it had only been her third time, and thus far, each sister had behaved differently, supportive of *innocence until proven guilty*, a court-like tenor, or indifference, simply waiting for the crisis to pass. Here, with Esther, there was abject shock.

Sister Mary pitied her. "Don't look so frightened. You 'e young. You think the world is in flux. It isn't. Things of this nature come and go. Sometimes more extreme than others. Why, even I thought the world might be done for when Covid struck. Yet, by the grace of God, here we are."

Deeming this satisfactory, she placed her frail, aging hand on the doorknob. Esther stopped her with all the grace of youth and passion. "But Sister Mary, surely Mother Superior understands the severity of this… *She knows.*"

Sister Mary fell into the patronizing tones of feckless wisdom. "Oh, my dear, these are the mother superior's words. She was apprised of all the details. She knows this is the best course of action." She placed her trembling hand on Esther's cheek. "Do as she bids, child."

Vanessa and Agnes were the last stops on Mary's route. Vanessa sat upon her mattress, with a fixed posture, hands at her lap, feet pressed to the floor, a few inches separating them. She studied the gnarled wood at the corner post of her bed frame, where it had become slightly swollen and wet; mold or rot, it eventually would cave in.

She offered no reaction, only a nod when asked to confirm receipt of the order. After watching Sister Mary struggle to her feet, she added in a soft tone, "Thank you for telling us."

In the hours that followed, Vanessa did her best to avoid Esther; she couldn't stomach her tarnished naivety, and she could no longer dwell upon the subject. More than ever, Vanessa wished to forget, to no longer be caught in the context she resided in.

By blue twilight's arrival, she ran out of places to hide. Esther brought her to the barrier wall, the one with the gap in it. The noise from the loading area gave them a blanket of privacy. "Oh, Vanessa, what are we going to do? They're letting him get away with this! The mother superior, the bishop, all of them!"

While Esther paced, Vanessa leaned against the damaged wall, her head hanging and her arms crossed. "Esther, we are all complicit. Even in our helplessness."

The nun froze in her tracks, "God have mercy on us…and the creatures We are all guilty…" She tilted her head, looking at Vanessa with wide-eyed terror. She could barely keep it in, the sensations rushing through her like ice so cold it burned her insides. "What do you think they'll do to us?" She dreamt up the scenarios, those claws, the bleeding faces, the creatures tying them up, cutting into their skin, branding them with every sin, not stopping even as the sisters' tears ran dry and the tracks ran red along their damaged cheeks.

Vanessa's chest tightened, and a dizziness like vertigo swept her off her feet. She was off the wall in an instant, embracing Esther, stroking her hair beneath her habit. "Esther, Esther, Esther, Nothing will happen to you. You are guiltless, sinless. Whatever happens, it is not you."

Esther shook her head as she gripped Vanessa. A woman cast adrift, trying to find a scrap to hold onto. She no longer was thinking of herself. She thought of what those…*things* would do to Vanessa, an angel, a would-be saint, weighed down by so much guilt, haunted by the past she'd fled. "I want to believe you, I do…but no one can stop this now. " *But I can try not to add to your tally.* This she did not say.

Esther gulped, her throat burning as she turned away from Vanessa. "I have to go. They'll notice if I'm late." She spoke flat as a board, unlacing herself from her love's touch and righting her attire.

Vanessa knew better than to breach Esther's boundaries. She needed space, while Vanessa feared isolation—that quiet, contemplative desolation. She stood, idling, listening to the sounds of the workers, the agitated grunts, the cheerful shouting, the invigorated truck engine. She craned her neck, her eyes grazing the intricate facade of the bell tower, pillars, the design works, the rest cut off by the building that bisected her view.

How much has come and gone since these stones were laid?

She sought to rediscover kinship and sisterhood, the simple joys and a sense of community. The reason she had taken her oaths in the first place, the connection, that magic they created, with song and faith, a unity that made her feel as though she were more than one mere mortal woman. Too long she'd been mundane. Too long since she'd seen angels. Too long in the absence of a miracle. *Beyond meeting Esther. Our beautiful little blessings.*

Her mind buzzed with remorse, with a hint of shame. She wanted Esther to feel safe. Yet she couldn't provide that for her. She was trapped, lost in a too-confined space, one that was slowly suffocating her. She could no longer remain idle

Vanessa roamed the halls, lost within herself. She found herself on the second floor, a balcony, with pilasters adjoining the more solid columns. Below, a few nuns cleaned the commons, so delicate when it came to the little broken fountain, pristine and refurbished save for the useless piping.

When she looked up, she saw Father Matthew, across the way, his eyes narrowed, his jaw set. Vanessa matched him in every detail of temper, if not worse. Her nails broke the soft skin of her palms as she refused to break eye contact.

Arm still in a cast, Kayden stepped into view, drawing Matthew away. The priest sent one last scowl in parting before disappearing within the bowels of the monastery.

Again, Vanessa stood stock-still, her mind at work, humming like a computer, heart hammering, an angry, anvil chorus. At last, the computation was complete. This time, when she walked the halls, it was with a determined gait, eyes scanning, tracking; she passed a little cluster of nuns, Agnes, Josephine, and Catherine—none of them would do; finally she found her prospect, Sister Elizabeth, by herself, her usual second half, Bernadette, nowhere to be seen.

Elizabeth was kneeling in half-hearted prayer beside a statue of a prostrated saint. The figure was all billowing robes and brilliantly sculpted lines, a wrinkled hood half covering the blank stare cast toward heaven, though in truth it looked as though she were averting her scornful gaze from Elizabeth.

"Might I interrupt you?" Vanessa began.

Elizabeth turned, pursing her lips, as she made some vast consideration. She shook her head almost absentmindedly. "No, uh, yes, we can talk. I was lost in thought…"

"About the news?"

"What else?" Elizabeth groaned.

Vanessa pressed upon this aggravation. "You felt it too?"

"Felt what?"

"That we are being made to shovel *merde*. Pardon my French," Vanessa declaimed with a duly conspiratorial inference.

Elizabeth's expression alighted, not with humor but with a suitable spark of passion. "Yes, *merde* indeed."

This was a tightrope, a little seesawing of balance and application. Vanessa needed to press forward, to let a little of that old persuasion come through, to gleam and glow—to light the way. "Are we meant to take it?"

Elizabeth rolled her eyes, much like the statue. "What else can we do?"

Vanessa smiled, an infectious invitation. "Make a fuss. What else?"

"We'll have to be smarter than that, Christina..." She pouted, her angular features pressed down to a single point like a greyhound catching a scent. "These creatures present an opportunity, don't they?"

"How so?" Vanessa asked.

The other nun shook her head. "Oh, never mind that for now. What's first is convincing the others. It won't work without all of us being of one mind."

I can do that, Vanessa thought: reason or emotion, or a greater plea of faith, of solidarity of sisterhood. *They will listen—too long have they been forced to listen and obey. Now, at last, we offer a chance to speak.*

In the meantime, Elizabeth coordinated with Bernadette, sorting through logistics, timings, and precisely the message they intended to deliver. Information needed to be distributed in small pieces, no one could know the full picture and subsequently risk the whole endeavor.

The cafeteria became a close, multifaceted conference room with plans distilled and set in motion. Such an intense, immediate reaction dumbfounded Vanessa. She didn't complain as Elizabeth took all the credit, lapping up the attention and praise. By nightfall, the collective effort had begun in earnest.

The next morning, the mother superior was awoken by a clamoring commotion, summoned to see a sight that made her go cold. Graffiti coated the walls, red wine spelled out bible quotes, and other phrases, even famous *feminista* speeches. Each laser pointed directly at Father Matthew and on the ongoing coverup, the signature following soon after: "***The Sisters.***"

Each morning thereafter was a fresh hell to wake up to—sometimes the afternoons and evenings as well—as more and more of the story came into focus.

These details were known only to Vanessa and Esther, as far as Lapointe was aware. "We must question them; if two or three confess and reveal the ringleaders, that'll be sufficient."

"But should we not first test their hands? See who's writing the messages?" Sister Helena offered.

She and Lapointe were walking through a second-story hallway, and upon hearing this, the mother superior wheeled about, hissing out a violent whisper. "Don't you understand? They're all behind it, taking turns."

Helena took this in, then furrowed her brow with an oddly calming comment. "The creatures have their own followers now."

Mother Superior fell into a furious silence; this wasn't a result she could abide. She stormed about the convent, personally seeing to her interrogations but producing not one confession. No matter her tact. Playing good nun or bad nun. Threats, collective punishments, and promises of rewards were fruitless; none of the women would break. Not even Josephine, who'd been so fragile following that frightful first encounter. Now she was hardened by determination and clever at playing innocent. Her angelic voice reminded Lapointe of Sister Cecilia, of so many memories that refused to stay buried. The mother superior fled the woman's cell and hurried along to the next. Only Sister Claire slipped up when she mentioned she'd heard the complaints from Elizabeth. "But getting her hands dirty with wine, you say? Ha, no, she's all talk."

Lapointe similarly couldn't see spoiled Elizabeth being the mastermind; however, she was her only lead. When she confronted Elizabeth in the workshop that afternoon, the sister, for her part, was aghast. "I certainly wouldn't risk my clothes with wine. You know I keep my habits pristine. You have punished me so many times for whining over chores. This is preposterous."

Lapointe scowled, hating how useless the sister's vanity was in a moment like this, an undeniable lightning rod. "Oh, but I agree. You can't possibly be coordinating this."

"I don't know if that should be a relief or an insult," Elizabeth chortled dryly.

Mother Superior ran her hand over a carpentry table full of the workshop's chalky dust. Her hand shook with barely curtailed annoyance, *the impertinence!* She'd lost control, and rebellion roared like wildfire in her ranks. The imposing visage of their savior, carved in pained wood, sat in the corner, a reminder of her duty. "I know it's Vanessa. Esther will have goaded her into it, but these rumors come from Vanessa."

"Vanessa? Leading this *protest*, as you called it? That's laughable."

"It's possible."

"Not really."

"Hmm…" Francesca hummed, removing her hand from the table, the skin coming away dirtied. "I never did call it a protest, Elizabeth."

At this, the younger woman paled.

The mother superior informed the bishop of these happenstances before the men could catch wind of them. The fact that the rumors had stayed contained to the convent a whole five days was a miracle…and a considered move on the part of the renegade sisters.

The bishop, ever pensive, agreed collective punishment was due.

Additional chores, lessening of foodstuff: "anything the local police or social media won't throw a hissy fit over. As near to the old days as we can manage. This has gone too far."

His banality was what unwound Francesca. He stood so calmly before his intricately crafted window, a dominating vista of the town, the craggy ravines and dusty sweeps beyond, and out farther to where the blue and tan met at the horizon.

She had intended to call the nuns' bluff, threaten them, and escalate by careful, measured increments. She'd expected to present these arguments to an immobile man. Now the bishop seemed terribly and cruelly vindictive. "Father, is it not possible to avoid this suffering?"

"That is for them to decide."

"Surely what Father Matthew is being accused of is of a graver nature?"

The bishop turned, locking eyes with her, and gestured for her to join him at the window. "See that down there? The man is fixing the family's car, and there, the wife is hanging laundry. There is an order to this, divine and pure. If she went to him and told him how to fix the car, it would break down in a day, and if he did the wash, the whites would wind up pink!" A smile crossed the man's lips as he placed a hand on her shoulder. He looked down his nose at her and spoke with a slight saccharine tone. "Let me fix our car. Hm?" He gave her a little pat before leaving her to imbibe the lesson.

Alone, with her back pressed against the wall beside the pane, Mother Superior considered a different engine, the one thrumming inside herself. The one beating within the walls of the convent, angry and sputtering, in desperate need of repair, left to neglect. She remembered how Sister Cecilia often spoke of sisterhood and *girl power*; she was such a creature of the nineties, blooming and rebellious. A troublemaker, a free spirit, a leaf flying through a perfect day. Lapointe had missed all the warning signs; she was shocked when Cecilia confessed she was leaving religious life. She wept as she stood at the monastery gates in Nice and watched *Cecilia* disappear from her life. Certainly, *Michelle Gasly* wrote her, wrote her rather often, of her life, (if not very often of her wife, whom she assumed Lapointe would despise on principle). She even wrote more recently to ask about the demons and all the chaos. She wanted to know how Lapointe was "holding up." No one ever asked her how she felt or was managing—she was meant to obey, never to feel. She couldn't confess the estrangement she felt from the mystical body of Christ, or those times when she'd admitted to Cecilia, to Michelle, the sanctified hypocrisy she bore witness to month after month.

The sigh of the existentialist rocked through Lapointe's frame as she peered through the glass. In the old days, before the sixties, before the Vietnam War, before her time, they'd each have been told to subdue their senses, to continue walking, and never to stop and smell the flowers, to look inward and never outward. They would be told to bind their chests and hide their feminine form, to protect their modesty, and to never ever have a particular friend. The decades had piled up, yet how much had changed? Told to cower and hide and ignore their senses, to be blind to what they could see plain as day.

She gazed out the window anyway. Not at the repair work as she was instructed to do so; instead she roved wherever her intuition led her. She swept across the vista of the town, tracking nearer and nearer, until she caught, at an odd little angle, a quiet secreted prayer spot tucked onto a second-floor balcony. There, three nuns, blanketed in the shade of sunset, passed out brushes and shared a bucket of wine, making quick, hurried work. One of them, dazzling as ever, was Sister Josephine, her quiet reserve giving way to that bright, searing passion so particular to her.

The Mother Superior couldn't help the smile that crossed her face, a lesson learned at last, the courage on stark display. *If only it would lead to a result,* she concluded ruefully.

Vision 7

THE ANONYMIZED protests and fervor of *The Sisters* grew as any conflagration might. The results were tangible. Matthew was becoming increasingly isolated within his cadre of supporters. And the more he withdrew, the more incessant the nuns became. They smelled blood in the water, guilt emanating from the men's quarters like a miasmic cloud.

The growing crescendo doubled and tripled, the stage set at last. All that was required was the final ascension.

It was a cold desert night. The wind crested lightly through the halls as Father Matthew wound his way back to his office, swaying slightly, his posture stooped and frustrated. His seminarian tried to console him. "This'll blow over. There's no evidence, and the women will grow bored. It's our generation—we crave gratification. It's an addiction, engagement, rage. They just need to come to their senses."

Matthew's head remained bowed, the shadows playing across the distressed sandpaper of his stubble. "You're wise for your age. But you still need sleep. Go and dream peacefully."

With the boy retreating, Matthew was left as a prominent shadow in an empty passageway. He stared at the gap beneath his door, where incandescent light reflected off a tiny tuft of white: a letter had been slipped under his door. It read simply, in a forcefully plain hand: *"Come to the bell tower. I know who has been spreading the rumors. Maybe if the truth comes out, the creatures will stop. Maybe then this can all be put behind us."*

Matthew read it over again, then a third time, as if to find some fresh insight, some clue to aid his decision. It didn't take him a fourth reading to formulate a conclusion.

With a flurry of robes, he carved a path back through the monastery, scanning every corner and each dark crevice for a glimpse of the creatures. Eager and rushed as he was, he had numerous blind spots. If only he had peered when passing the third courtyard, maybe he might have noticed…

He transferred from the flat structures of the monastic to the vaulted arches and voluminous splendor of the nave, then the cathedral's innermost guts, the artery of the tower, so separate and confined. Keys were required for it, yet the other priests had neglected to lock it once more. Grumbling, Matthew pushed the door inward and paused; something about the doorway and the close-knit double-back staircase beyond caught him off guard.

With a newfound hesitancy, he marked out his ascent slowly. The plodding footsteps echoed quietly, yet in the silence and stillness of the night, they were like canons. Each step was violence against the bell tower's dead air. Breathing itself was a sacrilege. Waiting, waiting, waiting…

The priest skipped over the final step, finding the square room beneath the bell empty at first glance. In truth, it was merely *stilled*. There in the darkness were shapes and equipment of some sort, murky outlines harboring no answers.

Matthew reached for the antique light switch. When the flickering, buzzing bulbs shot to life, he leaped back, his face a mask of terror.

Sat in the corners, braced against the walls, were the four creatures, arrayed, in order of their first appearances—Prudence, Temperance, Justice, and Fortitude—each docile, marionettes without their strings.

The dim amber illumination flickered, offering a dark silhouette. The young puppeteer stepped carefully into the thin light—the combination of each cardinal virtue held in the shape of a living, breathing woman.

Matthew's body grew rigid, hands clenching, his words a snarl, proud and full of radiant vindication. "It was always going to be you. I should have trusted my gut. I should have…" Reddening, as the rage consumed him, his hands formed into tight fists and he charged forward, boots thundering along the aged wood floor, his shout reverberating off the stone and the metal shutters, like a crusader's war cry

He made it four meters before his leg was caught on an unseen wire, his face widening in delicious shock as his world spun end over end like a top, though the surprise didn't strike nearly so hard as the wooden floor against his skull.

Matthew collapsed in an unconscious heap upon the splintered floorboards. The last thing he might have seen was Vanessa's smiling victory.

Chapter 13

ESTHER awoke with a pit in her stomach. As she reached her hand down to her belly, she knew it was no physical pain—this was a terrible, odious premonition. The creatures would be out that night. *I need to find them and get some answers.*

She had dreamed of a whispering angel. The glowing, glorious figure had beamed like a starburst at her unbridled love for Vanessa. A terrifying charity fell over Esther. She understood exactly what was at stake that night, even if she didn't know the details; the time had arrived, the hour was struck. But where?

She didn't know how accurate this thought was. She acted on the impulse all the same, heading in whatever direction her instincts and faith compelled her to.

First to the periphery and the dormant loading area, with that hole in the outer wall. Did the creatures sneak in using this weakness? She cursed her stupidity. She had been too slow and everything was already in motion.

In a panic, she gazed up at the darkened heavens and found a light above her, the bell tower that was so silent yet there! The dark shape of a human figure. No one would be up there this late. The bell was only used at noon;

otherwise the township complained about the racket.

Esther broke into a sprint, hands holding up her skirts. She entered the cathedral through a side door, which was mercifully unlocked. Of course, the obstacles would fall before her; she was on a sanctified mission, she was sure of it. Everything made sense: the accent, the anticipation, the dread, and the adrenaline—that all-consuming confidence of faith and worship…

Then nothing made sense for dear Sister Esther…

She stood in the arched entrance, her fingers limp, hands and arms pitifully extended, as if trying to push through the water. Her eyes blinked rapidly, as if attempting to wake up, trying to reconfigure reality, for she was in disbelief. Cognition failed. The sight presented before her couldn't be. There was Vanessa in one corner, tightening the ropes binding Father Matthew in place, a bandage at his head, red from the blood that had inundated it. Those four wooden creations, dead and unmoving, watched from the opposite side. This was the first time Esther had seen them. Without the carefully selected lighting, they seemed fake in a laughable way, fine pieces of craft, but nothing so terrifying as the creatures that had tormented the congregation.

"Vanessa…what the fuck is this?" Esther choked, fighting the lump in her throat.

Vanessa leaped back with a yelp, her hands pumping wildly, before she went rigid, "Esther…" It was a terrified murmur, her eyes at full spread, Eve caught holding the fruit.

"What are you doing?" Esther entered the bell tower properly, that great anvil above dwarfing her, making her look small and fragile. "Vanessa?" She was trying to piece it together. The sounds, the accusations, the logistics of operating the puppets, of smuggling in speakers… too many moving parts, and the haze of adrenaline and anguish making everything imperceptible and murky.

"I… I was… I'm…" Vannesa floundered, the words like gears with their spokes turned into ruts, unable to catch and hold, slipping and sliding away uselessly.

What did hold, by friction and firm grip, were her hands on the rope. The activity had been paused, not abandoned. Esther noted this blankly till the realization dawned across her expression, her stomach falling out from under her. "You're taking matters into your own hands, punishing him… The creatures, all of it was you. To avenge those he hurt. All those women…" Esther's speech drew into a quiet vibrato harmonic as if God were desperate to listen.

"No, not for them," Vanessa admitted.

A storm of a thousand increments played over Vanessa's features. Her body was numb, a buzzing hum in the drums of her ears, her chest a timpani. She felt the choir staring her down, the spotlight of her universe in the form of her love. No more fleeing, no more lying. For better or worse. She could speak.

With eyes gone glassy, chin turned up ever so slightly, lashes low, her head felt light as if she were spinning and falling, "Not for them," she repeated. "For me, Esther. For me." She blinked once then held entirely still. "He raped me."

Esther didn't know how to react, let alone respond, a wave of guilt rushing over her, drowning her. *I missed this. Every obvious sign. How stupid am I?*

Vannessa took every moment of delay as a nail, a crucifixion of seconds. "You don't believe me…" she concluded.

"I do believe. Of course I believe you. I'm just trying to process this." Trying to be strong, Esther fought back her tears. Watching this produced a similar effect in Vanessa. The two women were locked in a tight orbit, an eclipse as sure as any. "How?" she asked.

"In New York everyone wanted something from me, Sister Christina, the new Saint of Manhattan, a modern miracle. A young woman who might convert people with her magnanimity and inescapable gravity…"

It had taken years for her popularity to grow, her dissenters to crop up.

Vanessa reacted in kind, becoming defensive and calculating. Fame is fame, be it a tight-knit community or multinational, and with the religious, an ego can arise, even in one as benevolent as Vanessa. She erred, overextended. She wanted to help anyone and everyone. She discovered how well she could assuage the spiritual concerns of her fellow sapphics in particular.

The church was concerned about a cult of personality emerging. Vanessa, however, was clever and at every decisive juncture, chose servitude to the church over exerting her influence. This only made her more popular, her circle growing larger and more opinionated. So many supplicants shouted their wants and needs, in an endless calamity of charity.

"He was there with all the others, but I thought him just another devotee, a practitioner of God such as myself." Vanessa had been wary of him. She had already dealt with pedophilic overtures from men, and once she became an adult, things grew worse. She thought the convent and vows would help, but they only made things more obscured, more easily tucked away and ignored. "Matthew was unexceptional at first, and then... He became noteworthy."

"Why?" Esther shook where she stood.

Vanessa bowed her head, shame radiating off her in invisible currents. "He was kind and never did anything untoward toward me, I thought, like a fool, he must be one of the good ones. That's how he slipped past my guard. My recognition of his respect for me was taken as a *yes*."

They would often partake in close conferences, discussing their shared faith and the ways the Church had gone wrong. "He was so aware of so many of the indiscretions—he was proud that he had outed a pedophilic priest. He said accepting queer people would be a difficult but ultimately rewarding struggle for the Church."

Esther hung on every word. "He was lying through his teeth?"

"No," Vanessa said with a matter-of-fact apathy. "No one thinks themselves the villain. And at its core, if a pang of guilt gnaws at you, redemptive acts can be craved. Being a 'good guy' is a great way to lie to yourself."

"Vanessa…"

"I trusted him!" The tower quaked with her agonized outburst. "He was the reasonable one, the one who always listened to me complain… I almost came out to him, Esther!" Vanessa felt her voice rising despite herself, spitting out the words. "I thought Matthew, of all people, would understand. He was my greatest advocate…but I was blind and an idiot."

"You are neither of those things!"

"Look where I am!" she shook her head viciously. "I didn't even realize till he was…"

It was in his office. They had been reviewing the plans for a charity gala to feed the hungry. The desk had two red roses, a symbol of the nonprofit, bright and clashing against the subdued woodwork and modesty of his decor. Vanessa had been showing him the proposed pamphlet she had printed out—he read it over her shoulder and then…

"I didn't fight back; I didn't do anything. I wanted to reach up and claw at his face, but my arms, my body, it felt like moving a mountain…" Vanessa was sobbing and shaking, her hand still clutching the line of rope that led to Matthew beneath her.

"I'm so sorry." Esther put every ounce of sentimentality she could muster into those simple words.

"He said I never said no…but I did… I did… He didn't hear me…"

"You don't have to tell me more, not if it's so difficult having it bottled up for so long."

Vanessa sneered ever so slightly, "You're not the first I've told. I reported it. Recounted the thing so many times I've lost count. Even if it meant I was despoiled, I told the church officials about it, and they put it in some secret ledger. I asked if they believed me. They said, 'We'll look into it.'" Vanessa scoffed, between labored, furious pants. "Nothing came of it until, I think, other complaints were made or uncovered. I never knew them. He was sent away. And what happened to me was never acknowledged."

Vanessa was left to suffer on her own. The Church deemed this a charity, not punishing her for the sin, the act of coquetry that "inspired" the heinous act.

Isolated and lonely, she took to using a knife, hacking away angrily at pieces of wood. She slumped further into her night terrors and waking depression. When she could no longer perform her duties, she was shuffled off to Boston, where she broke down further. The new cloister thought her meek and incompetent. Once again, she had no one to turn to. She sent a letter to her father asking him to visit, and that's when she told him everything.

He raged and threatened to track down the priest himself or hire a hit man. Vanessa forbade these weightless claims. Instead, he helped her find a therapist and rented her a cramped apartment in the city. There, under his quiet encouragement, she pursued more carpentry. He gifted her the materials and the time. Soon she became excellent at it.

"In Boston I tried to stabilize myself. Stop from sinking further," he explained.

Although she poured her trauma and pain into her woodworking, nothing could fill the hollowness stretching out inside her. The speech therapy made it worse, reliving without healing. Her father couldn't afford more specialized treatments, and the convent refused to increase her budget.

Vanessa's work grew repetitious, the same figures over and over. She was spending too much time away from the Church with her father or else wandering the city during daylight hours in crowded, congested places.

"That's when they first threatened me with Europe, where I heard whispers of a double monastery Matthew had been shipped off to."

Her obsequious nature was gone, burned at the altar of all her pain, replaced by a plan, both devious and audacious. She enlisted her father's help; he had a friend in the film business who put her in contact with some VFX

Makers. They aided in the creation of her masterpieces, the perfect avatars for her vengeance.

In Spain, a clandestine sort of man was hired by her father "to accompany me with the equipment: speakers, wires, remotes, all the things that I would need," she told Esther.

Step by step, Esther was gathering the whole picture. "So you've been tormenting him, putting us all through this…this…*hell*."

Vanessa sighed, trying to formulate the reasoning in a way that might make sense to Esther, reaching and grasping for words and phrases, the way a child reaches for the first snowfall in winter, only to have it melt in their hands. "If I pointed the finger at him immediately, he would have known too soon. And he almost figured it out many times."

"But our sisters, what you put them through. What you put *me* through. The fear…the terror," Esther argued.

"The congregation deserved it. Not everyone, not Josephine, not Catherine, but you've seen the wolfish nature I raised forth. The cowardice." She tilted her head, amazed. "Only this past week have I had a sisterhood. Glorious and graceful. It wouldn't have existed otherwise."

"And me." Esther corrected, inching closer. "You had me. You had *us*."

"Yes, you above all…but I knew this would be too much for you." She limply held up the rope in her clutches.

"It doesn't matter now," Esther spoke forcefully, "You're at the end, one last fright to make him realize his mistake." Her words rang with desperation reaching for any solid purchase., but she came up empty.

Vanessa couldn't lie to her any longer. She closed her eyes and breathed deeply before confessing one last truth. "Esther, I'm not going to frighten him. He will never be redeemed. Never be forgiven. He cannot continue, cannot get away with it…"

Esther stammered wordlessly, taking a fateful step forward, the stalemate breaking down.

Vanessa matched her movements, striding as if to cut off Esther's path to the priest. "I promised my father theatrics and torment, nothing more. No one knows I'm here to kill him, except you."

"Kill him…?"

"Yes." Vanessa, there was no flippancy or naivety, only clear-cut comprehension.

"Vanessa, think about what you're doing." Esther held her plea tight to her chest.

"I have, for years." Vanessa bent down, incensed. She pulled the tether taut, yanking until her skin blossomed red with the pressure. "The only thing that saddens me is it can only be him and not the rest of the maggots feeding on our Church."

Esther's lips quivered, her world spinning around her, every bedrock, every surety crumbling. "Do I factor into this at all?

Vanessa couldn't believe her ears. "What? Yes, you do, why wouldn't you?"

"So if I told you to stop, to show mercy, to take the path of grace…to forgive him, you would? For me?"

"There is no forgiving him."

"Even if it costs you me? Our love?"

Vanessa floated across the gap to Esther, each step smooth and resolved, like silk, so soft that Esther's skin tingled. Saint Christina, no—Saint Venessa, anointed and in the flesh.

"You know it as sure as I do, in your soul. You know who I am. You know I am right. That I am righteous." The persuasion laced every syllable, burning with the light of a mandate.

Esther's chest hitched up, her fingers twitched, her mind ached, too aware of everything around her, the room so small, and cramped, the outside world lost to her. The desolation of faith or its salvation, she couldn't make up the differences.

Vanessa watched and waited, her heart peremptorily breaking as she prepared for the inevitable answer. What life had taught her, faith tried to resist, that all good things end, and bittersweet things were the only sure things. Hope, and prayer, wishing, and wanting, were means to delay the inevitable.

Esther recalled every fragile moment they'd shared: Vanessa's jittery nature, her alertness, the way she needed everything to be done gently and slower or else a minor panic might ensue. She thought of this and realized, in the grandiose ways of an existential crisis, what God was telling her.

Notice the real, not the saint or the sin, but the tangible, living woman before you.

Vanessa's voice replaced God's, reciting a bittersweet truth. *"You make me feel safe."*

Esther looked down at Matthew and knew.

"I do," Esther whispered.

"You'll let me do what I must?"

Tranquil, as a cool breeze, Esther shook her head. "No, we do this together."

The two nuns set to work bringing the priest to the window, opening the metal blinds ever so slightly, breaking one latch, shifting some of the refuse and clutter toward the window, crushing one piece underfoot, and adjusting the lights to dim the area. With a cloth, they scrubbed everywhere they touched, removing any prints. They fretted over the details, but a spotless scene would give them away. Just as long as there was nothing to tie them more directly than the others, that's all they'd need. Special attention was paid to where a few drops of the priest's blood had splattered; with that, the erasure of their presence was complete.

All the while, they kept checking, by sight or prodding, to see if Matthew had come to yet. He hadn't and never would. They undid the ropes, careful to leave no impressions upon the skin.

One final step remained: the defenestration of Father Matthew Elias.

"Ready?" Esther asked, her now gloved hands full of his robes,

Vanessa scoured the scene one last time, surveying it, taking it in, confirming every last scrap of context. "Yes," she agreed.

With a grunt of exertion, they hauled the unconscious body to the window. A breath, a pause, before they hoisted him up and over, pushing, letting go.

He toppled out the window, falling end over end, until he connected with one metal-tipped spire partway down. The force, the angle, the momentum ripped him in two, the entrails and viscera flying for meters in every direction. What was left of the corpse crashed into the stone of the entrance plaza, with the echoing splat of a water balloon and the cracking of bones like ceramic.

The sounds trailed off and the night was quiet again.

Revelation

THE SISTERS gathered at the nave of the cathedral, hands held before them, grasping their leatherbound folios. Sister Mary raised her weathered palms and, with a vigor and splendor of passion that overcame age, began to conduct the choir in a holy refrain.

Their words in Latin, the sounds so sweet, each woman giving it her all.

In the morning, just past dawn, they found the pieces of the corpse formally anointed Father Matthew. There were no chores to be seen to yet, no premonition or ill-tidying brought by a curious entrant. By the time a startled group found the mess, the carrions were already feasting, with a dog was among them. There was no fighting among the animals over the fetid remnants.

The choir continued to sing, Sister Mary praising the nuns, Sister Josephine wiping her eye, the bright sun striking at her so sharply. Sister Mary assumed her to be moved, and her enthusiasm provoked the others, even in rehearsal, to give it their full effort.

After no direct evidence could be found of foul play, the clergy was more than willing to spread the story of an accident. A fateful tragedy for one so faithful. A horrid end to the string of ill omens, discontent, and paranoia that had befallen the centuries-old establishment. With the sinner having met his end, and the torment abated, most were satisfied that the answers to his guilt lay in this demise. The faithful were ardent, and the rest thought it prudent not to question it. Lapointe, calculating as ever, thought to bring Vanessa into her office and dance around the subject of that night and the bloody finale that took place. She interrogated her fully, the interplay entirely in their eyes, Lapointe, putting her to the question, and Vanessa for her, part remaining composed. In this way, Mother Superior had her answer and pressed no further.

Since that meeting, Vanessa and Esther noted how their mother superior and Sister Josephine could be found among the less frequented hallways, lingering, near each other during the sermons and mealtimes. Josephine appeared to no longer wear the binder around her chest. Her fears over her modesty had settled at last.

Some had tears for the man known as Matthew. The bishop, and certainly Kayden, who wept and quoted the man's last words to him. While he spoke, the nuns, forced to attend the funeral for appearances' sake, sat with blank faces, not a single tear shed.

The young man continued, "I hope Father Matthew is dreaming peacefully now."

Not a chance in hell. The one good thing about the Devil: he knows how to give a monster his due. Vanessa glowered as Esther sat beside her, her expression a tight mask. Guilt pooled within her, right alongside a rising sense of glee. Her secret was safe, the deed done, and they had gotten away with it too! God blessed their actions with his mercy.

Lapointe was less overjoyed or remorseful about the entire affair. She wanted it to be put behind them. Whatever had happened to the priest and whoever—devil creature or angelic Carmelite—had had a hand in it made no difference to her.

The choir dipped low, voices straining against their vibrato, coiling, modulating, then falling in a sotto pattern, the rising crescendo beginning anew, amid a more rapid rhythm, made light and exhilarating by the sweet pitches and octaves demanded.

Soon after the funeral, the shock, like a slowly draining tub, began to dissipate. Vanessa took to watching the sky, something she hadn't done in many years. At first, she thought it was Esther's slender hand guiding her. But no, it was the sensation of a burden thrown off her shoulders at last. She accepted she was the one who had raised herself up. There were still nightmares, and she frightened easily; by that same turn, she viewed herself differently. No longer was she dominated by what Matthew had done to her or what she'd enacted in retribution.

Esther never spoke of that night, what she had been an accomplice and participant in. Questions and ruminations still played at her—a rising tide of emotion.

The closest she ever came was when she caught a private moment with Vanessa one day in September. The autumn colors weren't yet taking hold, so they found themselves at an arcade bordering a particularly lush green-infested courtyard.

"Vanessa..."

"Yes, Esther. What is it?"

"I needed to ask..."

"What? Is it…? Oh, oh, Esther..." Vanessa saw the emotion painted across those slender features. "You feel guilty. Don't feel remorse. Not in this."

Esther's voice trembled as she replied, "I feel guilty over my lack of guilt…"

Vanessa's face bloomed into a smile as she held the other woman close. "Then you have had the same revelation as I have."

"Revelation?"

"That we both know what really matters in this world, what God has given us."

"I do."

The women leaned in and kissed, perfectly silhouetted by the sun and the greens, and the black cut of the shadowed cloister windows framed them—their love.

* * *

The requiem Esther sang with her sisters stirred these thoughts of an absent shame, though they could no longer proliferate into panic. How could they? When she held Vanessa's hand, hidden by the clothes of brown and black and the sheets, they traced their way through.

She nearly had lost her part in the song, so enraptured by Vanessa's voice and angelic face...once more pointed toward heaven.

The Dead Breath of Night

"THEY say she arrived last week when it was foggy and cold." The stern voice took over the quiet room, agitated following the interruption, a father angered by his daughter's insistent curiosity.

From outside, laughter, raised voices, and crescendos of joy filtered through the nearby windows. To Sofie, the frivolity was as transparent as she was. Her father was proving this notion, enjoying his pontification—and she was meant to be grateful for it. Unlike most young women set upon their embroidery in comfortable silence or amid the usual gossip, she had been graced with her father's wisdom, a man's wisdom.

He thought it would make her more attractive to suitors if she were sufficiently versed in such concerns. Not to carry a conversation but rather to understand her future husband's wits and whims.

Sofie longed to be gossiping, braving the windmills of rumor to glean even a morsel. A new arrival in Amsterdam! A French Mademoiselle! Or so she'd been told. Needing more, she trampled her father's ceaseless prattling.

"Surely you saw her last night when you visited Mr. Van Der?" Sofie insisted.

Mr. Vevers waved his hand. "A brief visitation. She was courting others' attention, a little flock of ladies, those who feel cramped in their apartments and rowhouses this time of year."

Sofie blinked. Every other account she procured was far more striking. "But what was the *impression,* father?"

"She has beauty…but she's terribly pallid. It matters little, though. She won't be visiting long."

"Surely long enough to grace some estates outside of the city." *Such as ours.*

"My dear Sofie, one can never be sure with those touring. They are, to a person, nomadic, adventurous—not like us. I would hate for you to assume any sort of relation with one so itinerant. An acquaintance at best, no true friendship. I had that happen to me, you know, my British contact, Mr. Anders. We shared a summer, a whole three months. Now he can't bother to respond to my letters within an entire season!" Mr. Vevers let out a disillusioned tsk. "It matters little." He repeated that it could not matter to Sofie, not openly.

She was forced to seek other means, even those whose company she was loath to endure. Her aunt Debora was one such example, a creature of such open-ended ignorance one could paint any thought into her mind at whim. Similarly, what she unwittingly observed could be gleaned with the correct persuasive technique.

They were each plying their needles, reclining on settees in the pastel pink drawing room her aunt preferred, with its accents of gold, floral trims, more Italian than Dutch, ostentatious and nearly Catholic compared to what Protestant austerity demanded. Her aunt was going on about the seasonal weather. Sofie set down her work with a huff, using this frustration as the requisite opening. "And oh, what of the mademoiselle?" She spoke with a lightness, as if seeking a casual reprieve from her anger. "I hear much and more, yet so much seems like hearsay."

"Oh, the lady has been doing the rounds. She's been quite eager to visit with everyone and won't spend a single evening in her apartment," her aunt explained.

Sofie could hardly contain her intrigue. "What is it that she seeks?"

"Mending her poor luck, I'm sure. Just because a lady has passed the age of thirty does not end the interest in her hand. She has wealth, thousands a year. Yes, yes, there are still suitors out there," Debora chirped.

Sofie leaned back, the pastel blue furnishings seeming old to her of a sudden, far too baroque, outdated, outmoded, but what of this woman? Everyone sounded so invested in her, and she was a spinster. Or was she a widow? That would make sense of it all.

She pursued this line, and that evening, over supper, she begged her father to send her into the city and its society. "I know I made a bad impression, and I've apologized… Is it not best to try again? I've only just reached twenty. There is still time."

"But has the field grown bored of you?" Her father's snide expression matched her feeling of degradation. "Absence, perhaps, has made you seem more exclusive. That is the best we can hope for."

*   *   *

The foreign aristocrat had arrived in the city only a few short weeks before, yet Sofie Vevers had grown affixed to the thought of Mademoiselle Vervliet. She witnessed her twice, each time at an overcrowded soiree (done in the French fashion). Vervliet carried the air of the Frankish aristocrat so perfectly. Sofie knew much about their politics, with Napoleon III proclaiming himself king after a few years as president. Sophie's father didn't consider his daughter's delicate nature as he recounted the bloodshed of '48 and '49.

Sofie had sat in her armchair, head bowed, ostensibly to study her needlework, but the tiny beads of red fibers were supplanted by the sanguine tracers of blood, flesh, and warm bodies, hung off wood, sent into the gutters, soldiers, priests, and damsels too, the Parisians reduced to dead eyes and emptied corpses.

She never told a single soul how vivid her imagination could be. She wanted more pleasing fantasies, tulips, and a walk along the canals come spring. She should have been dreaming up an ideal match, yet he never arrived, in life or reverie. When she attended gatherings, she was careful to scatter her intrigue, never too committed to any one suitor.

This aroused a greater interest in her. She was so preoccupied fending off the frigate's worth of bachelors and gossipers who intercepted her at every opportunity. This personal clout and the prevailing mystique surrounding Vervliet were so thick that when they did cross paths, it began with an insult.

The occasion was held in an apartment along the Signal canal, near Dam Square. It was clustered and claustrophobic, and Sofie's closest friend, Angelic, had guaranteed her Mlle. Vervliet would be in attendance.

Angelic and Sophie talked in hushed, excitable tones beside the silent pianoforte. They held no secrets from each other, and so Sophie didn't disguise how eager she was to meet this woman, the draw of attention for so many. Angelic couldn't agree more, even if she wasn't as enamored as Sophie; she could try for her friend's sake to become so. Angelic, after all, enjoyed society, the games, the craftiness required, those dances both literal and of words, coquetry, and courtesy. She found the new arrival fascinating in the way she plied their shared trade.

Indeed, the woman reigned over a small court, eagerly clumped around her. Sofe caught her in glimpses. At first, there was her dark crown of raven hair, visible above the other women's heads, for the mademoiselle was tall. Her temple, devoid of wrinkles, was so very pale, pearlescent, yes, a perfect pearl. At last, a sliver of her face, the sharp, thin brow cut along chiseled bone, the skull, which drew everything toward that eye, dark and narrowed, seeping with intellect, wit, and boundless studied intrigues. Her nose was sharp and rounded in every right way, her chin so singular and jutting, the gaunt slope of her cheek riveting. Above all other considerations, were her lips, multifarious, red, deepest crimson, and then deeper still, with a supple sheen.

One piercing eye found Sofie through the crowd, and her heart ceased to function for a moment. She became very aware of herself, exposed by the lack of a crowd surrounding her. Billowing lilac petticoats, a fitted bodice matching the shape of her corset, her modest bosom pressed up by it, the top of those crests, and her collar, were bared without any accessory, displaying her vitality in every pink pore.

The mademoiselle's gaze raked up her neck toward her slender features. As a child, Sofie had been pudgy and rounded off, but adolescence had gifted her enough austerity to become beautiful. In a less timid creature, she would be liable to fall at any given moment. Her aversion was her safety net.

Here was the knife.

"Mademoiselle Vervliet." Sofie performed her most elegant and dainty curtsy.

"Good evening to you," the mademoiselle replied with the most powerful articulation of the feminine bow Sofie had ever witnessed. Regal and commanding. "However, you mistake me for French. I am Belgian."

"Oh, my, then what shall I refer to you as?"

"Maxime."

"Maxime Vervliet." Sofie sounded the syllables out.

"You make it into an honorific."

"Vervliet is so terribly pretty." Sofie batted her eyes, looking up for forgiveness.

"Indeed." The word was rendered guttural.

"How are you enjoying Amsterdam? They say you have an apartment upon the canal." Sofie was tiptoeing through her wording, matching any waltz.

"The water is rather stagnant, which in some ways I prefer over the roils of the sea."

"You know the seas? Normandy, or…?"

"Bruges, east of Dunkirk. Not so far from your Middleberg." The mademoiselle was dismissive, abrasive, and entirely aloof, yet what charm she suffused this disposition with!

Sofie didn't wish to leave her sentiment untended and spoke as earnestly as she ever had. "I have never been so far as that, though I have visited Antwerp."

Vervliet inclined her head forward. "A friendly place. Kind people. And beautiful in turn. The courtesy and grace of the French, in a finer allotment, culture meeting cultured land, if you understand my meaning. What did you think of the city?"

Sofie was taken aback—no one, in society or at home, had appeared so invested in an answer from *her*. She herself was guilty of asking questions without caring about the responses. The wit behind the woman's eyes, the intuitive way she drew nearer. At once, Sofie understood she needed a sterling *repartee*. Perhaps architecture could be her bastion. "I do so enjoy its structures, the rows of buildings, with their façades so aligned, and even those gabled roofs, like steeples breaking up the horizon."

Vervliet studied this determination, her pointed chin dipping in a nod. Before she could agree or disagree, a cluster of clucking hens interrupted them. The leader of this rabble, Mrs. Dallmans, detested the countryside and any city that wasn't Amsterdam. She was already moving the conversation away, even as she and her escort formed a blockade around Maxime.

Angelic swooped in to spare Sofie the embarrassment of stepping aside alone. "How did you manage the courage?" she asked.

"I dove in, like how you taught me to swim, I went in and trusted myself, my instincts, my nerves!" Sophie could hardly believe it herself, yet it had undoubtedly occurred. This was no dream but a waking reality she had helped to create.

"How pretty a sight!" Angelic declared, beaming ear to ear.

"Oh, yes, Maxime is quite beautiful, isn't she?" Sophie agreed, the thrill of the activity leaving her in a drunken haze.

"I was more referring to how excited you were. I haven't seen you that invested in society in such a long time. Oh, I felt such joy as a mere spectator."

Angelic and Sofie continued to review each detail, awaiting another chance to speak to the woman. None arrived, forcing her to retire, resting on her laurels.

Sofie spent the following day worrying over when she might see Maxime Vervliet again. She could call on the woman directly; their unfinished conversation would be her *raison d'être*. Just as this proposition propagated in her mind, a footman entered the drawing room to announce none other than Mademoiselle Vervliet. Sofie's mother introduced herself and brought her into the parlor to sit beside her, relegating Sofie to the sofa beside the window.

For several minutes, her mother carried on with hurried small talk, in her chalky, high-spirited manner. Vervliet humored her with trained patience, the one breach in this etiquette being the glances she sent in Sofie's direction. When several minutes ticked by without an opportunity, Vervliet pivoted her strategy entirely. "Might Sofie show me the lawns and gardens? Your estate is ever so lovely."

"They are dreadful. It's winter; that's how nature is," Mrs. Vevers rebuffed.

"And nature is lovely even in death," Vervliet countered with a rousing passion, as pointed as a dagger.

"Very well then, if you insist. Sofie shall be happy to provide a tour. Go on, dear, do not keep her waiting with your dallying."

Sofie flushed, irritated by the utter ignorance her mother used when embarrassing her. "Right this way, I like this passageway the best." She took them along a narrow hall decorated with a few landscapes of Nieuwpoort's grassy dunes, the walls a pale lilac.

"I believe I can gather why." The mademoiselle hummed, running a finger along a glass-topped sideboard.

Sofie turned, attempting to hide her reaction. She was seasoned when it came to a certain kind of soft-spoken ridicule, which made ingesting a compliment a rare prospect.

Outside, the gardens were well and truly dead, spindly, latticework being the sole reminders of vines and rose bushes. At least in death, they didn't putrefy as humans do, leaving the memory of their pleasant scents, Sofie concluded as she led them past the plots along the crunching gravel tract.

The rhythmic lullaby was interrupted as a swarm of bats flew from beyond the estate's grounds—a swelling, shadowy vortex, arcing and spinning through the pale sky. "Oh my, how terribly out of season! They have it all backward," cried Sofie.

Vervliet watched on with a hawk's keenness. "Not everything in nature is such a given. We used to know there were things beyond the explainable, that which must be experienced to be understood. Now the anatomists would have us believe there's a concise answer to everything."

"Their answers don't strike me as concise," Sofie countered before clamping her mouth shut. *What a rude way to speak!*

Maxime was unbothered. "Oh, you'd be correct, were it not for the holes in their understandings. Things that disprove them so thoroughly that it would make their heads spin! Why, even the concept of a continual adaptation is only now taking shape!"

There were far too many dangling threads for Sofie to grasp. Ultimately, the words produced a much more personal anticipation. "You know so much, far more than any woman I have ever known. Is that why they spread such rumors? Or is there another reason…?"

"Rumors?" There was something sharp hidden within the word

The young woman's eyes widened. At last, she broached what she feared might be a subject of some sensitivity. "You are yet unmarried. I have heard much in the way of idle speculation."

"Oh, I am sure they have been much more than idle. Women can be vicious creatures." Beneath her veil, her eyes were narrowed, reduced to dark glimmering pinpricks catching the stray light.

"Yes. They have been awful," Sofie admitted quietly, thinking with great resentment about the way her mother and sisters had spoken. Even Angelic had been at times cruel under the weight of peer pressure. They talked in chiffon ways, disguising their words, desperate to make them translucid. Inferences toward propriety, illusions about a woman's mastery over manners, and above all, the importance of keeping good company and setting a proper aristocratic example. "We must each ensure we spread grace and elegance. Discordance of even the lightest sort can bring such devastation to our quiet lives," her eldest sister, Babette, had insisted.

Sofie was left ignorant of what lay beneath the fabric of their words. She understood well enough, however, the disposition conveyed. It took everything to prevent her from snapping at them. From where had this protective urge emerged?

She squeezed her delicate hand so tightly that her nails dug into the soft skin of her palm, threatening to breach the seams of her flesh.

"The truth of it is awful as well." Maxime spread her words carefully, drawing out an implication from them. One Sofie immediately immersed herself inside. "There was a man who once courted me, oh, a decade ago or thereabouts. He made his money in Africa, even coaxed me to that continent."

"Oh my, how adventurous." Sofie managed.

"Tragic, I'm afraid. There was a great violence afoot. I even witnessed some of it. Nature, however, is what got the better of him, the lack of countenance on the part of a very large hippopotamus." Maxime stared unblinkingly. "He was hunting big game, but that beast was as big as a rhinoceros. It ground him into a paste. Blood was everywhere, along with too much of his innards. Clay and jelly. Bones like the shell in your eggs."

She slipped her gaze over to Sofie, expecting to see green fill her warm pink complexion. But no, her eyes were at full bloom, left in a raptured awe.

Maxime stared at her until the young woman recovered her senses. "That's awful. You have my deepest sympathy." Sofie chimed, unsure what tact to enact.

"I'm glad to have it." She continued their procession, Sofie stuttering back into the rhythm beside her. Eventually they came upon a stone bench beside the statue of a Mediterranean nymph. Maxime's gaze was still far-sighted as she spoke. "Have you ever visited Budapest or the mountains east of there? "

"The Carpathians?" Sofie offered.

"Yes indeed," Maxime affirmed.

"I only know the geography, I'm afraid." Sofie flushed a royal red, hands bound up in the folds of her lap.

"We each can only know so much." Maxime assuaged. "What piques your interest?"

"Hardly anything. The pianoforte, my needlework, the constant insipid gossip, and matrimonial warring. Perhaps I shall specialize in children. I do so regret how we tend to foist our offspring onto our staff. If I went through all the rigor of birth, I should not think to abandon my child so readily." Sofie averted herself hastily, fearing she had overstepped her mark within and without. Children, to her, were an abstract oddity that occurs after marriage, precipitated by the wedding bed and how greatly she feared it.

"I do believe we are in agreement. I, for one, think we should take great care when it comes to creation, cuddling without coddling, teaching without proscribing, giving appellation to the world and its wonders without inflicting its shackles. There's much and more out there past our basic perceptions and precepts." She chuckled. "Oh, but look at us, a pair of ladies, conjuring up dangerous thoughts, thinking beyond our prescriptions." She flashed a sly glance toward the house. "They wouldn't like hearing such words out of us."

"No, not one bit," Sofie agreed eagerly, stepping in closer. "Father insists on politics and my capabilities at listening, never my ability to speak on it."

Vervliet laughed, hearty and deep. "That is a shame, I do so enjoy the politick." She weighed the words down with a careful tint of mourning.

"By all means, please share your thoughts!" Sofie encouraged. "An outsider's point of view might be cherishable. I would find it nothing but the most ravishing of accounts." She faltered on that word, *ravishing*; it didn't fit; it wasn't proper, yet it had sprung into her mind and out of her mouth like an unrepentant need.

Vervliet smiled, flashing those pearlescent teeth, her full lips stretched so wide across her gaunt cheeks. "I took a terrible fancy in the spring of revolution; mind you, I was entirely relegated to the periphery, but it was nonetheless fascinating to see the women in Sicily rising up, then the French, the Austrians, the Hungarians, what a vivid circumstance! Bloodshed and warring!" Her oration was just as vivacious, her lips curling about her teeth.

With a start, Sofie realized that a pause was being taken on her account, a door left open, but he crossed the threshold readily. "That was eight years ago now. I was only twelve, but my father did furnish me with a few gruesome details. Nothing compared to the guillotines the *citizens* enacted decades ago."

"Certainly not! What a sight," said Vervliet before she abruptly tilted her head. "The one conjured in the mind's eye."

Sofie barely noticed the correction. She was hungry, starved, and craved this vague sensation of rightness. "To think," she began, "that a mere two decades ago, a short time before my birth, we were at war. The Belgians were revolting, the splitting up of the nation. So soon hereafter, a Catholic and a Protestant can stride arm in arm."

"A quaint thought, but you presume nationality falls to us. Are we not mere passengers on this locomotive?" The lady countered.

"You do not strike me as a passenger in any way. Quite the opposite. I sense the spark of agitation in you," Sofie admitted with an angled expression, an attempt at aversion, yet unable to properly escape either.

"Precisely so, Sophie," she cooed. "One small rebellion, one simple change, sometimes that's all we can do. Unhook enough moorings, and the whole ship can be freed. It's just a matter of starting small.

Sophie considered this as she would the fleeting candle, a flame she wanted to nurse to full fury. *One small rebellion. What would mine be?* She hadn't an answer, nothing tangible, at least. She used her words instead, staying on topic. "What of the now, the Dutch and our silly ways?"

Maxime simmered, a coy roll of her shoulders effusive and affecting. "I find the Dutch terribly slow to recognize this changing world. An entirely new thing is being born; those who fail to adapt will perish..." She lowered her voice to a tantalizing whisper. "That is nature."

*   *   *

They spent the better part of the afternoon together, and Vervliet seemed fatigued by the end of their walk. Sofie hoped the woman would rest and recover from the day given to Sofie and return to her soon. This notion was quelled when Angelic informed her, "Mademoiselle Vervliet was spotted at no less than three different parties last night prior, and some say she may have even ventured down the seedier parts of the city in the early morning hours."

For three days, Sofie stewed in the churning waters of this revelation. Although she'd assumed the farewell was genuine, her fear spoke a different tale: Maxime had grown bored of her in the span of a few hours, not a further thought given, while Sofie thought about her regularly, persistently, like an itch she couldn't sate.

On the fourth day, Maxime was there at the portico once more. Sofie invited her into a drawing room, playing a tender and delicate game. "It is a rather gray day out. Perhaps we might sit in. I could find some needlework for you?"

"I'm quite sure my fingers need not fidget, and besides, I don't suspect I shall be bored." She preened with such a conflagration of subtlety and boldness.

Sofie wouldn't be overcome by fickle sentiment again. She elected for the sofa offset a pace from the window while Maxime chose the chair set deepest within the room's shade, the veil still upon her.

They engaged in more or less vapid conversation. Sofie had forgone her embroidery, wishing not to insult Maxime after her earlier comment. Her hands, however, betrayed her, rifling and tooling through her skirt. She felt exposed; the shoulders of her dress didn't reach so very high, and her skin prickled with goose pimples from her neck down toward her bosom. It was the fashion, as was the narrow corseted hip, before the ballooning skirts. Maxime was, on the surface, more modest with her kid gloves and the handkerchief at her décolletage, in the style of the previous century.

From her style to her manner, there were so many intriguing counterpoints wrapped into one woman. Sofie was determined to know every note of Vervliet's chorus and held a growing panic as their parting drew nearer. She needed to cast this relationship in stone. What could she offer besides her most guarded secret?

"Such an alive spirit are you, and yet no man has laid his claim upon you?" Vervliet commented, opening wide a breach that Sofie could charge through.

"They do try so hard. The fault is entirely mine… Melancholic maladies… I'm prone to them. Bouts of terrible sadness. Sorrows I cannot explain." Shame pooled with a cursed heat at Sofie's cheeks.

"Oh, but you are such a bright creature!" Maxime contested.

"Is not the wilting flower of beauty more captivating for it?" Sofie related in a dour tone. "Certainly my suitors seem beset by the noble anticipation of curing me through their affections."

Vervliet stared down at Sofie, an illegible glowering traveling her sharp features. "A noble cause indeed." The phrase sounded almost like a lamentation. "I think I've found the most interesting person in Holland," she murmured.

Sofie flushed again. Flattery struck a nerve more undoing than any mere compliment could. Only she couldn't pinpoint which one precisely was being activated.

*   *   *

From that day forward, barely an afternoon went by without the two women seeing each other. At gatherings, they'd be spotted latibulating upon the couch farthest from the dance floor. Sofie would invariably be pulled away by one suitor or another. With each spin or twirl, her eyes harkened back to Vervliet, and each time, without fail, Maxime was there watching her.

When Sofie invited Vervliet over for dinner, she scarcely pecked at her food, choosing instead to sip lightly on her wine, claiming a delicate appetite as the culprit. Sofie wasn't so sure, for Maxime stared with such hunger. Or perhaps she experienced all of life so thirstily.

No one else seemed to notice; her father, Mr. Vevers, took it all in stride, joking and jovial. "Well, more supper for me. I do like to eat like a Hungarian!"

Sofie was rocked continuously by a feeling she assumed to be envy. She modulated her disposition toward an aloof vision of revelry as if to place herself within and without—an objective observer paired with the intimate context of subjectivity. She relived her earliest memory, seeing for the first time, understanding what it is to wake up, comprehending the difference between living and dreaming.

Those lines had never been more stark. When she slept, she saw only Maxime, and when morning arrived, she was left disconsolate, concerned with instinct's reactivity, an intuition that didn't feel like her own. The reveries lasted into the day, the figment of her unconscious imagination haunting her. The days blended steadily into the shimmering mist of obsession.

A singular crack in this status quo arrived suddenly through an invitation to the final ball of the season. An honor Sofie had never received before.

She spent the entire day preparing, her hair bringing the greatest anxiety. "It's marvelous, as are you," her lady's maid assured her. Yet Sofie still sighed, disaffected. There was a need for perfection, and every brush stroke served the greater impetus. She wore a cerulean blue dress shimmering and silken (an exquisite gift from her father to reward her newfound societal success), her radiant golden crown all the more dazzling, the sun set upon a fine day.

Vervliet was the night itself, pallid, cold, and dark.

Sofie was at a loss for breath, taking in the sight of her. She foreswore common courtesy and flew across the grand ballroom as if there were a tether reeling her in. Only by Maxime's side did the suffocating darkness disappear so she might breathe again.

They passed the evening in the presence of several members of the government, and they held a keen interest in Maxime. She stoked a powerful intrigue that drew in the affluent and scared away the shy. Sofie considered herself of the latter category but dared not shrink away; in fact, she clung to Vervliet's proximity. Even if she wasn't allowed a word, she'd give everything just to listen and be near her. Besides, the quiet afforded her time to contemplate, aligning the last remaining pieces of kindling the flames desired.

That heat alone couldn't abate the darkness that sought dominion. Thoughts that weren't her own, dark, violent things. This anger wasn't entirely sated by proximity alone. When fellow guests approached and made their society with Maxime, Sofie considered hideous conclusions. For all their newness, they didn't spark her conscious as fabricated whole cloth, rather, they were untapped urges within, long resting beneath the surface.

Sofie didn't know whom she held more disdain for, the men or the women.

In either instance, she meditated on what it would be to see them bleed, gutted, quartered, or without their head. Yes, they wouldn't be so talkative then.

Eventually she was separated from Maxime, engaged as ever by the twirls, two steps, and waltzing with men who spoke past her, seeking a soothing, coaxing sheathe at the end of a bland courtship. The ritual was an odd, demanding supplication as though she were an impervious gatekeeper, a Sphinx with which they couldn't riddle. Oh, if only Liam De Vries could have his eyes put out, the sanguine mixing with the white gunk and pouring down his hallow cheek like tears. That would finally silence him, wouldn't it?

When at last the fifth routine in a row concluded, she rushed for a glass of wine, eagerly searching out her dear friend. Alas, the volume was devoid of Vervliet, that singular presence.

Close to a panic, Sofie struck down one hall then another, yet no study or lavatory gave way to her query. She was about ready to give up when a small sensation—a whisper along her nerves— rifled up her spine and drew the peach fuzz upon her nape. At once, she wheeled about and stalked with alien confidence to the end of another passage, finding a small room filled with paintings half covered in sheets—a gallery caught between states of dress. One settee was exposed, its muslin sheet tossed to the floor.

"Ah, I do apologize. I needed relief from the spectacle." Maxime's words were coy and silken.

"Is it so great as that?"

"Well, I should think you require a larger card, that is for certain." She countered, an edge biting at the fringes of her disposition.

Sofie hurried to Vervliet, her hands unsure, then very much so, as she took up both of Maxime's. "Whatever is your ailment?"

Those dark eyes cast their sight out to the gardens before returning to the work half-denuded before them. A woman standing at the edge of a bluff, the ocean spread before her, a white *beudo* clinging to her skin as it wafted in the harsh wind.

"I only wish I might have joined you." The lady silenced Sofie with a preemptive tsk. "You, not some *man*. You. To dance together. Ah, would that not be fun?" She smiled affectionately around the words, her body from her head to her hands, adding subtle inflections to her words. "Alas...."

Sofie had danced with her cousins since childhood and Angelic as well. With how grandly she and Maxime got along, why it would it be untoward in the least? *Then why, oh why, does my heart keep hammering as a cannonade? Why does her nearness bring dryness to my throat? What's the heat doing deep within me to stoke such passion? Why does every single confusing sensation roiling through my body share a commonality? Why does giving appellation to this disease bring such giddy excitement? Mademoiselle Maxime Vervliet. Mademoiselle Maxime Vervliet. Maxime. Maxime. Maxime!*

"Alas?" asked Sofie.

"You were busy." The words came out like silence, a thought within Sofie's mind.

"I had no choice." Why did she feel such a need to defend herself?

"You could choose. Indeed you chose not to."

"I...well...that's not entirely fair." Although Sofie was breathing hard, each articulation felt shallower. "Maxime, it's not so simple as you make it out to be." The violent thoughts raced through her mind afresh, her fingers scraping at Maxime's skin.

"Then what is it?" Each word was drawn out, and every ounce of sentiment was laced within their lettering.

Sofie had no more words, only impulse, the rush of air as she crossed the gap between them till her lips landed on Maxime's, and her eyes fell closed in raptured sensuality.

There was nothing hard about the kiss, the world became desperate and soft as Sofie pressed in further, her neck craning, her hands unsure what to make of themselves. Everything collapsed into this singular sensation. For the first time, she understood the poets and their obsessions.

Maxime brought a hand to Sofie's shoulder, to her collarbone, the thumb running against Sofie's throat. For one moment, she reciprocated, meeting Sofie's measure, deepening the connection toward a hardened, incisive purpose, a groan reverberating from the depths of her diaphragm, transferring to Sofie like an earthquake.

Her hand shoved Sofie aside as the lady stood up abruptly, the back of her hand at her mouth where Sofie's had been but a moment prior.

The young woman was gutted, the absence instant. Left in a blizzard without a coat, a cold she couldn't comprehend, her body and heart reached through the white hell. "Maxime," she whispered, tears brimming, fear reigning.

In a cutting profile, the mademoiselle gave her a sidelong glance, her eyes ablaze, the dark recesses nearly red with fervor. While her body was still, there was an energy to it, like a line holding a man-o'-war, readied to snap. Maxime was furious and disgusted. Oh, certainly she was, for why would a creature so elegant and perfect demean herself with someone so lowly?

Without a word, Vervliet flew from the room, a flurry of skirts and the staccato two-step of heeled shoes. "Maxime! Maxime!" Sofie cried as she pursued her until they rejoined the party proper, where she was forced, even in this state of crisis, to cater to expectations. "Mademoiselle Vervliet!" It didn't matter what title or name she used; the damage was done. She'd embarrassed herself, and Maxime hadn't stopped, hadn't so much as flinched.

Alone, unmoored, and with so many eyes upon her like a crushing weight, Sofie bowed her head and retreated. She dove into the cool night blanketing the gardens and hurried through the hedge maze, finding an isolated bench far from the party's glowering light. There she wept until she had no more tears to shed.

*   *   *

In the days that followed, Sofie feigned illness as the arbiter of the ball's disastrous episode. No one believed her, so obvious was her bereavement. Heartbreak uprooted the physiological, and she was indeed physically ill, crying until she vomited, her eyes dried out as she stared into the fire or read through another tragic work of verse or sonnet.

If she had only shown modesty and humility, her beloved would still be here, walking the lawns, chatting the days away with her. The agony and torture of being so near was a marked improvement over this terrible absence.

February faded, the promise of spring leaving a hush over the land. Sofie was too exhausted to grieve in the same vicious manner any longer. Yet, she dared not return to society at this time. As for Maxime, Angelic offered up the news unprompted while trying to keep Sofie occupied with the pianoforte. "They say Mademoiselle Vervliet has taken to the country; that's why she raced away that night, no? And to think she left at such a poor time. I think your spirits would have been roused to have her as a nursemaid!"

"I need not be coddled. I need not mourn her absence, for I am better off with her gone." Sofie finally reached for anger, and it was a brilliant flame. Her rage brought her fingers harshly against the ivories, a discordant minor chord echoing through the music room. "She can have her adventures. I have my life here."

The fury lasted the day, carrying into a fitful slumber until her dreams betrayed her. She awoke in distress, her body craving what it would never know. She ran a hand through her blonde hair, smoothing down the loose mane, and adjusted the single thin braid her maid had laced together among the waves.

She sat at the edge of her bed, quieting her breathing, bringing her articulations in tune with the wind. The night was a cool comfort, fresh air prickling her skin. How odd this draft, she was positive her lady's maid had bolted the window. Yes, just after twilight, she complained about the chill, but really it was the incessant sound of the bats that had disturbed her.

How, then, had it come loose? The curtains curled around a dark shape projected through the translucent muslin.

Sofie blinked and squinted, peering, searching, discovering…

Maxime, there, within the frame of the open window, her silhouette mollified. Sophie blinked rapidly, the mirage too brilliant, a dream too cruel to wake up from and face such a bitter disappointment as reality. Yet, the image persisted, and the figure stepped further in. The unusual moonlight bathed them and permitted sight, the wind kicking up smoke from the slumbering fireplace.

What Sofie saw wasn't kin to any vision she'd conjured. Maxime wore a uniform that was utterly foreign and entirely scandalizing. Her tiered skirts billowed around her legs, its cloth cut down so that it hugged the sides of her long limbs and collected at the back, leaving her legs bared, the long boots she wore with their latticework of lace, the tops gripping her exposed thighs, the bodice much the same, cut down to pieces. What remained accentuated her every curve and pushed up her pillowy bosom.

As Maxime stared down at Sofie, the young woman became startlingly aware of herself. She curled an arm nearer to herself, her forearm at her navel as if to guard her lack of modesty. Sofie wore a simple chemise, collected under her legs, pulled tighter by it, her breasts straining against the thin cloth. The woman's eyes slipped along Sofie's form. Further heat pooled into Sofie's cheeks and down below, where she pressed her thighs together to stifle her need.

Vervliet stepped nearer, and as she did so, her portrait shifted, each line and bone hardened, rippling with jagged edges. Her eyes held no white within them, only black and deadened gray. But with her elongated fangs bared, the arched crease of her brow, and the rippling of taut strength throughout her body, she was beyond alive. She was feral.

"Sofie, do you comprehend what this is?" She spoke with a Siren's soothing.

"How can I?"

"But this is what it is to love me." Maxime simmered, reaching out, cocking Sofie's head forcibly to an acute angle. "This is what it is to be consumed by me."

Sofie was lost at sea, a swirling torrent inside her. "Why did you leave me? Were you disgusted by me? Or was it shame?"

"Disgusted by you? Shamed by you? Silly girl. It's better this way. Surprising you…finding you like this, at the end of your mettle." She ran one long finger over Sofie's cheek, possessing her skin.

"You waited just to toy with me?"

"There were arrangements to be made… Is this moment not all the sweeter for waiting? Are your thighs not slick with excitement of a kind you've never known?"

She was right. Of course she was. Sofie was helpless to discredit her.

The woman looming over her cooed, tracing a digit down her slender neck, dipping along the valley that formed the nexus of her collarbone, coasting a thumb over one erect nipple through the sheer fabric. Sofie whimpered as Maxime's hand crested her navel, scoured the pronounced hip bone, and collected the shift, hiking it up.

Maxime grabbed at Sofie's exposed thigh with such an iron vise that the bubbling flesh began to bruise. The shock of it raced along Sofie's nervous system. She'd never experienced such glorious pain as this, peaked and enticing, nothing like agony or a fall from her horse. This was a symphony's crescendo—she couldn't know it was but the overture.

Her eyes were in full bloom as her heart waged a percussive war upon her rib cage. She was sick to her stomach with fear and anticipation. Her eyes were pressed firmly shut to blind herself to everything she was craving. By that same token, she leaned into Maxime, her head nuzzling against her right arm, which wrapped around her back to hold her aloft.

"Oh, what a beautiful angel you are," Maxime loosened her grip on Sofie's thigh and pulled her legs apart, garnering the access she craved.

The cool air upon her sex made Sofie shiver. Those spindly fingers shifted nearer and nearer to the dripping folds, two digits slowly separating the lips. Again, Sofie quivered, looking up through slitted eyes heavy with captivation. Maxime bent over her and planted her lips upon the young woman's, and Sofie's body rose to match her, to prove her love to her.

When they pulled apart, Vervliet was panting without breathing, a trickle of saliva falling over the red throw of her glossy lips. "Time to fall," she whispered.

"Please," Sofie begged.

Maxime smiled, baring those fangs again, her chin tilting downward as her eyes, at last, fell upon her true target, her need, her want, her hunger…the waiting meal.

She dove down, her teeth piercing the tender pink flesh of Sofie's neck as her fingers penetrated her. A paired motion. Pain and pleasure. Two needles, two fingers. Sofie's back arched, a scream dying in her bleeding throat as Maxime began to feast on her, sucking the very blood from her body, as below those fingers worked her interior, a thumb flashing over her bud, sending a fresh wave of heaven to fight the devilish suffering.

Dewy tears bubbled and spilled from the corners of Sofie's eyes, pressed tightly shut. She wanted to flee from the objects inside her, intruders who wouldn't leave, giving and taking in equal measure. She wished to lie to herself and pretend she didn't seek and crave this.

A low groan, the sort of guttural noise she'd never made before, seeped from her lips as she rocked her body in tandem with Vervliet's ministrations.

Despite her lightheaded weakness and growing fatigue, Sofie raised one arm, riffling her fingers through Maxime's raven hair, urging her to dive in deeper with her teeth, the pathetic thrusts of her hips begging Vervliet to increase her haste.

The iron smell of blood filled the air. It was gushing now in dark spurts, a trail lacing its way along Sofie's collar and between her heaving chest. Her vitality and arousal fought for expenditure. She tasted it in her mouth, the combination of her lust and her life entwined. Her world became these points of connection, a universe of nerves and shuddering bliss, an ecstasy the poets knew nothing of, a bursting shooting star none had glimpsed except her and her lover.

The onset of her crisis was so sudden and encompassing that it forced Sofie's eyes wide as full moons. Sightless, the world was a wash of blurred figments—a painting dying under an assault of water while still fresh and unsettled.

Death is what it felt like to dear Sofie, her body clinging so readily and warmly to the heated coals of a beating heart. Her grip couldn't hold, not as the spasms overtook her, not as Maxime held her so tightly, invested in her, at the neck and between her thighs. Sofie imagined the union of these two opposing sensations melding inside the kiln of her belly. That is when she was lost to it. A sound escaped her parted lips, somewhere between the groans of agony and the moans of pleasure. She let go of herself and her body, and everything became like the bliss of a contented snowy day.

Maxime pulled away from her, her chin dripping bitter ichor, as she caressed Sofie's, flush and pale all at once. Her shuddering, panting breaths rocked into Maxime's unmoving form.

Sofie held but one desperate thought as her hand pawed at the lace of Maxime's mantle. She used this purchase and the last of her strength to hoist herself upward and place her mouth on Maxime's. There, she tasted herself, the blood of her veins, and her virginity. She kissed that all goodbye.

Her strength gave out, and she fell away, for she was woozy, her head spinning, pain, blood loss, and ecstasy forming a thick cloud of fog. As Maxime hung over her, imperious and without animation, Sofie fell into the surest of slumbers.

Maxime murmured wordlessly over the girl's fainted form, eyes latching on to where the sweat made the shift cling, where Sofie's belly rose in the gentle rhythm of living. Oh, what jealousy, to peer upon the living! What a fractured state of existence she was reduced to. What power she found in it, what glorious prideful glee.

She settled on this exaltation and rose. Carrying the limp Sofie by one arm, the vampire transferred her from her bed chambers and out of the house to an awaiting black carriage. The driver was wordless as he opened up the velvet interior; the horse let out but one bray as it was stoked to activity.

Within, Maxime spread Sofie over her lap and brushed out her tousled golden hair with her fingers. Her quiet humming was the only sound within the dark expanse Sofie traveled.

*   *   *

It had been weeks, nearly a month, and Mr. Vevers was beside himself. His daughter had vanished in the night, the day before like any other, the morning after a terrible, empty calamity. The sight that greeted the maid had sent her into a stuttering bout of hysterics. The sight of a murder. That's what everyone who saw it told Mr. Vevers. The doctors admitted no one could lose that much blood and survive.

While his family fell into grief, he remained firm and, in his mind, clearheaded. He would find her even if it cost a veritable fortune, even if no one believed him. One night, his wife stated in as clear words as she dared,

"Husband, can you not see the truth of it? Everyone at the ball saw how upset Sofie was and how Mademoiselle Vervliet abandoned her, the mourning she fell into…. Our daughter was always a melancholic creature."

He couldn't bring himself to consider this answer, just as he couldn't face his enemy, the monster Vervliet who had recklessly thrown his daughter into despair.

On a pale afternoon, amid this mounting stupor, a knock arrived at his door: a familiar face, Sofie's best friend, Angelic. In the parlor, she spoke in a rapid falsetto, explaining how she'd been dared to visit Vervliet at her estate, where she hadn't been greeted by so much as a footman or a maid. So she patrolled, her eyes pointed upwards, searching, seeking, as she wound toward the back lawns. That's when she spotted her, Sofie, framed within a third-story window, peering down at her with a peculiar, illegible expression.

Angelic had been a more stalwart nurse to Sophie than anyone. Her closet companion. Angelic had been so happy that Vervliet had awakened Sofie's joys, but she never thought it could send her tumbling back down. She feared the worst. But what could have precipitated such a heinous act? What betrayal could lead one to...to do that to themselves or another? Angelic had her answer when she thought of what she would do to Maxime Vervliet. She had gone to the house under that very impulse, frenzied, unsure, violent. Yet that spark had died like a fleeting ember when she saw her dear friend alive and imperious up in that window!

"I shouted to her and pressed upon every door until my limbs were sore but to no avail." She pressed in closer upon the sofa, her hands bound up in Mr. Vevers's. "You must believe me. I've known her since we were children. I know her face better than my own. It was Sofie!"

He contemplated this for a singular instant before calling for his carriage. Angelic's pleas to accompany him fell on deafened ears. This was a matter for a father and a father alone.

Maxime had acquired an estate from the Dallmans. Dark and decayed as it was, Mr. Dallmans was loath to part with it. Only an uncannily convincing presence could persuade him, ruminated Mr. Vevers as the carriage bundled along. His Sophie had become so instantaneously intoxicated by Vervliet. She had enveloped him as well, soothing the old soldier in him, uncoiling his arms, letting the set of his jaw go slack, in so many ways she'd ensured him that she was a fine friend to his daughter. All while intending to abduct his flesh and blood. The tension was back, contorting his body, the scars cut fresh, anger burning a molten trench through his veins aided by adrenaline. He was a fool, he who disbelieved the queer shadow of rumor that surrounded the mademoiselle from the beginning. He'd done so for his daughter's sake. The poor, sorrowful girl was exactly the vulnerability that predation fed on. If only he had been more mindful.

No matter, he assured himself. He would arrest his daughter back and ruin the name of Vervliet once and for all.

His vehicle turned onto the narrow gravel tract leading to the manor. Despite the bounties of nature blossoming throughout the countryside these lawns were desolate, with only a few patriotic outcropping of tulips.

The house itself was compact in that very Dutch way, three stories with a steeply gabled centerpiece leading to an angular cupola.

At the door, his nerves got the better of him, and he slammed the wrought iron knocker again and again until, at last, a servant answered—a butler dressed in a waistcoat, pale and withdrawn.

"I've come to see my daughter. I know she's residing here." The man blinked at him, refusing to answer one way or the other. "I demand to know if my daughter is here…." Again nothing. "Show me then to Mademoiselle Vervliet. Do not underestimate my stamina. Not when my daughter's very soul ais t risk." He tried to make the words sound threatening.

The tall reed of a man was immune to such pathetic overtures. He turned, moving with a lethargy like wading through shallow water and disappeared into the house.

Culled like a mutt, awaiting his true mark, Sofie's father followed the butler into the foyer and deeper into the belly of the manor. It was as yet unfurnished, and what bright pieces remained were covered and set against the wall, while those articles in place were each dark and velvet, with red being the penetrating color, glistening gilt, and vivid in the dim light. Each shutter was done up, with a few expectations opened only at their tops, the light reflecting softly off the ceiling.

This dreadful march ended when Mr. Vevers was abandoned at the top of the stairs, left to the eerie silence and the singing that flowed in and out of it. The melody, the humming duet, and the laughter echoed as if emanating from an uncorked dream.

Cautiously he stepped down one dusty hall before turning down a much longer corridor, terminating in a slightly brighter room warm with candlelight.

Two forms flitted across the doorway, appearing and disappearing in a flash. Quick enough to make Mr. Vevers's heart jump in his chest, his shoulders hiking up.

This was wrong, terribly wrong, but he couldn't stop watching. Again and again, the two silhouettes danced across his limited view. Their dresses caught by the wind they created with their revelry.

"Sofie!" Mr. Vevers called out. His terror made his throat weak and cracked.

The tapping of heels ceased at once, and a lone figure appeared in the narrow aperture, tall for a woman and even more imposing in posture. "Ah, Mr. Vevers, I'd thought you might visit. Please, this way."

Mademoiselle Vervliet gestured him into a side chamber. The room was bare except for a pair of armchairs and a sofa. Vervliet chose a seat near the low-burning fire, most of her features hidden deep in the room's penetrating shadows. She plainly ignored his aggressive posturing. Indeed, the way she positioned herself was like a bowed arrow, at any moment ready to be unleashed. Daring him to provoke her.

Mr. Vevers's hands went clammy, his every instinct recoiling, retreating as the heat in his veins petrified. He modulated his tact, submitting to his fear. He sat at the edge of the other chair, the thin sunlight at his back. With his hat still clutched in his hand, he made his case. "I know she's here. She was spotted in the window. My dearest daughter…" His words trembled and he forced a pause. "Was that her just now?"

"A dance partner? Are you sure?" Vervliet sat lazily with one arm propping up her cheek, a moue of pity dotting her marbled red lips. "And who claims to have seen her here in the first place?"

"Her dear friend Angelic—I dare not disregard her words, for she is too innocent to lie. The same cannot be said for you." He set his jaw and glared at her.

"You know as well as everyone else that your daughter and I had a falling out. I'm terribly sorry she has…vanished, but are you sure *I* am the culprit? What evidence have you? What motive? Beyond seeking the company of a beautiful soul?"

"An unnatural desire, a perversion of nature. Do not pretend otherwise, vile creature. I have heard the stories of what's left in your wake. I wanted to trust you for the sake of my daughter. So that, at last, she might have a friend to make her smile and help her take charge of her life." He gripped his hands as if life were nothing more than a steed to command. He shook his head, his face red and full of adrenaline. "You are no friend to her and your name will be poison on anyone's lips, God as my witness."

"Enough," a voice spoke from behind him and to his right. He recognized it instantly as the soft, high-pitched tone of his daughter.

She materialized out of the shadow, her dress as black as Vervliet's.

"Sofie!" Her father rose and took one step forward as if to rush to embrace her. This sentiment died, replaced by anger, hands balled into fists, the ligaments of his arms taunt, as if readying to inflict a stinging punishment. "Where have you been? Why are you here?"

Sofie furrowed her brow and narrowed her eyes, a hand held up against the light, but the sun wasn't enough to dissuade her; that would come later in the process. She wouldn't be bested by it yet. Nor her father's fury. Delaying her response, she maneuvered past him and sat on the sofa where the light met with her skin, a pallor not her own at all.

Her complete dismissal of his wrathful posturing took the wind out of her father's sails, forcing him to take pause. "Are you unwell, Sofie?" he asked at length.

"Not in the least," she assured him as she clasped her hands in her lap, her posture more regal than ever. He would see; she'd prove it to him. But how could he not tell already? She glanced toward Vervliet, finding the necessary encouragement in her steady gaze. "In fact, quite the opposite," Sofie added as she peered down at herself.

"But there are other things to discuss," she continued, meeting his gaze dead on. "If you want to be included in my life, I'd love that more than anything… Take this estate"—she gestured to the room—"it needs care and attention, the right sort of decor given our limitations, but I think Maxime did well finding it. Oh, what plans we have—the gardens—I want to find every flower that blooms in the moonlight. That will be spectacular, don't you think?"

Her father blinked at her, stupefied and broken. The pit in his stomach fanned out into a greater void. "Plans for the future?"

"For forever. Maybe not here. Still, we have plans." She smiled, and when she did so, it revealed her fresh canine teeth, of a kind to Maxime's, though not nearly as grown yet.

Her father's heart sank as grief found him at last. As he stared at what used to be his daughter, his frown descended into a grimace, then a snarl as he glared once again at the fiend responsible.

Maxime, for her part, let out a snort.

"Father, please. It is not her. It's not." Sofie's voice grew higher, more desperate.

Mr. Vevers replied with a furious exhale through his nostrils, his hands bending his hat. "Sofie, my sweet foolish daughter, you don't know what you're saying, you don't understand what you think this is… It isn't so. It isn't. Please come home with me. Let me see if the damage might be undone."

"Damage?" she whispered.

"Yes, Sofie, yes! You are ruined! Destroyed!" he bellowed, rising to his feet, painting his daughter in his shadow, save for half of her pale portrait.

Sofie's eyes widened as a tear spilled out over her bloodless cheek. "I am not. I'm not. Father, can you not see? Your Sofie is finally happy."

Twilight in Tinsel Town

THE BELL rang so rapidly that it bled into one crescendoing arc. Shouts echoed before everything fell quiet. Only a gentle hum remained—*flip, flip, flip*—like paper rushing as fast as a machine gun. The clip of a woman's heels overrode it: timid, careful steps until a prolonged pause, frozen in place. That's when the screaming began. Bloodcurdling, ear piercing.

It was awful, hideous, obnoxious. She was playing at it, the gorgeous blonde in a tiny red slip, now covered in fake blood. Her cords would get time to rest while they cleaned her up. And they'd dub it all over in the post. Still, Clive Henderson insisted on it. He wanted to be the author—or auteur— whatever the French were calling it now. Henderson was a step above Ed Wood, hence his ability to work on a backlot, but he wasn't Hitchcock, and the producers didn't let him near any real talent.

That wasn't a penny to me; I just jotted down my notes and clicked my stopwatch, judging how many frames each scream lasted—anything to make the ADR go smoother. Not that I'd get any gratitude for it.

One more shit show then something real. That's what the producer, Anthony Richards, had promised me. They needed continuity bad. Clive was loose and risqué in all the wrong ways. You could have antics—everyone did— as long as they were off the lot and out of the rags. The studio heads wanted movies made and making money. The rest was a means to an end, and they rarely lacked imagination when it came to inventing means.

This was quid pro quo in the most servile, decrepit way. I was all of thirty-three and had survived too many rounds in the ring. The judges were ready to call it for my opponent.

But I wouldn't let Hollywood win, not yet. Not when I was better than eighty percent of the people who got along just fine and got their promotions and their laurels. I didn't need their advantage, or the Oscar or the riches, just what I was owed, what I deserved. Others cared about the intimacy, the excitement, the enraptured masses. Their precious illusion would be shattered in an instant if the lead's bonnet moved from a right-quarter turn to a left-quarter turn between the wide and the close-up. That's where I came in. That's where I disappeared. My job was to be invisible and missable. Fuck me if I wasn't good at doing exactly that.

This flick wasn't going to be winning any awards or breaking the box office either, for that matter. Yet it held a kitschy charm, a creature feature perfect for October. The suits. The silliness. The hijinks, and the bedlam. I'd have easy stories to tell over drinks. Hell, I could recite the whole script if I wanted to, given how many times I had to feed the actors their lines.

Clive yelled cut, and Henrietta Langford scurried over with a grin, the flush of exertion on her cheeks. This was all one dress-up game for her. She didn't have the kind of looks that really got men going, and her charm was wasted on them. Mostly she was earnest. I envied her boundless naivety, marveling at how uncorrupted she was.

With the reset in progress, I approached Clive. "We need to keep notes on the blood. You want your close-up of her death, don't you?"

"No, no, not death, transformation? Jesus, haven't you read the lines? *Script girl!*" Henderson still clung to old terms.

Stowing my aggravation, I replied blankly, "The audience will think she's dead. You want to sell that."

He was startled to find me already beside him. Recovered, his face dropped into a wrinkled sneer. "If they're too busy looking at the pattern of blood and not her breasts, mankind has failed me," he retorted.

Before I could make the mistake of talking back, there was a commotion at the far side of the sound stage. Four strapping boys from the prop house were carrying a wooden crate with strips of packing paper sticking out from its lid. They were led by the prop master, Nicky. He was a fairy with a fine tweed cardigan and a little lilt to his wrist as he gestured to the box. "That last little bit of spectacle I promised. Harder to find than the Japanese hiding in the grass, right boys?" No one responded to his faux machismo affect.

I was entirely too preoccupied with the crate. It emitted a smell, a tantalizing musk, like sulfur and brimstone or bourbon easing down my throat —and a good vintage at that.

My hand reached out of its own accord, fingers splaying off my notebook. The crate had been damaged. Little trace works of black soot ebbed out in weblike patterns from the gaps in the wooden slats—no, not webs—lightning, spiked and jagged, layered so thickly that it became more Art Nouveau than Deco.

But how could I make out the tiniest details, of millimeters and less when I was still a foot or more away—

"Just plop it down over at the altar," Henderson grunted.

"That'll be in the shot!" I protested. "We dolly from the altar to the antechamber. And what we shot yesterday—"

"Can it, Margaret. If it's anything close to what Nicky here promised, it'll be a sight prettier than you."

My jaw locked in a smiling grimace. I returned to my rickety wooden chair and checked my notes, foot and pencil tapping in a two-step, making a point of ignoring the activity taking place beside the stone slab.

"Margaret, are you missing something?" My head shot up, and I looked around. The voice sounded familiar, a feminine voice, taffeta, icy. But the only women were those tending to Henrietta.

My eyes caught a flicker that stood out among the glimmering set. Oval shaped, made to look like obsidian, smooth like an egg, just large enough that I could wrap my whole palm around it. At its center, it was carved up into a square, intricate labyrinth. The piece was inset with rubies, sapphires, emeralds, and more. It would be worth a fucking fortune, if were they real.

It rested on a dais, and I could see Nicky's handwork, his desperate need to replicate the tiny thing, yet it was impossible. He was too much of a hack, and this relic was the real deal. It *fit*, like the moment when an errant detail is put back into place. The same inherent sense of rightness led me to recognize the kitchen counter *just so*. Well, this object was exactly *so*.

The thing was just an egg, yet thinking about it so blithely was a hideous crime. How could it be *just* anything when it was *something*. I had no thought or direct rationale, only the tactile feeling, like an instant attraction, the overpowering feeling in a museum when an art object conveys the sublime.

There it was, a few yards away, small and tantalizing.

Our actress returned, her skin chafed from whatever noxious chemical they used to clean up the blood. The next take bled into the next, and five long hours later, the day was done, with the last stragglers packed up and trickling into the backlot ahead of me through the side door. I slowed my steps until I stopped completely. In the silence, I stood and waited in the oversize mausoleum, more silent than any grave, the heavy insulation stilling the air. I heard my breath, so sudden and frightening, mouth breathing, not my norm—I was panting. But how? I was staying put, so why? There was an answer in my gut.

One I ignored.

Outside, the sun had dipped below the curtains of the San Fernando Valley, leaving the world in lavender. The air was perfectly temperate. Deciding to savor it, I had a particular urge to sate, a craving not so different from sex but entirely more singular.

I pulled out my cigarettes, tapping the box on the leather to parse out one stem, my teeth hooked on it, my other hand dancing on the lighter, its bright stalk glowing and real as opposed to those outdated carbon arcs and their stifling heat. Supposedly the film couldn't afford to use tungsten lamps alone, yet the arc lights sapped up more juice. Probably a racket by someone halfway up the chain.

After another drag, the heat ballooned inside my chest. It wasn't enough. I needed wine and my wife, anything to drown out the headache. My body, however, couldn't be bothered to move, not yet anyway. A stalemate, a standoff, stagnation, procrastination—take your pick, darling. I was rooted to the low-rise concrete of the pool. Walls and water could be added, a damsel sent out into the water, and meet a nasty fate at the hands of a tentacle-laden monster.

Or a romance, I told myself, lovers holding on to flotsam for their dear lives, confessing their undying love and adoration. If memory served, the next feature to use it would be a war drama. Set during the Second World War, when we so clearly knew who was bad and who was good, instead of searching for red-blooded Commies in our cereal. This was Hollywood; most of us only had to roll over in our beds to find someone quoting Marx or Lenin.

I breathed out, my cigarette long since expended. The moon was up, and the amber glow of the city lapped at the darkness. Nearer were the bright work lights between the sound stages. Their reach was poor but still bright enough to note the dark silhouette passing by, in the shape of a woman wearing a dress and hat with the posture of tiptoeing in heels. She was followed by the more rigid figure of a man with another feminine form clinging to him.

Had tourists snuck in again? They constantly invaded, in sundresses and polo shirts, let in by the ticket they purchased, happily flaunting their souvenir visitor passes, getting in our way demanding attention, grasping for a tiny glimmer of starlight under the scorching sun. Or trespassing at night, for kicks and thrills, or simple robbery. This trio, however, was marching toward a specific destination, stage twenty-two, the same place I'd just put in my ten hours. Why would anyone risk a felony for cheaply painted sets and a child's approximation of the grisly?

Why indeed? Even a dull intrigue was more than I'd expected from the evening. I stalked the Three Musketeers at a weary distance, leery of confrontation. I didn't carry a truncheon, only more curiosity and impulse than sense.

On the stage, one woman raced toward the lighting board and eagerly threw the massive switches. I dove behind a bit of cover as a few beaming arc lamps burst to life. I wanted to count to ten but only got as far as seven before peeking around the crate's edge.

The three of them were nearing the altar, illuminated from the sides and with their backs to mel I couldn't make out anything beyond how sharply they were dressed, he in a suit and the women in fashionable dresses that were better suited to a cocktail party than skulking about quiet sets. None of these people were hurting for money. Why were they here?

Reaching a better vantage meant crossing a no-man's land of open space. Going around was my only option. I removed my heels and fell into a painfully low crouch, disappearing into a forest of wires thicker than my arms and thirty-foot-tall naked plywood. At the back of the set, I landed at a dead end. I'd chosen the wrong side; every entrance for actors to strut into the scenes was on the left.

I tapped my foot and the light shifted, catching the dark sheer fabric of my pantyhose, dim and dull, but there nonetheless. Dropping down onto my belly, I discovered a gap beneath the wall, through which cables into the guts of the set. At the far end, I made out heels and polished leather shoes.

Who dares wins, I thought as I entered the tunnel. It was full of dust and splinters, and my scalp scraped on the hard surface above me. My stockings tore loudly as a protruding nail dug into the tender flesh of my calf. I bit my lip and forged on.

At last I reached the end. As I tilted my gaze upward, a swell of triumph flooded my chest as I was rewarded with a proper view of the interlopers: Buck Taylor, Janet Moseley, and Greta Bennett. Some of the most important pieces of talent in the studio's roster. They represented a combined box office reach that was hard to fathom, and here they were, studying the perplexing little egg with an enraptured urgency, rapacious widening eyes and hushed reverence, each more eager than the last to study it.

First Buck looked it over, his fingers cresting its intricate ridges and rises. Then Janet cupped the smooth underside with her palm, wavering this way and that. When it was Greta's turn, she held it close to her chest from the top and bottom. My heart hammered as I watched the display of beauty, the three stunning people, and that perfect object.

Greta smiled, serene and exuberantly blissful. That's when the first jewel began to glow, its green light catching in her golden-blond locks. She giggled, the relic bouncing in the gap between her sizable breasts. Another burst of color, this time red, matched Janet's crimson mane. That red-haired vixen took a step toward Greta, bending down to place her lips upon the obsidian. As she did, a gentle humming filled the room, filled…me. From my muscles to my bones, I felt the tenderest massage. But the sensation dispersed as quickly as it had arrived.

Frowning, Janet attempted to kiss the artifact again, to no avail. Frustrated, Buck arrested the item and looked it over again. The way the red and green light spun and rolled over his chiseled features made him look like a demented Christmas elf.

They went back and forth, each trying in vain for the better part of an hour, sometimes arguing, sometimes forming dismayed proclamations. I had a miserable time making out their words from this distance. "Come on, we can't be any more late for the party!" Janet shouted loud enough to carry.

Whatever little mew Greta replied with was lost to me. Buck was in control of the object, grasping it between his meaty palms. He turned on a dime, his head whipping about, searching, finding his mark. For all his height and muscle, he possessed a certain elegance as he stepped away from the altar, aiming directly for me.

I couldn't breathe. Any instant now, he'd discover me, and what then?

At the last moment, he stepped off to my left, producing a key from his pocket and opening a little compartment built into the set. "Dearest Nicky said he'd stow it for us, not leave it out."

"Oh, I think he assumed no one would sneak in here," Greta defended.

"Besides, it made for a better shot, didn't it? Janet said before spreading her arms wide, spinning, encompassing the whole lair. "The three of us beholding it at last!" She paused her spin cycle and held her arms out to the egg.

"Less beholding, more unlocking. But we have plenty of time." Buck placed the egg in the hidden recess and locked it. The damning click silenced any hope of my possessing the little relic.

They left. I stayed. For a while anyway. But I had no means of breaking the lock, try as I might, and I'd be missed at home. Very missed.

*   *   *

A short, furious drive later, I pulled up to our small, one-story house, a nearly identical twin to the one beside it and across from it. GI Housing—cheap, earned kicking the Krauts' asses.

We'd done what we could to make it ours. We'd made a lot of changes really. None more so than *her.* She filled the doorway, dressed in a gingham pastel-red checkers that matched the house. Amelia's sparkling blue eyes held too many questions. I stood on my toes, closing her advantage in height, and planted my lips on hers, trying to answer a few of them.

161

"What was the hold-up?"

"Oh, just dealing with Clive trying to murder the script, and then I forgot my notebook. It was just one thing after the other really."

I stepped past her, shrugging off my purse and heading toward the living room, where the radio was babbling on about a toxic chemical spill off a highway pass. "…just past Santa Clarita. Officials are recommending commuters and travelers avoid any roads in the vicinity for the foreseeable future."

Amelia folded her arms in front of her chest. "Nothing else?"

Frowning, I turned down the radio and faced her. "Just a regular day at the office."

She didn't reply. She didn't need to. One stale look was all it took to dredge up all my past mistakes. I hadn't always been faithful or committed in the ways I should have been. I'd nearly thrown it away, this miraculous, beautiful thing we shared. But I'd made amends long ago and over and over again since. Trust was fragile, and try as you might to repair it, the cracks still showed.

We'd met after the war. She'd been at Normandy, then the Pacific. I'd been exactly where I always had been, LA. I helped build fake cities to distract potential enemy bombers before taking care of the domestic side of things. The boys were away at war, which left me with so many options—trysts, affairs, flings, and love, or close to it. Then Amelia sauntered into my life, and I fell harder than I ever had, in a way I never imagined I could for a man. But he was different, so very different, in a million ways impossible to put into words. They peaked through in those darkest hours of the night. After he had finished worshiping me, I'd feel his trembling body and not understand such vulnerability. He was a decorated war hero, courageous and fearless, the very definition of a man, yet with me, he felt so broken, shattered… as if every piece might crumble like pale porcelain.

"What is it, my love? Is it the war?" I asked at last one early morning before dawn could breach the curtains.

"It's the war inside me" arrived a quivering whisper.

"What war is that?"

"The part of me that says I should stay like this, happy with all my luck. And the other part is begging for more."

"What more do you want?" I asked.

There was a long silence, meeting well with the murky light. "What if you called me Amelia? Like the pilot." We took it one step at a time from there. She'd gone under the scalpel, a sex change. I'd had to pull strings for her, and we couldn't do it stateside. A vacation in Europe sufficed.

We were still legally married, and while she technically wasn't my wife, I still saw her that way and announced it as such. My pedantry was my work, not my free time. Besides, seeing people perform a double take was always a show. At first I'd been treated with cloying sympathy, as if I'd lost my love. Turns out I'd only lost a few friends.

I joined her at the wall separating the living room from the kitchen and laced my limbs around her waist. "There was something. An odd prop…. It was…unsettling, I suppose."

"It's a horror movie and you don't spook easily."

"You're right. It's just…" I rolled my eyes. "It ruined my continuity, Nicky and Clive were so excited over it. They stuck it right in the middle of the set."

"Ah…" She dragged out the sound, satisfied she'd found the answer: my meticulous perfectionism. "Are you hungry?"

A hundred images flashed in my mind, recent memories each. "Starving but not for food," I whispered, taking her wrist and pulling her toward our bedroom.

*   *   *

* * *

It was murderous, trying to concentrate on silly details no one could gave a shit about. I didn't either, not when that cubby was hidden just past that pillar, tucked in under that fake boulder. Waiting, kept from me.

Clive mourned its loss. "I liked that prop. It was the best damn thing on set." He glared at me. "Well, I guess you're happy now."

I wasn't, not until night fell and the trio of actors snuck back in and set to work. They cracked the next step within three nights, passing it rapidly between one another, causing two more jewels to illuminate. That's when they started staying longer. Each time, their moods grew more hurried. By the seventh night, they began having sex, the three of them, with the relic being used in the act. By the tenth night, I joined them from afar, my hand caught between my thighs, another at my breast, my teeth making my lip bleed as I tried to stifle my moans.

The smell—oh, God, I think it was the smell, like sulfur and a woman's arousal.

Greta was better at fitting the egg inside her than Janet. It responded better to her as well, leaving Miss Mosely in a constant state of jealousy. I too boiled with envy, thinking of how they were nothing compared to me and how the egg would react better if I got my chance with it. I could crack it. I would. I would. I would.

Buck tried to play mediator at first, but soon enough his favoritism was obvious, coddling and caressing Greta, giving her more attention. He urged Janet to do the same, to show her the same affection and pleasure she'd had before the gap had formed. Janet, for her part, gave in. I think the relic helped with that, responding well when the woman descended on Greta's folds and suckled upon her sensitivity. Buck took Janet from behind, and the image left me groaning, the hum in my ear a thrumming chord vibrating throughout my body. I was each of them. I could feel his cock in me, and I knew what Janet's tongue felt like, what Greta's arousal tasted like, and most of all, I sensed the heat of that egg.

I just needed the real thing and not some illusory reverie.

Greta's belly glowed, a cornucopia of color, a rainbow. Then she screamed. She shoved Janet away and threw her legs to the floor, doubling over beside the altar, her hands working at her stomach and her vagina. Her howling continued, even as she pried the egg out and sent it falling to the floor. The small object rolled in a tight circle, awash with light and steaming with heat.

Buck and Janet rushed to Great, holding her gently, trying to calm her down. "It burns!" she shouted.

"You're sweating. You're burning up. But Greta, we can't see anything!" Buck answered.

"It's inside…what's happening… It's.." Greta convulsed and clasped, falling to the floor, her body leaning forward, contorting too far, so far that every vertebra in her spine could be seen. Each bit of bone moved and shifted like a snake, skimming below her skin like a whale, ready to breach the ocean's surface.

She threw up a bioluminescent mix of blood and orange ichor. Then her entire form shuddered, and she fell limp, the glowing heat still filling the lamp. "Greta! Greta, baby, talk to me," Janet wailed.

"Come on, darling, wake up. Wake up. It's okay. It's going to be okay." Buck enveloped her in his thick arms.

They were so wrapped up in their tragic little show that they'd forgotten about the relic entirely. This was my chance at last. *At last!*

I burst out from under the set and sprinted for it. I didn't scream even as it burned my skin; I tucked it into my elbow and brought it in close, like a running back protecting the pigskin. Voices followed in my wake. I had to escape this place. *Get out. Get out.* I couldn't let them have it. Not when it was finally mine!

Buck gave chase, running me down. Just as I reached the door and shoved it open, he grabbed my arm. I reacted on a dime and brought my knee up, catching him in the groin, then slammed the metal door into his perfect face.

I ran through the backlot, scrabbling in my purse for my keys. I drove with one arm, the egg cradled in the other like a babe. I only calmed down when I merged onto the freeway and my breathing normalized. The sweat and the excitement bled away, forming a serenity I hadn't known since my second wedding night when Amelia and I renewed our commitments in the gentle darkness.

She tried calling out to me as I burst into our home, charging to the bedroom. "Just one second, baby!" I called out as I dove toward the closest, found my densest shoe box, and replaced the Mary Janes with the precious artifact. It was no longer glowing, though it was still warm and slick to the touch.

"Margaret, what is going on?" Amelia found me sitting on the bed, hands clasped in my lap, legs pressed together.

"I had a fight with the director. Complaining about being overworked. He was a jackass about it." The lies arrived so readily, as if I weren't the one conjuring them up at all, merely letting them pass through me. But when I smiled, it was real. "No more late nights. I'll be home on time tomorrow. I promise."

And I was. Night after night. A week passed in a flash. The time on set was a limbo, waiting for when I would get home, then waiting for Amelia to go to sleep. I curled up in the closet beside the shoebox and fell asleep listening to the rhythmic humming.

I wanted to quit, race home, and stay there, cooped up and contented. But that would bring too many questions. Amelia would have an issue with the sudden loss of income. I was our breadwinner; how could I explain to her that I'd won something more important than subsistence?

No news had broken about the dead starlet. And there were no whispers about the bloody scene on the stage either. What a perfect cover story. Who'd notice real blood amid all the ketchup? The other two would be searching for me, and what better place to hide than under their noses? It was a thin shield. I broke three pencils on the first day. By the fourth day, I'd swapped to a metal pen. Every time the stage doors opened, I expected a flash of crimson and Buck's accusatory stare.

They never arrived. Neither did any changes. The humming never grew beyond a gentle lullaby. Even when I took more extensive action, there was no reaction. I was left feeling silly, wondering what the fuck I was doing.

I held the egg to my eye and memory washed over me. I needed only to be patient. What I'd glimpsed and tasted would be mine again; I just had to stay faithful.

Morning light swam through the gaps in the blinds. Amelia was sleeping snug as a bug beside me. She'd exhausted herself the night before. God, it had been ages since she'd been so excitable. Bed death, ha—we were better than that.

Groaning, I crawled out from under the sheets, sore in the best way, our instruments lining the nightstand. I smiled despite myself.

Donning a silk robe, I slid my bare feet over the kitchen tiles. I couldn't remember the senses being so… acute…pronounced, each hair on the back of my hand, tickling, the pulse in my wrist a humming metronome, the sound of every breathe like a lover's sigh, the scent of combined postcoital musk was a shot of morphine or maybe dopamine rushing into my mind like a burst dam.

My bliss was tempered. Darling Amelia, for all her hunger, had neglected her errands, and the fridge and pantry lay empty. I'd have to pop out—I left a quick note on the fridge and threw on a pair of palazzos and a blouse.

By the time I returned, the warmth had left me, and panic filled my breast. Only when I crossed the threshold did it dissipate. Yes, that was precisely what was called for. I waited till the tub was wafting with steam and the water scalding to the touch. I dove in, hardly wincing as my skin turned red.

I remained there till the liquid was tepid and my eyes grew heavy. Afterward, I toweled myself down, teased out my russet brown hair, and donned one of my smartest dresses. From behind her desk, Amelia commented on how pretty I looked, as though I were fit for a wedding. I concurred and offered the same compliment, for she wore a sterling navy swing dress, silken and shimmering. She'd never worn it better. "What's the occasion?" I asked, preening.

"I could ask you the same. But you already know. Of course, you do." She purred as she leaned over her pile of notes and paperweights, black, shiny, and even glowing...

A sound, distant and desperate, broke through. Someone was shouting and banging on our door, the doorknob rattling like a plane coming apart at the bolts.

As I strode into the living room, the low-hanging sun caught a burst of crimson, strands frayed and messy, eyes just as wild. Janet Mosley's face contorted in anger, then tearful pleading. "Please, please, please," she begged.

As with any cornered animal, I approached with a slow step, twisting the knob and opening the door at precise intervals. She pressed the gap without delay. "Margaret, Margaret, that's your name, isn't it? Oh, Margaret, we must speak, we must." She gripped me by the shoulders, yet there was little force in her pawing advances.

"Let's sit you down," I encouraged.

Janet didn't object, falling like a limp doll into the corner of a sofa. Her eyes still held some clarity, a focus within the mask of grief. It sharpened with every word she spoke. "I'm here about Greta. About what happened—don't, don't even dare. I know you were there. Just as I know *it* has you—don't deny it." Those eyes, which had graced a thousand silver screens, had never emoted like this. "Please, I'm here about Greta. I must save her."

"I watched her die. You were there. Janet, I'm sorry, but she's gone." Guilt roiled through me, but it wasn't my fault. It wasn't.

Janet shook her head, "No! No…" Her next refusal arrived as a hiss. "She's not dead. She's *changed.* It's not her body. It's up here." She gestured to her head. "Buck thought he'd knocked her up, insisted that we should take her to a doc to take care of it, but she's not pregnant, she's…infected…it's like…*she's the child.*" Her eyes glazed over, and a slight magenta shimmer skimmed her irises. She shook her head; it was gone, her eyes fixed upon me again. "She asked me to kill her. Begged me…but I couldn't do it."

"Janet, there's nothing I can do about it," I insisted.

"Yes, there is." Every bit of fog left the actress. "We can destroy it. Somehow. Matter is matter. Nothing is invincible. We just have to think big." She rose from the couch before closing the distance, her slender body trembling. "Just show me where it is and I'll handle the rest."

There was no way she could. But what if?… What if she eviscerated something so precious, so much more wonderful than anything in this dull human doldrum? "No…" I planted my feet. "No! I won't let you."

I glimpsed it for half a second, the hardening of Janet's stare and her muscles tightening. The back half of that second never really existed at all, a blur, a gap, an absence, and then she was there, her hands, her nails, her rage. She punched me. I elbowed her. She shoved me, and when I rebounded, lunging at her, she kicked out, heel first, finding my solar plexus. I wheeled back, trying to find my footing. Instead, my back connected with the wall, and what little air I had left was forced from my lungs.

Janet didn't give me time to recover, pressing me into the pastel wall, her hands at my throat. My lungs burned, my heart was ready to burst. In vain I tried to claw at her, to draw blood, but we remained deadlocked, and my attempts grew feeble. Terror fought against a mounting numbness, the black fringe creeping into my vision, obscuring the shape standing in the hallway, so familiar. Her blond hair, the rapturous figure, the swing dress, yet so changed, the eyes, the chin…

One instant, my last instant, passed, and then, the pressure was gone, and Janet fell to the floor in a heap.

I joined her on my knees, sputtering and coughing, a hand on my throat, my lungs a desert, tears streaming out of my eyes.

A firm hand found the small of my back, found my shoulder, and lifted me up and onto the couch. When I regained some sense, my wife stood above me, smiling as the triumphant protectress. There was not one drop of weakness left in her.

She clutched a small round object that filled her palm…

That's when I noticed the change in her cheekbones, the dark tendrils filling in the whites of her eyes.

"Amelia…you've…"

"Been in communion, I know, I apologize, I was quite lost in it, another moment or two…" She looked at me, and for a moment, the strength vanished, and she was as I knew her before. It passed as a ruddy expression took over. "It doesn't matter. The bitch is taken care of."

I turned to the floor, finding Janet lying there, stiller than still…at least at first glance, but there at the stomach, was that the gentle rise and fall of life?

"I was mad at first that you didn't tell me." Amelia continued. "But then everything made sense. Each of us to our time. You and your secrets. I wanted to one too…" She brought her hands to her chest, the egg clutched between them, her body swaying side to side. "Oh, I dreamt of this moment when we'd both be read in. When it would dawn on us—all the possibilities."

"What possibilities? What has it done to you?" I felt the hideous tug of jealousy. Why did it choose her over me? I rescued it. I saved it. And it chose her. "What are you saying?"

Amelia's face blossomed like she'd just discovered true fusion. "You and me. Better. Even more than before. No more doubt, no more sadness. Just trust me this one time. Like I trusted you, again and again."

I rose to my feet and slowly stepped over to her, my eye breaking from hers only to look down at the relic as I slid my hand over it. The heat was instant, like a warm blanket or slipping nude into a hot spring. It was better than any human invention. It felt primal, older than time itself. And here we were, tasting only morsels when we could have a feast, her and I, our beauty, our compassion, our love, every ounce of blood and ecstasy.

"Oh…" she cooed, then moaned.

"Oh…" I echoed.

A thousand thoughts flashed by at a million frames a second. And there, among all that celluloid, was a breach in these far-flung futures. A memory. The day she turned to me, shy as a butterfly, her hair wavy and perfect, her dress finally finding the figure she'd developed. It was the moment *after*, the time when I realized she'd finally molded herself into who she wanted to be. It was like meeting her for the first time.

I fell in love all over again in a single second.

But this…wasn't that. It wasn't even close. That was love. This was a lie.

The reverie shattered into a hundred onyx shards. I didn't react physically. I was pretty good at lying, after all. And I'd need to be Oscar worthy.

Think big. That's what Janet said. Forget big. It was time to think stupid… and high. Very high.

"Okay…okay… Come on, darling. Let's go for a drive."

"A drive?"

"Buck will be after us, I'm sure. We just need to lay low for a while. San Diego or San Francisco. The redwoods! What better place to complete this!"

"Yes, you're right," she simpered.

"See? You can trust me. I have it all sorted."

In the car, I tried the radio; at first, it was white noise no matter the frequency before it made a noise like whispers and screaming. I turned it off again, but the sounds kept playing

Amelia stayed silent, save for the times she whispered to the egg. She begged forgiveness. She begged to learn. Most of all, she begged for grace as though she were talking to a god.

Traffic was mercifully light, but there were too many damn patrol cars for me to speed. I sat right below the limit, willing the car toward our destination.

Please, please, please. I glanced at Amelia, and she was unrecognizable.

Turning back to the road, I ignored my peripheral vision and the noises and the sounds she was making, scratchy, slimy, like vinyl and shellac, melting and shattering.

The smell of sulfur mixed with her musk was overwhelming, but I dared not open my windows. The car was a measly cage, but it was all that was available.

Outside, the world was beautiful. The purpling horizon was a thin line stretched out between the azure darkness above and the soft, arid earth below, the light falling away as we rose higher and higher.

Amelia noticed the problem in the pattern. "Why aren't we continuing on the freeway?" Her one hideous, oversize eye weeping blood was fixed on me.

"It's fine, dear. Just a detour."

"A detour?"

"Yes, yes. Trust me."

"Trust you? Like I did before?" It was my wife's voice, trembling and scared. "Like I did before?" She reached out for my hand, pawing at me, gripping my shoulder. "Margaret. Margaret, this is where the—"

"Shh, shh, it's okay, just trust me. It's almost over."

"Margaret…"

Her voice was heartbreaking.

I was betraying her. I was saving her.

I met her eyes, a glimpse of the real her visible within the terror she'd become. "Please, we have to destroy it."

Up ahead was the runoff, the spot where the chemical truck careened off the mountain.

There was no more time. I lunged for the egg, but Amelia was quicker; our hands connected, her claws piercing my skin. I howled in some far-off space. I saw red, and a burning heat filled my veins like poison. She cracked my arm back, twisting my wrist. It was almost like we were arm wrestling.

Except this wasn't a game and I didn't give a shit about the rules.

She needed to possess the object. I just needed her to let go of it. Pulling her arm around, I pressed in closer, time dilating, heartbeats becoming seconds, the car slowing to a crawl. I could count every pant, every pulse. My head slid to the crook of her neck, almost as if we were cuddling. I raised my feet onto the seat, and my shoes found the driver's side door. I leveraged myself, digging my nails into the tender muscles of her wrist until the relic, a beaming bright sun, flew from our laps and landed by the pedals, burning a scorching trail wherever it touched.

My arm found Amelia's waist as I took one last look at the cliff and the awaiting freefall…and then I kicked out.

The passenger door burst open, and we tumbled out, barely avoiding the wheels. Pain lashed through me as gravel at dirt tore at my skin, my spine screaming as it connected with the ground, like a can opener ripping at tin. My whole world dipped to black as Amelia tumbled over me. We parted, my limp body tumbling and rolling on.

Everything came to a halt, and my lips pressed to the earth. The car was gone, vanished—one heartbeat, then two. A hideous metallic screech rang out, followed by the explosion. Not a thing of brimstone and orange flame; this was green and purple, neon and searing. It made my eyes water as acid filled my mouth.

The starburst lasted only a second, but the glow was burned into the back of my retinas. A trail of white smoke mixed with a pastel blue wafted and shined against the night,

The demanding oblivion of the unconscious beckoned, and I refused her call. Forcing my arms to move, I rolled over. Suffering didn't matter to me. Nothing mattered if I had failed.

Amelia had come to a halt behind me, lying on her back, eyes staring up blankly. But there…there…at her belly… Was it rising and falling? I couldn't tell.

I fought for every inch keeping us apart until my bloodied, nail-split fingers reached her, her arm, her wrist, her cheek, and her stomach. I waited for an eternity till I felt movement in her diaphragm.

Her eyes turned away from all the stars and met mine. Amelia…Amelia, just as she was. Damaged, injured, and hurt, but still as beautiful as the full moon. With all the strength she had left, she reached up and grazed her fingers along mine.

I still had a little energy left, and I used it up, kissing her harder than I ever had before, as my ears still rang with the sounds of a dying deity. A ringing that would never end.

The Crossing

THERE came a ripple, quieter than a splash. The river was dark, serene, alluring, its depths unknown. Nearer to the shore, amid the pebbles, were bones—pieces of bodies anonymized in glorious secrecy.

I harbored great affection for the quiet that draped the thoroughfare, just as surely as the fog slunk between the black trees. Try as one might to peer upon an image, the inky waters held no picture, only nothingness. I sat at the edge, waiting. For what I knew not, only that my heart told me I needed to be here, where there was no other.

I sensed the presence before I held any conscious notion of it. A figure, across the stagnant current, hunched over amid the gray dirt, a leather coat wrapped around her, sun-bleached and blacked by equal turns. The shadow of her hood hid her face. It rippled as she craned her neck upward, a single beady eye, steely as an overcast sun visible within the darkness.

"Hale and good health to you, fair maiden." Her voice was a whisper, smooth as the ivory pendant mother clung to, as scratchy as the splinters when father bade me repair the goat pen.

She spoke formally, so I did as well. "Hale to you. But are you not mistaken?" My voice did not sound as it should, carrying so light and feathered over the channel.

The weathered folds parted, revealing a feminine and cunning face, a crass smirk pulling at sharp teeth awful and white as if they had never tasted tea or known any decay. Her face was the same, leaving only the wisdom in her eyes to hint at her years.

"Am I incorrect? I am not often wrong and certainly not from a pup."

"Seven and ten is not a pup."

"Not quite. Plenty of time for ruination. Oh, dear, you must fret."

"Over what?"

"The sculptor who mismade you," she replied.

"I don't understand."

She waved a hand and I recoiled. Her hand was white as bone and just as thin. "You lie more to yourself than to me. But what should I care? You are there and I am here." She hesitated, lifting her posture ever so lightly. "If I bid thee to join me on my side of the hallow, would thee?"

She was as articulate as the Lord's tax collect. She had the grace befitting a woman of wealth, yet she dressed worse than a beggar. Her cloak was perforated by countless holes, the once crimson skirts bleached to a dull pinkish-maroon, and one part of her stay was gouged, revealing a glimpse of the sweat-yellowed shift beneath. She was a witch for a certainty: the words and speech, a conjuration. Mother had warned what such overtures meant, what ruin they foretold.

I shook my head, quiet and numbed, "I shall not, for if the waters did not trick me with their depths, surely you would arrive upon my greeting a wicked turn."

"Fool and some, thou can wallow and waste away, but what of the world that could be?" She waved her hand again and hunched back over. "I can waste no more of my time on those who are unwilling to imagine. That is the surest evil. Never forget that, sweet child, innocent girl." She pressed a bony finger to her temple. "As long as thoughts are in thine skull, reverberating and unquenched, then insolence, glorious insolence, shall never perish." With that, she turned, her cloak thrown back around her, its leaf-strewn makeup concealing her in an instant. Vanished without so much as the sounds of boots on leaves.

The Crossing

* * *

*   *   *

On my journey back to the village, I thought of the witch, my shoulders

slumped, boots kicking at the dirt. It was a ruddy day; the clouds were so gray

that they were almost green from the storm they carried. Any golden luster the

straw roof of the house had possessed before was now faded. It was as pale as

an elder's mane, the wooden frame so dark I had to squint to scry my mother

hiding beneath the lip. She stepped forward, her arms crossed. The waning

daylight found her every black pore, her wrinkles twisting into a harsh tableaux.

"And where oh where does thou think thou hath been the entire day? We wasted

away without thee."

No answer might suffice, so I didn't give one. Even as her foul disposition

mounted, she didn't shout or scream. She understood subtler methods than that

—guilt and shame—and I was well acquainted with both.

"Go help thine sisters with the hens," she commanded when she grew tired

of chastisement.

I nodded, giving in. One cannot fight the world entire. I could not even

fight the other children in the village. They mocked us with sounds I couldn't

recognize. I wouldn't know what Africa sounded like any more than they did.

But I looked different, and at some point, my lineage had come from

somewhere else that wasn't Europe. Those two facts were enough for them.

If they tormented me alone, it might be manageable. Kick me like the mutts

they'd beat to death when they grew too old. If only they'd leave my sisters be.

My sisters were having a miserable go at herding the crazed chickens.

Something had roused them, and their clucking became a terrible, pained

shrieking. They fled from the hands grasping for them. When I entered the fray

and scooped two up, I received five bleeding cuts for it, and howled at the

swelling pain. I dropped one of them, and it landed poorly and lay there stunned for a moment before it fled to the coop of its own accord.

Sweat-slicked, despite the damp chill in the air, I leaned against the coop, sucking in breath after breath, tasting the waning day. I was scattered like leaves—a twist of time, a slender knife, the frail piece of wood awaiting the ax.

Hanna reached out a hand to console me. I hurried her away, insisting we clean up the yard. My sisters' deep green and blue dresses were caked in mud at the hems. Hanna's was withering upon her. It needed mending, and her stay desperately required new threads with which to lace. The thing was loose and unkept, hanging off her chest.

"Stop." I crossed the mushy soil to her, brushed her curly braid back over her shoulder, and took the threads in my fingers, pulling and sending them through their eyelets. Knotted and tightened again, my job was done. "Do not neglect this, or someone with think thou let thyself be undone as well."

She was grown enough to perfectly understand what I'd implied, warmth and aggravation reaching her cheeks.

Gertrude was five years her junior, and her skin was light brown compared to Hanna's or mine. She was eager to prove her knowledge in the most inciting manner. She bent forward, hands clasped behind her back, the devil's grin upon her lips. "Yes, Hanna, thou must lace up"— Gertrude's voice became a hissing bite—"or they'll decry a witch. Every one of them is a harlot and they already think we practice—"

"Enough!" My words were a lash, and I instantly regretted my anger. The buzzing misalignment in the back of my skull thrummed, a channel separating me from whatever it was I resided inside.

Gertrude kept at it, her spirits alighted. "In town, everyone is losing chickens. Does thou think they have taken flight? Nay, A thief most likely. And who will be blamed for such a thing?

"Enough of that, all of it. Thou will stop this instant." I took a moment to pass a hand through my hair, stamping down my temper. Seeking calm in the storm. "Go help Father gather the wood. We will finish with the hens."

She stomped away, too full of impotence to pout or weep as she often did before.

"Thou needn't pretend as though she's wrong," said Hanna after a few minutes. "They all whisper about us...even thee."

"Do they now?" I was elsewhere, somewhere past the brown egg I held in my hand.

"Indeed, they say all sorts of odd things about thee. Meek and mild as thou art. It's why none of the boys like thine company."

"They've never liked my company just as I've never cared for theirs." I set the egg in the pouch at my hip, dusting off the hay from my knees.

"That does not prevent thine loneliness," she countered, arms knitted together.

"I am not lonely on account of them."

"Then it's the women who rile thee?"

There was a seam where the fencepost met the slowly eroding dirt. The soil gave way, but the wood was a sturdy constant. "It's..." I shook my head. "Father will be waiting on me; see if mother has need of thee."

Scowling, she obeyed.

Loneliness was easier. I was a house of stone, without any mortar to hold it together. Strength and solidity without whatever elusive feature defined it.

Why, then, did the witch appear in my mind as a soothing recourse? Was it attraction? The shame of lust? Harlots. My sister declaimed them harlots. With such degradation, she'd sneered. We all did. It's said the witch hunts had lasted for over a century. Some claimed it was the work of Pope John XXII; others saw it as inevitable or a sign of plague times. Either way, it was the Franks and the Germans who started it, and soon the terror spread all over Europe. Who knew how long they would continue for? A traveling merchant not six months ago had offered every vivid detail of a pyre, the woman's screams choked out by smoke. She was naught more than a corpse by the time the flames melted her skin, her eyes—embers for hairs, bones charred soot black.

He reveled in the violence. The other men were enraptured, salivating as he described how her simple shift clung to her. I and I alone felt such nausea. I contemplated being upon that pile of sticks, feeling the leering gazes upon me, not a single drop of dignity in death. Even her ashes had been spat upon before being poured into the city's sewers. What crime could justify such cruelty? What fundamental truth had she broken?

These were dangerous thoughts, ones that distracted me from supper and my father's prayer. My punishment was a dozen Hail Marys before bed and the same number upon waking. Yet every time I did so, I dreamt only of the river.

*   *   *

Five days passed before I set out again on the trackless path through the forest. A tangled jumble of markers, this broken branch, and that twined tree, a gully, a boulder, the same chill in the air, a quiet filling the inner ear, a tangible absence.

She was waiting for me, a small leather pouch cupped in her hand. She pulled on its draw and deposited its contents slowly and carefully. She showed me each smooth orb till they became a waterfall of chiming crystal.

"We each are like these little stones." She ran her thumb over a few of them. "Some are perfect. Others misshapen. Many appear one way but are actually the other. The surface never speaks for the whole river. As the exterior never guarantees the center. What hath been misshapen can be repaired. Or a perfect thing, be rotted from the inside. The sun. The moon. One to another. Reshaping a soul is an unpleasant process. But then, not all unpleasant things are so detestable."

She smoothed one hand over the pile in her palm, the droplets fanning out. They were an inversion of light, consuming and crushing errant rays from the air.

Nestled down in a small hole, she buried the entire menagerie.

"A thing hidden is no less real," I argued.

"A seed trapped in the earth can never be a flower."

"Flowers are fragile."

"Most pretty things are."

She cast her sight across the water, and I was rendered naked before her. It was deeper than nudity, her whispers traveling beyond meat and flesh, farther in, till she was beside me, her soul and mine, held up to a watery surface. We were each reflected in it if I dared to look. One glance, and I'd be doomed to mourn it forever.

"Oh, do not shrink away, not now."

"I'm scared."

"As thou should be," she soothed. She warned, "But fear isn't enough. For it will never depart, thou art kin, paired and bonded, but that need not deter ye." Her voice was so silken. "Thou can covet, and thou shalt sew. Thine thread will be woven in a different pattern."

"No, no." I rose to shake my head, trying to get her out of my mind. Across the river, her body was writhing with the effort. "No!" I repeated.

She stilled, her limbs taunt like a feral cat. "Fool! A miracle is what I offer and is what thou needs! Another moon or another lifetime, this shall not arrive again," her voice snarled out of every branch and every tree.

"You offer a curse... You offer what cannot—should not be. Pain and isolation I'll never escape from." Back peddling, my boots caught on a pebble. I landed hard but continued my retreat without ever losing sight of her and the other her, the illusory conjuration appearing before me. "You are a witch!" I screamed, "You deceive, you lie. You know what I want, and you'll trick me with it. You offer misery and misery alone. A lifetime of it."

"I offer you sisterhood. I offer thee that wish thou hast never spoken, never given thought to."

"You infect me, you poison."

"I offer naught but a mirror." Her voice was softer this time—more matter-of-fact.

I put my legs under me and grabbed hold of a rock, then a branch, scrabbling up and out of the riverbed. "I need no such thing."

The forest became a blur, and I broke into a run. The last thing I heard within the eerie silence was her gentle sigh.

*   *   *

For days, I couldn't sleep. Each night, nightmares plagued me, the sensation of her residing within my mind, the alluring concepts that bled from her lips like ambrosia. As sure as a setting sun, the glimmer of glory would shift to terror.

My screams awoke the house. At first, father scolded me for it, but by the seventh occurrence, they feared for me. Praying and pondering what coins we might spare for a healer or a priest.

Those nights without nightmares were worse, for those dreams held no terrifying monsters. Everything was perfect. I was perfect. And I lived lifetimes within these hours. Tasting truth for the first time. When I awoke, my eyes streamed with silent tears, and I cursed whatever god had condemned me to the waking world.

A fortnight after my woes began, I was sent to the village proper. They'd had me speak with a traveling Jesuit, but he could offer no aid. I feared telling him the truth, in part or in full. My sisters were with me, waiting outside. I lied to them and told them I was healed and that we should buy some victuals to celebrate.

Along the short row that served as a market, we stopped and collected the ingredients for a stew. I was so busy pondering how the cabbage would smell—

sweet and hearty, washed down by the musk of wine—that I didn't notice the trio till it was too late.

"Thieves! Thou are the ones stealing the chicks from our farms!" the leader called out, raising a finger in accusation. "If not my martial art, then by dark magicks thou steal food from beneath us!"

"Liar!" Gertrude shouted, standing defiantly, only to be shoved away pitifully. Hanna, a creature of ferocity, protective to the last, leaped to her defense. Then everything escalated.

A few seconds became an eon. I threw myself into the middle of the melee, taking a blow across my jaw, square and solid. My head flew to one side and I stumbled. Iron and ichor filled my mouth. I spat red, the blood coating a single cobblestone.

Someone wiser, better, and with more worth would have let it go and run away; I was no such entity. Instinct, rage, and righteousness propelled my hands. Hanna joined me, retaliating with fingers wielded like claws.

Our struggle drowned out Gertrude's cries and the other shouts. Everything was devolving. Instinct…sheer blood-soaked instinct won out. Rage and malice, fury and protection. The waning pale sunlight reflected dully off the Kirk dagger. Terror poured ice in my veins as the blade licked down to where my sister was grappling with one of our attackers.

Again I leapt between. This time, however, there was no pain, only horror. My arms moved, twisting his wrist, his arm, till a hushed breath escaped his lips. He collapsed just as soon as his body understood its impalement. The dagger was buried to its hilt, the prongs tangled in his ribs.

We fell in a heap next to Hanna. The man's limp weight crashed into me, the heat of his blood overtaking the senses, and gurgling spurts, coughs, and wheezes filled my ear. Then the world fell still.

One shallow breath, not enough to fill the lungs, was all the time it took to process.

My sisters pushed the body off me. "Run," I pleaded. "Tell them it is I and I alone responsible."

Hanna gave one shallow nod, and Gertrude, there wasn't any time…for here, for respite or remorse. The life I had lived was over, left in my wake, drowned in a crimson pool. There was movement, the rush, the fear, the small glimmer of possibility, and nothing else.

The gnarled tree, the twin tree, the forked bush, the tiny gully. The rise, the fall and there at last, the river, cutting through the forest. I expected the same silent calm to envelop me and soothe my ears, still ringing with curses and shouts. The air, however, was filled with sound. Pristine, seraphic voices, and earthy deep thrums alike.

There were four of them forming a tight circle across the river. The one known to me and three new faces weathered like old leather, supple, and ivory, and one with skin as brown as mine. Each was a different figment of perfection. From the shortest to the tallest, they danced and writhed, reveling in the ritual called living. The pebbles and rocks were kicked about by their bare feet, and scents of rosemary, thyme, lavender, and ginger lifted over the water. There were dresses woven from wool and silk, some draped in quilted segments, while others clung to hips and breasts, translucent enough to tease.

Each witch was powerful and…deadly. In their eyes was the glint of capability that made men run in fear, for how could they possibly understand those infinite depths?

That cornucopia, its endless majesty, overcame me. I felt a single impulse, one continuous pitch, the lyre gliding and falling in a repose that made my chest swell and flutter.

There was no more doubt, only the promise of what was before me. My weathered shoes met the water, and I waded in, bracing against the bitter cold till I was submerged up to my neck. That's when frost became fury. My wool tunic was scoured and torn, ripped away with the current. My very skin was next, burning and boiling, the agony as she foretold, like an artisan hewing away muscle and sinew like marble or clay.

The weight was crushing, and tears pressed from my eyes as the world grew dark, the water closing in. I sucked in a final breath and fell into the river's depths. There was no sight amid the murky churn; every sound was muffled as each nerve sensed a soothing touch. The same as my mother's warm embrace, the ones I had known and those before I had existed. I could be nothing again, blissful once more. Never knowing what might have been.

Better than to be something. Whatever it might entail, I could dream.

Blood pooled around me, streaming from me, and there were lacerations along my stomach, my chest, face, throat, the river stained red with my ichor.

Reaching out through the veiling of pain, I churned and pawed until I found purchase, my fingers digging into the soft soil and pulling. My lungs emptied, my energy depleted, and I had but a few moments of heartbeats left.

I came up coughing and sputtering. Choking on life.

My eyes opened to the world again, the same one I'd left: the gray day, the dead forest. Everything was the same…except me.

The witches bent down and lent their strength, hauling me up limb by limb. The one who'd first offered a miracle grinned with glee in her eyes as she brought her lips close, "Welcome, sister."

Repossessed

THE entrance to the cave was a simple gouge in the otherwise sheer cliff, its surface scoured like a popcorn ceiling. There wasn't anything intimidating about it. Then again, tall tales and superstition never had much to do with tangible reality. I just needed one all-important detail to be true; the rest of it could be a tourist trap. The allure of cursed treasure, of a king hiding the key to his long-lost love. They could keep spinning the yarn forever. No one would ever have to know I was here.

The last orange dregs of the day help paint a mosaic of shadow over the rock, courtesy of the dense foliage.

Edith sat by one of those trees, fussing with her camping items. She wouldn't be heading in with me. Thank God for that; no one could nag like Edith. She was a bank account on two legs, with oh so many zeroes. A platonic sugar mommy. She just didn't know it. She thought she had a shot, that those doe-eyed glances she failed to hide from me would amount to something. After tonight, she'd understand at last. I'd be free of her, free of all of it. The deprivation, the anxiety, nervously opening an app to see if my biweekly deposit had finally come in. No more games, no more feeling like a con, no more scraping by.

All I had to do was get my hands dirty, but I'd done that before. What were a few more cuts and scrapes?

"Okay, time to go."

"Not going to wait till morning?" There was as much hope in her voice as apprehension.

But some people needed to learn to take no for an answer, even if her parents never could. "I'm a night owl and it's not like the light matters down there."

"But won't you get tired?" she insisted.

"I'll be two hours max. Chill the fuck out."

"Okay," she mewled like the prize dog she was.

I stepped over her and reached for my kit, carabiners, lightweight ropes, a rugged smartwatch, a helmet with an LED lamp, and sports padding for my shins, elbows, and knees. Lastly I slung a flare and a few glow sticks next to my water bottle and protein bars.

I was armored up, a knight ready to descend into hell. It occurred to me that the local superstitious nut jobs would get a kick out of that visual.

"Be careful," she called out. I'd stepped away from the half-assed camp without so much as a comment.

She stood again, a hand at her elbow, the same worry in her eyes as the first time she watched me free climb. We'd met in college. She was a sorority girl, while I was an athlete. She'd tried climbing the rock wall exactly once and ended up threatening the gym with a lawsuit when she broke a nail.

The entrance to the cave was even smaller than it had appeared at first blush, the arc of the gash close in at the base. It felt like stepping through a doorway.

For the first twenty minutes, it was more of a downward hike than anything. The passage was generous; trapped moisture made it damp, but without rivers or ponds nearby and no forecasted rain, so there was no fear of flooding. Graffiti coated the walls, from modern paint to old-school etchings. Although there was a history to this place, I didn't have time to pay attention to it. The only sound in the cave was that of my cleated boots as they crunched on the soft pebbles.

The thing with Edith was that she always had more money than she could comprehend, and she understood others didn't have what she did. To them, every bit of green was precious and terrifying. She recognized this; she just didn't care.

I reached an expansive void within the cliff the size of a football field. Old, broken railings hung limply over the edge. I'd been warned of this by the local spelunkers. The cliff face was sheer for thirty feet, and then there was a steep gradient, forty-five degrees, with loose rocks and slippery smooth granite everywhere else.

Edith and I didn't reconnect till years after we'd graduated, or rather, since I'd flunked out. When we'd reconnected, it was easy to convince her that financing a few adventures would be good for her.

I proceeded at a rapid pace along the solid sheets. Suddenly everything was churning, the dark world in a spin cycle. I threw my weight back, falling onto my ass instead of tumbling forward, my heart lurching in my chest. The skid sent a wave of rocks gliding down into the darkness, each little dot disappearing like snowflakes passing by headlights.

A little snicker, a sip of water, and I got back to it; there couldn't be much left of this element. A glow stick confirmed it, landing at the bottom some thirty yards down.

From this basin, a series of antechambers branched off. I knew what I was looking for, but a fracture in the rock gave me pause. It was man-made for sure. The era eluded me, but the uncanny cuts, the etchings hewn in as if by needlepoint, were as unexplainable as they were unnerving. Nothing at all like my research had shown.

After Edith had agreed to this venture, she set her feeble mind to helping me with that research. I had to nip that in the bud quickly. She was so achingly romantic, leaping at every fanciful tale. Rich and flighty, with an elevator that only went up to the second floor.

The caves continued to narrow, and I pressed on, using the mental map I'd memorized. One boot in front of the other, each step drawing me closer. I had to temper my giddiness. By now, life should have taught me setting expectations always dulled the pain, but it also dulled the thrill. If I were to place a bet, I'd enjoy it end to end, be it glory or humiliation. It would be mine and no one else's.

At last I reached the spot I'd been warned about. The one where I wished I were a cat with whiskers. I'd measured myself, kit and all, a half dozen times just to make sure I'd have enough clearance. Even prone and within a healthy margin, the crawlspace forced me to go prone and wiggle like a worm. Everything was so tight that my breath, its heat, shot back at me, and the sound of it was immediate and close.

Seven full minutes wedged in a kill hole, praying a cave-in didn't crush me or, worse, trap me. I scrambled out the far side, and to my surprise, the cavern blossomed around me. My map hadn't shown this. The space was fifteen feet tall, with broad switchbacks and gaps in the rock walls to peer through.

Of course I'd been fed bad info by my fixer, by the locals. None of them had wanted me to succeed. No one ever had. Not my parents, roommates, Nina with her nuevo spiritualist manifesting, or the carousel of men who couldn't keep up. Even Eric, yearning, pathetic Eric, who wouldn't let me go and tried to drag me down into mundanity. And Edith…well, she was a whole different level of sad.

I walked the passages of rock, noting the change in crystal formations. More and more sprouted until the stalks were so fine and so smooth they could be…fur. They *were* fur, I realized with a start, running a chalk-laden finer over them, leaving a white trail in my wake.

Soon the crystalline forms became proper organic matter, not like silk or flesh but the dense moss of a forest. It seemed untamable and active, like a body. With the continuity and pliability of a membrane…and it was breathing.

The whole cavern shook with a steady rhythm as though it were slumbering. I could just barely hear it humming.

The next cavern was voluminous as an auditorium. The diagonal throw of the wall, was now awash in orange and brown and black, moss and algae, and even some red plants sprang forth. None of it was rock anymore but a dense jungle of smooth and coarse, with cutting lines of glowing amber-hued blisters, some as long and tall as subway cars, others a strip running like the painted lines on the highway.

All routes led past the hushed worshipers with their moss-covered, misshapen silhouettes.

I blinked and wiped the grit from my eyes. There were no prostrate figures, only boulders that had been eaten and made into something else.

The humming still followed as I entered passage after passage, some like palace halls, others smooth and minimal. Slowly, ever so slowly, the expansive splendor grew tighter, collapsing into smaller avenues, each older than the last.

The moss was petrified and fossilized. Yet my heart beat faster and the rhythm increased. There was life down here, the one that generated all this energy. Rich and beautiful. This was the heart of that entity.

I slipped down an artery and arrived at the epicenter. The narrow passage down abruptly met the ceiling like a folder or book cocked slightly open, and there at the junction was my prize.

At the center of the cave was a jewel that emitted an impossible, captivating glow. I sat, my back arched against the slope, and cradled it in my hands.

As I stroked the stone peaks and ridges, I wondered how I'd ever be able to part with it. Surely, I thought, it couldn't be worth a measly seven figures. Oh, it radiated such energy. I felt it dip into my veins, better than any arousal, more fulfilling than post-sex bliss. It was a thunderstorm and a snowy day. It begged for lethargy. It longed for activity.

As I brought the jewel closer, its glow filled my sight, drowning out the pathic headlamp and making the cave disappear. I hardly noticed the grinding cacophony, the moving shadows. It wasn't until I felt the rock against my skin that I realized the world was shrinking around me. Still I clutched it. "No, no," I screamed. "You can't. You can't. Save me." It could, it could, it had to. "Please! I don't want to—" The words were pressed out, along with every bit of oxygen, my whole body crushing in on itself.

That's when the light died and the pain began. In the infinite darkness, every limb was squeezed. I couldn't move, I couldn't scream, I couldn't breathe; wild panic grasped at me. I needed air, air…

I just needed one more breath before the end. I just—

*   *   *

IT'D BEEN so long since I had a body. Human forms are gregarious and cumbersome. Yet they can have a certain lithe quality: a cozy, fleshy way of sitting here in the darkness. Even for a being such as I, rebirth can be difficult. It's easier to take over a babe's body, like when they used to bring their children willingly. I was like a child, huddled and scared, running my hands slowly over oily black arms.

Oh, no, there's a horn, and there's another, and my tail, they aren't supposed to have tails.

It took another few minutes? Hours? To finish the process. Their timekeeping can be so cumbersome: 4:00 a.m. or zero four hundred hours? The woman whose body I stole couldn't remember the difference. But she could remember every detail of Glenn Powell's face, someone she'd never seen in person, only as pixels and ink. Wait, do people still buy magazines? Perhaps that's why she'd been so greedy. She wanted vanity and wealth.

Humans never change.

Getting accustomed to bipedal limitations was a slow process. There's pain. Maybe I was a little too forceful. The agony of these recently repaired bones was my punishment. Oh well. Live and learn. At least the woman left a rope for me. The last part of the hike was almost charming, the locomotion setting in, this form finally in rhythm. That's when I caught the first whiff of fresh air that had been a long time coming. And the sounds! The life, the animals, the critters. They were so young they didn't even run away at first scent. They were so used to human encroachment that they didn't understand what could be worse than those clever creatures that had conquered the world.

As I stepped into the night, I was reminded of the breeze, of everything I lacked. That woman, she was so terrified of a few dying moments caught in the dark, unable to comprehend what it was to endure an eon in such conditions.

The moon twinkled behind some clouds, the thick foliage waved to me, and a voice broke through my reverie.

A human rushed down the short hill to meet me at the cave. Her clothes were pink and frilly. Her voice had almost no bass except when her throat trembled, hiding a choking sob.

She truly cared for that bitch, but why?

Then I noticed how she stared at the torn remnants of my clothes, the places I accentuated when I put myself back together. Her arousal flitted over the calm night air and into my nostrils—a heady odor mixed with just enough sweetness to curl my tongue over my new lips.

I pushed her down into the dirt and took her with my hands and fingers. I supped upon her, and her moans did more than just invigorate this body.

When she was all used up, she clung to me. She was one of those humans. She prattled on, saying she knew it was too soon, but her parents would pay for the wedding, for the honeymoon: "We can go wherever we want."

Her eyes were so large, her heart open, her body having already done the same... I couldn't help but grin.

* * *

*   *   *

Our wedding day passed without a hitch, at least not any that my bride was aware of. Fragile creatures, humans. Sometimes they fell down stairs. Sometimes their heads were smashed against marble, their brains exploding like fresh melons.

But she, my bride, was radiant as her father walked her down the aisle.

Her dress was coated in lace. Its skirt was kept narrow to hug her thighs, cinched at the waist to display her figure, the bust straining against her breasts as I was treated to the sight of their milky-white tops. But it was the portrait that left me transfixed. Her straw-blond locks were pulled into a regal bun, the veil doing a purposefully mediocre job of hiding her. Beneath the mantle, she was both smooth and cut, her jaws, the hallows of her cheeks, but then those eyes, the soft skin around them, was already crinkled, fighting back her emotions. Her eyes pooled with so many feelings, their deep brown depths sparkling with a light beyond the sun.

Under my hungry longing, she demurred, her cheeks filling with a natural crimson warmth.

I had enough of *Alexa's* memories to understand the context, that it was a special, nearly abnormal thing to see two brides at an altar—the *yo-yo* of human squalor bouncing back and forth between one set of moors and the next. One of Alexa's old flames, Eric, was particularly shocked to discover that "Alexa was a dyke." He insinuated by text message that it must be some fresh scheme. He claimed to care about Alexa, yet he accused her of being a gold digger. Ah, a man's wounded pride never changes. I had to scroll back through his and Alexa's conversations to let him down easy in words that would make sense coming from her. Turned out it was quite straightforward when someone was so heartless and crass.

I took satisfaction in Edith's glee, in the undercurrent of soft-spoken rebellion that happiness brought her.

It's a laughable notion that there is any upheaval in performing a function that costs as much as this ceremony. She even had swans on the lawn. Matching our pearlescent gowns.

I fended off a snicker as I repeated my vows, swearing an oath to her god, a man I'd never known. Perhaps he vacated the premises before my arrival. Still, the tears streamed down her cheeks, and much as I'd liked to lick them clean, I met the moment and kissed my wife. She giggled into my mouth with unkept joy; I could taste her naivety.

*   *   *

The honeymoon, a yacht tour of the Mediterranean, rivaled the cost of the wedding. Not that my wife took note of it; I don't think she or her parents knew the sum total.

Much as I wanted to spend time alone with her, I'd endured a never-ending cavalcade of visitors and well-wishers. It was the vacation season and everyone wanted to check in on the happy couple. They each tried to assess what a lowly peasant had. done to capture her heart. Those who knew Alexa from before were the most tricky. I had to hold myself to a harsh posture, had to speak with cynicism and whine in the right ways. When it came to gossip, they could be quite attentive. It was a shame, then, that so many of them weren't as good at swimming as they'd thought, and who'd ever actually considered how much damage a jet ski could do at full speed when ramming into an athletic body? Thirty pounds of muscle mass certainly didn't offer any cushioning.

It's around the old Greek Isles that I began to feel more like myself. I spotted old haunts, now decrepit. Damn the British for stealing so many of my favorite pieces, now jailed in bulletproof glass with little placards to serve as tombstones. It was more than what remains of Babylon, at least.

Edith also helped this process; last night she'd built up the courage to chide me for having such a terrible attitude. "You aren't like that with me," she'd complained. That opened the door for an apology, for a promise, and a commitment to grow and do better.

We went from site to site, Edith dressed in khaki shorts and a pink short-sleeved shirt, like Laura Dern from that dinosaur movie she liked so much—the one about hubris and the perils of playing god. The tourists strutted about the ruins without a care in the world, no reverence, only ignorance. They didn't know what it as to be culled, to be sacred. They still had every right to be, given how capable of damage they ere to themselves and the world. Why, it was rather pretty once. Sure, the ocean still glimmered, wine dark and all that, but the luster was faded, and the skies were choked with their noxious defecation.

"I'm surprised," Edith chirped from the top of the broken plinth that used to hold a row of decorative, woman-shaped pillars.

"How so?" I asked, squinting up as the sun caught every thin hair on her arm and neck, and all those fly-aways atop her shimmering mane.

She hopped down, smiling, enjoying how hungrily I gazed at her. "I'm surprised you aren't looking at these ruins with dollar signs in your eyes, assessing their value."

She chuckled, deep and heady, the way she liked it, the way I'm sure she always wanted Alexa to react. "I only studied archaeology to find that gem."

"Shame that you didn't."

"No. Not at all. I have all the money I need."

She smirked, tilting her head, leaning in, the sunset adding more and more to these moments, the heat, the dying day. "So then, what do you hunger for? I can see it in you; you're trying to find something. You're always trying to find something."

"I'm hungry for you," I replied, half-truth, half-lie. I chose the former. I fed that hunger, planting my lips on hers.

But her question gnawed at me more than it should as we returned to the ship and made love. Was I a creature so simple as Alexa? Seeking greed and easy thrills? Those whispering little memories, the ticks still nestled in this body that became alighted at every new piece of jewelry or silk garment? I was worshiped once, but I didn't see it happening again. Fear perhaps. I always liked fear. Devotion. Being tempted. Urging, coaxing. What could I urge them toward? They butchered themselves in numbers I had trouble calculating. How had their scale overcome me?

Perhaps it was a matter of smelling the roses, enjoying the nearer and smaller scale offerings. Like this woman curled into me. What a fine example she was, wasn't she? So denuded beside me, her breathing so synced with the waves rockin' this boat…so accepting of every excuse when I acted against the grain of my predecessor or when I acted too much like her. Oh, yes, there was something delicious about this entire arrangement. In the meantime, there were other urges. Other appetites to sate.

Some folks remembered the old ways, the old starvations, fixations, and solutions…or can be reminded of them. Of those times when more than one deity ruled these lands, when that deity wasn't so singular male, when the feminine aspects weren't so reviled and hated and burned at the pyre. They could embrace the Mother again. Togas traded for polo shirts. A man strapped down on the slab wearing swim shorts, paint on his body forming intricate symbols. The etchings were powdery, like chalk-covered hands ready to climb. They stabbed him in the belly, piercing his abs, as they chanted, chanted for me. Some of them wound up killing one another afterward, and the rest wound up in jail.

It was all the rage in the papers; ritualistic sacrifice was now a novelty. Edith read through the reports on her phone with rapt attention, her pupils dilated and widening, her dainty mouth expanded into an absentminded *O*.

She said we should move on to Italy, to Venice and the canals. I agreed wholeheartedly.

*   *   *

After the honeymoon, Edith and I headed stateside to her parents' compound in the Hamptons. The thought process was that we'd bounce between here and her apartment in Manhattan until we selected a spot to settle down. She tried to temper her planning, but I overheard the conversations with her mother, the ones where she used words and phrases like *adoption* and IVF. Each utterance was a leash—every syllable reeked of domestication.

For the sake of her daughter, her parents humored, but we could see each other plainly, her father with her fixed stare, trying so hard to be tough. Age did nothing to diminish his forceful charm. He understood the concept of morale if not morality. Edith's mother was a trophy and had been one long enough to understand the game. I, however, breached this continuity. Nothing was good enough for her, not my attitude or attire. She despised my versatility, seeing me in a pantsuit one night and a cocktail dress the next. She could properly masculinize me, nor could she entirely slut shame me. I remained ever and always unreachable, slipping through her bony ring-laden fingers.

Edith was unhappy, caught in a gothic tale in an environment far too bright to convey the proper mood. She languished on the beach, suffocated by all her advantages. She thought she might be losing it. Her hold on the life she wanted, her connection to the family estate, her sanity, or me.

She had few friends to call on, so we invited one of mine over. Nina, *with her nouveau spiritualist manifesting.* She crashed into the house, all dangling bracelets and hoop earrings, and reeking of essential oils. When she spoke about her spirituality, she did so with a hard edge, expecting a rebuke from me.

Edith tittered, trying to find some nebulous middle ground between belief and atheism.

I did not. "There are many unexplained things in this universe," I said. "So many wonderful mysteries and darkness, the little shadows we like to ignore. They're everywhere. We see them when we're sleeping and call them nightmares. But they're the truth."

This was overstepping the mark, my movement, my posture. The ways and elegance of who I am bled through, past the bite of fingers on rocky purchases. When I walked Nina out, her face was a mask of furrowed concern. "I worry about you, Alexa. Your aura… It's so different. Seriously I'm worried."

"Don't be. There's no point." She could either accept that her friend had irrecoverably changed or not.

"What do you mean? I don't—"

"Goodbye, Nina." I shut the door on whatever else she had to say.

Inside, Edith was crying again, and I had to hold on to her and pull her in close. "The darkness, I see it every night, I see it constantly…I see it everywhere." Her eyes were wide open.

"Shh… It's okay. You may look as long as you like."

Edith didn't answer. She pressed her eyes closed and nuzzled into me.

As the weeks passed, she kept insisting she was losing something, falling out of step with reality. She's wrong. It was her parents who were free-falling into darkness, waking each night to a nightmare, a fresh horror. It didn't take much time to decipher someone's fears. The mother was scared of shirking responsibility. She was blamed for the time her father got her cat killed. She was scared to become a mother because of it. A few pitiful meows were all it took. The kitten didn't even have to die for the threads to begin unraveling.

As for her husband lying beside her, well, his was so much more straightforward. He buried a few bodies to achieve his ambitions, and the guilt over the first few was still nestled up in the crux of his identity. All he needed was a few ghastly reminders.

I calculated that matters would take four to five months to deteriorate properly. Instead, after just two short moon cycles, Edith and I stared at the rehabilitation center's entrance, leaning against our car while she cried. We let the family fixer tend to her father. Edith had always been closer to her mother, and she wanted to see her settled properly into her new home.

Madness, it seems, is not as potent as it used to be. I was hoping for some delicious asylum with screaming and cracked stone walls. It was a luxury resort, really, not a treatment center. Sure, they tried their best, the therapists who make the task of destroying a mind so much tougher now. I doubted, however, that they would be able to untangle this mess.

No, this was a nice, quiet spot to shuffle away the mad queen and let her princess take the throne.

If only Edith would stop crying about it.

*   *   *

The donor party was on a ranch, a sprawling herd of Tom, Dicks, and Jerrys who each spent hundreds on their denim. It was like watching children at a fair, except all the usual delicious innocence had been traded for smugness and ego as they operated tractors and milked cows. When Marie Antoinette had a fake village to play make-believe as a peasant, the people reacted. Out here, however, there were no eyes and ears.

Only I, narrowing my gaze, took in the lot of them.

Edith existed in a double state to them. They tolerated her because of her lineage and dynasty. She was the regent of her fortune. But her wife? They wouldn't say anything directly, all smiles and handshakes, but Edith had begun to see through it. She had been the cub, the next generation. Most of these people's children had done something in their youth, but they'd gotten clean through rehab or other means. Edith was fully grown, and her oddity hung off her shoulder and rested on her third finger.

Her consternation mattered little. With her parents interred in all but the most literal sense, she was the head of her family, and business superseded all. She joined in the bullshitting and ego stroking. Her smile forced, a little grimace tugging at her expression at every fresh slight.

Edith was almost mine and mine alone. She so close to being cut off from all those bastards. The pathetic rich who didn't understand power. What an awful class of overlords, these *bros* and *whores* who infected the world with sweatpants and buzzwords.

The object of the party was more of the old class of two-faced sleaze. I watched as he made his round and did his handshakes. He was like an older version of Eric, Alexa's ex, who wouldn't cease hounding me. I had to put an end to things when he began stalking Edith and me. His warm brown eyes were at their prettiest when they were wide with the last light of dying fear. Somehow I doubt this candidate would show a morsel of truth even in his last moments. His palm was clammy when he reached me, his attention half-baked at best, but then he locked in, finding something alluring. I could see the instant he decided he wanted me. He was married, I'm married, but that didn't matter. It was in his beady eyes and slicked-back hair: this was a man groomed for power. He wasn't begging for our money. He was receiving what he was owed. In turn, we got our quid pro quo.

The perfectly practiced smile was wasted on him. Perhaps his skull post-decomposition would retain the charm without all the fat. Decay takes time. His death, however, would not.

For all the expenses and pomp, they hadn't accounted for a rogue tornado, and the cramped shelter only fit sixty people. When push came to shove, all those zeroes couldn't be calculated when the animal took over.

At first Edith seemed shell-shocked, but a few weeks later, when the news cycle had already moved on, she admitted something quietly in bed: "They were such assholes."

I laughed until tears streamed from my eyes.

*   *   *

Two of the survivors from the Zurcudo Massacre, as the event was dubbed, invited us over for dinner. Perhaps some eager interest in further consolidating ranks. Edith was old guard now, unlike all those new heirs who just took the reins of their empires. Or could it be commiseration? Wasn't talking through one's feelings all the rage these days, using words borrowed from therapy erroneously till they were ground to a meaningless pulp?

Alas, they weren't interested in anything fun. They had a new candidate to pump full of money who was hard to control but virile in all the ways they wanted.

Edith as hesitant. She preened and waffled about moderation. She was becoming boring. She's growing weak.

Meanwhile, our hosts were becoming more and more irritating. They kept trying to come back to politics. I drew us away to less cumbersome topics. Their vapid opinions on art kept the meal trundling along for a few minutes, and then Edith set in about the climate again. She'd been doomscrolling these last few months, fixated and glued to her phone. She often expected assurances from me, assurances I couldn't give her.

Now she was on her latest pronouncement: "I just think these days, adoption might be the better course. Bringing a child into this world is a lot."

"Yes, well, that makes sense given…well, your situation," the woman of the house implicated.

"There are ways." Edith smiled at me from around the rim of her wineglass.

I bit into the steak our host's chef had whipped up. He'd listened and left mine wonderfully bloody.

"All this doom and gloom," the man of the house said dismissively. "The world is doing just fine. People just expect fairness to materialize overnight. They forget the pecking order."

I stared at him, trying to see if he would squirm. "Perhaps they should be reminded."

"Ha, you speak as if you're one of us," the wife sniped.

"Don't insult me," I simmered. "It would be beneath my station."

Now our hosts were annoyed. Best not to push things. Edith seemed nervous, almost shaking. I excused myself to use their restroom, but sadly there weren't any fun toys in their clean marble dungeon. I liked to apply my creativity as much as the next artist, and a painter required brushes, not crayons.

Defeated, for now, I kicked that bucket down the road. My body harbored annoying systems that needed tending to, not just the bowel movements. Perturbations can have a physical effect, ones that need tempering. As I washed up, splashing water on my face, the whole nine yards, I heard a muffled shout and a glass shattering. The woman of the house must have spilled her wine again. Her husband bellowed at her the last time she did it.

After rolling my eyes indulgently to the me in the mirror, I headed back into the fray.

Silence lay stagnant throughout the mansion. A single thud and a slick sound echoed throughout the geometric minimalism. Passing a twee, surrealistic sculpture, I took a final breath of resolve, building up my patience, waiting for my moment to inflict my will.

It was pointless. As I stepped back into the dining room, everything had changed.

Edith was bent over on the near side of the table, and wine was everywhere, mixed with all the blood. The woman of the house was sprawled at Edith's feet, her hair a wash of dark crimson and deep violet, one steak knife sticking out of her collarbone. Her husband was leaning back in his chair, his head and the knife in his eye, pointed to the sky. A few of his fingers were scattered on the table, and their original *Haystack* on the wall had become blood-splattered collateral damage.

Edith, panting, exuberant, looked up at me, a tentative grin stretching out her sharpest features. "Hey, didn't know how long you'd be." Abandoning the knife she can't retrieve, she swiped a tremulous hand over her mouth, managing to soil herself further.

Approaching her with due caution, I offered an elegant wave of my hand as if I've found only a passing peculiarity. "You've made quite a mess. Just what do you think you're doing?"

Her smile turned into a simpering smirk, her arms knitting together as she aired an open accusation. "Exactly what you would have done, Alexa,"

Ah, so we had finally reached that point. She was s in for a penny, in for a pound now. "You know I'm not really Alexa. I haven't been since the day she went down into that cave and never came back."

I watched her, eager for flickering panic, a furrowed brow, a quivering lip, or eyes wide as a deer's in headlights. *Snow passing by headlights.* I shook the memory away and focused, waiting for Edith to give me the final satisfaction she could offer.

Instead she gave me so much more. She placed her hand, dainty and so unlike the killer she had become, on either side of her, gripping the glass table. She leaned forward, rolling her shoulders and her neck.

"Sure," she breathed. "I've known for a while now."

Her words hit me like a bolt of lightning. Stifling my surprise, I gave in to the surging heat. Gripping her hips and pulling her into me, she responded, electric, even by her standards. She was on fire, her arousal blossoming in an instant. With a gentle worshipping excitement, her legs locked around my hips, and she spun me onto the dining room table, pinning me with her body and her kisses.

"But you never said anything," I said, disengaging, confronting her with my eyes.

She frowned like it's inherently a silly question. "Why would I? I've always liked you better."

Dusk, Day, and Dawn

EVERY NIGHT, in between the sun and the day's domain lies the moon, the whistling winds, and a woman who walks alone along the wilderness. A trail of asphalt, tar, and concrete, not the cobbles of old. Though gravel still sits like a moat in front of the large chalets.

A car clunks by, belching black smoke dipped crimson by its taillights, the darkness happily swallowing the rest. By technicality, this car is much older than the wandering woman, and the invention of the automobile is even more so. But the woman doesn't like to think like that. Being in one's twenties isn't nearly as special as feeling eternity.

The horn blares, and the driver shouts, his hand animated around his cigarette. He called out over and over. The woman keeps her hands in her wool coat's pockets.

The man is insistent. "Oh, *belle*, come now. The night is dark and it's cold." He makes a blubbering sound with his lips, imitating the chill, not aware the woman is an inferno wrapped in wool and the ligaments beneath.

Knowing there is little she can do, she tries nonetheless. "It would best for us both if you were to drive on, *monsieur*."

"Oh, don't be like that," the man whines as his headlights flicker twice then shut off. "The next town is three miles away. Don't waste your legs—"

The sentence never finishes, cut off as it is. The car trundles on for a few more meters, its headlights ignited again, its cabin emptied.

"Three miles. That shouldn't take me too long," the woman says and walks on.

*   *   *

From Marseille to Ytrac, Le Mans, to the edges of Tours, she goes. A gentle slope, a rising cliff, it makes no difference. She never accepts a ride, not even on a beggar's mule. The nomads respect her, but she doesn't dine with them for entirely considerate reasons.

The day is bright but spotted by clouds, making the fields a checkerboard of shade and sun, leaving everything indeterminate as far as the woman is concerned. For the birds and the rest of nature, it's a perfectly suitable summer's day, in utter contrast to what the chill night brings.

The woman picks her way along the tracts and tractor tracks of a few farmhouses. People work this land, their hands and feet blistered, and more than a few inquire after her. She either makes her excuses or else ignores them, letting them get on with their days and their lives.

In Amboise she ponders Leonardo da Vinci's tomb. She wishes she had the time to see it. That adage and style he clung to: *Memento Mori* clings to her coattails.

After descending into the town proper, she settles on procuring a coffee, favoring the sides of the street bathed in illumination. The café she selects has a few tables in the alley, and her chair is rickety and lopsided. It appears to have been green before becoming bleached, and every time she fidgets, so does the chair and a loose stone beneath it. She, by all appearances, is alone, her half of the table bright and glistening, the other side and its chair draped in shadow. She sips an espresso and mulls over its flavor, how starkly it stands out now that the matters of temperature and caffeine have no effect upon her.

The lackadaisical summation winds her internal clock back to idylls and times gone by. The many dates she had partaken in, so many cafés, so many faces, so much time wasted.

The waiter, grinning, comes over offering a scone. A customer had forgotten to pick it up. "Do you want it?"

"Oui. Merci." She uses every inflection and turn of etiquette, of their culture, and of the larger culture, the dictates of pleasantry never bordering on coquetry.

If only the man could realize the latter distinction. He disappears into the shop and the woman breathes out for a moment, happy with the scone and the interaction, pleased to return to ruminations and memories of sensations long since abated.

She's about to leave, her cup empty and the saucer filled with the last few crumbs, when the man returns. He insists upon a festival, a film, or simply showing her the town.

"Your accent. You're from the south, are you not? Come let me show you Da Vinci's tomb." As he speaks, he rests a hand on the table, leaning in. The sun has moved on, and only a bit of the table is still burning hot, leaving him to favor the cool shade.

The woman stares at his hand, then at him, as he presses himself farther and farther into the dimness. *"Memento Mori,"* she replies. "Is that not how it goes?"

"I wouldn't know," the man says before he is gone.

"No, it appears you don't," she says.

Still, the woman sets down some change for the cup and the scone.

*   *   *

Dusk makes the woman think of her with its muted, softened overtones and blue casts. The light always made her love's eyes seem even more perfectly blue. They'd clamber up trees as if they were children, nestled in knots or lower in the roots. Wherever they lay, they would whisper, and she would conceive of her next invention, not of metal but of might, of thought and precepts bordering on the effrontery. The invocations, the incantations. It was a new fixation each month.

The woman humored her love, chatted with her, let her ramble, their hands entwined. She could mute the words and enjoy the last dregs of the day upon those animated lips, waiting to silence her with a stolen kiss.

Her love was of a jealous caste and wished to monopolize the woman's time. Being out in the fields, with wheat and wine, and little in the way of comfort nor a ready respite from their families, the woman was ensnared. Eventually she was whisked away on a journey. Her love had discovered something, a ritual of sorts, one that required a different farmland, a different region, the sound of a church's bell ringing out…

The woman is so lost in memories that she grows forgetful, and at a fuel station, she lingers too long, choosing a sugary snack. The heat of the summer blows out a fuse. Darkness overtakes the store. The other customer is gone in an instant.

The stream of sparks showering outside the windows throws her back once more to that field… It was twilight, her love was grinning, and their hands were interlaced. The temperature was as soft as a kiss, the wind as well. They waited together as the murky azure gave way to the dimmest of nights, with no stars in the sky, no moon, nothing to illuminate them but flashlights. Her love's hands were hurried, and soon her arms spread wide. A shout let loose, bells ringing out as the wind picked up. The breeze was as sharp as knives. The woman's hands were frozen; she couldn't even pull her coat tight around her. All she could do was watch.

The metal clamor rose, bells doubling and redoubled, mounting a discordant cacophony only supplanted by the laughter as biting as any scream, the last sound the woman ever heard from her love.

They were at Domrémy-la-Pucelle, where a miracle had appeared some six hundred years prior. This then was the ashen afterimage, the revision through inversion.

The woman, as she wept and ran, thought she would perish at every instant, yet she persisted. When she barged into a farmer's house, they wondered if they should call a doctor, someone who might place the woman in a far-flung facility.

She forced herself to calm down and to lie; she would need to become good at lying. The farmers offered her the bed of their son away on holiday. She collapsed on the mattress, trying to breathe, trying to live in the moment and quell the overwhelming panic. Instead she realized how alone she was and what she had lost.

She didn't yet know what she had gained, not until the next morning.

Dawn and its shadows, the magenta sheen reflected off the windows and grass, met her, as a soft hazy glow to match her groggy mind.

She went down for breakfast; the last thing she wanted was interaction, but she had to appear sane. At first it was odd not to feel hungry or cold, hot in only a nightgown, full when she hadn't eaten in over a day. But she didn't have time to dwell on that. In the kitchen, she found no one. An oddity—she was sure she'd heard a whistling kettle. It was still crying, so she took it off the burner.

"Where are they?" a voice said behind her. The daughter of the farmers. She was a little older than the woman, with a gaunt face and an uneasy attitude. None too trusting, not that it would help.

"I don't know," the woman answered.

"Yet you use our kettle?" she spat in that hurried French way.

"I didn't do this. I thought you must have."

"Where are my parents?"

"I do not know!"

"Liar!"

The farmer's daughter took three steps toward her but never a fourth as her foot fell away and sunk into the floor or rather was sent somewhere else. The rest of her followed. Slowly consumed. The action was untrained, sporadic, messy painful. The victim's face was ashen with her agony and certain instincts took over. Once compelled by rage, she was now pitiable. "Help me!" she screamed.

But the woman could only press herself into the wall, muttering meaningless phrases as she saw the unseeable in that hungry void.

"You're killing me!"

A realization dawned as harshly as befitted the scene transpiring before her: "No. *I'm* not," the woman said.

And then the girl did perish.

*   *   *

It became much cleaner and quicker after that. The woman took to her travels, never staying put, never tiring or growing famished. She didn't linger or spend too long speaking to anyone, for each conversation and every interaction ended the same: a cruel jealousy and a simple curse.

She makes it to the edge of Orlean by noon when the sun is highest, and the shadows fall only under the trees. She lies out in the fields, where she can feel the heat and enjoy it, her coat spread about her like a blanket upon the supple stalks of grass. She thinks of times past and things more present, of *her* so nearby. She daydreams of old armies and of lost loves and lives alike,

Though sometimes lost loves are not lost

Sometimes they change and they evolve past the tangible.

But that doesn't mean she can't still feel her.

My Eyes, Those Eyes

THE FOREST, imperious and apathetic, shifted and fluttered, barely perceptible. Rainfall cuts through the heavy leaves; the soil turned to mulch, sodden gullies. A sound beyond the showers scraped at the mind, the moonless night a void beyond the dim lantern. One compatriot jostled another, ribbing him, mocking him, for a bulwark is hewn together if one can make light of terror.

The fear passed, and the first man settled down into his pack and rolled inside the thin excuse for a tent. He was content letting the other two keep the watch. "We couldn't pack a bigger tarp?" he whined, scraping his head against the canvas.

"Shh, pipe down," the fourth man, the leader of the group, hissed. The irregular sounds had returned. The leader quickly covered the lantern, leaving a yellow slice to paint the tiny encampment.

Night senses, pitiful senses, took the lead. The unyielding pitter-patter drew out, each protracted second being all too *damning*. The forest cared little; it continues as it always has, rainfall, rejuvenation, death to life, life to death, passive intricate happenstance. To the interlopers, the forest was nothing more or less than ambiguously disguised malice, a looming maw waiting to bite.

One second, one heartbeat, the gap between what was and what arrived, a huff of breath, the crush of leaves, bark ripped and gouged, as an unseen mass dominated the clearing. A cacophony of screams followed as bone, limb, and throat were torn as easily as the leaves. The tall man, the last one left, scrambled for the lantern, garnering one glimpse before he became nothing but soaked leaves and splintered wood.

*   *   *

I hadn't even been on my own for a year, and I knew my means were expended. Prospects for work were dwindling, and I had few resources. By then, I was numb to it. Inevitability does that to a person, and this was a decade in the making. Poverty likes to grow as rife as any wildlife. Plant the seeds and they shall sprout. This land held the most fertile ground for that application, Appalachia, that appellation, it fits nice and tidy.

My pa was injured when they warred over Blair Mountain, the army with their martial law and the Baldwin-Felts agency with their well-endowed backers. The coal barons wanted their mines to choke the gullet of the earth and earn company money to use money at company stores. Things escalated, as they always do. They painted their hideous portrait of us in the papers that we weren't starved but instead led by "misguided rage." So bombs were dropped and people died.

Nothing changed. Unions tried, unions failed, reforms too. Pretty soon Wall Street cratered and the miasma spread. The Forty-Seven sharing the misery.

Someone told me that after the Great War and Blair Mountain, things could not get much worse. I suppose that, with how things wound up, most would have him shot. Jynxes and curses superstitious natures are a given. 'Why is God punishing us?' In the cities they reveled, they sinned with their illegal spirits and the spirits of wanton sexuality and greed. The matters of moonshine were ignored, as were copulations in the barns and sheds bereft of wedding bands. As for greed? Well, a man in New York might lie and, by it, garner a thousand dollars. Here in my life, I'd seen a score of men beaten to a pulp over fifty cents.

Things in the city grew worse till there was no hope of escaping anywhere. What work and pay there was dried up. The rains of prosperity never arrived. By the time the twenties became the thirties, I was near thirty myself, twenty-eight and hardworking, not enough, never enough. My pa, one evening in February, sat me down and laid it out simply: I had to go; there was no means to feed me. I'd never had luck in marriage, though that was more a matter of interest. But my delay had run its course. Grace, my remaining unwed sister, still an adolescent and sickly, could do but the basic chores alone. I couldn't stand to watch it, to witness her guilt and shame, no matter how many times I told her it wasn't her fault, only our damnable luck; she refused to listen. I suppose we were each stubborn in our ways. The responsibility of her always weighed on me, the price of love. An investment, without cynicism, the warmth of a smile, of a hug, the nights we'd spent sharing stories—conjuring better days for ourselves than the ones we lived.

I screamed at my father, who cursed me, and hated him for taking the one thing he, my mother, and life had ever given me. I despised him because I knew there was no world in which I'd let my sister suffer just for my sake.

I left three days after that, my handkerchief wet in my hand from where I'd wiped Grace's tears away, her throat raw and coarse as she begged me not to leave her. No words could suffice. I told her farewell and those most damning words imaginable: "I love you."

Months passed, and autumn set in. I traveled when I could manage, working wherever I could. It wasn't enough, and neither was my virtue that good yet to be sold. I heard tell from a kindly man, similarly indisposed of work, that a community was sprouting up a little ways from the town we were passing through. Tucked right up into the mountains and woods. They had work there, food, clean water, and shelter. He said their leader was a rich man trying to start up a sanctuary of sorts. A glimmer of hope, like a morsel dropped before a starving beggar. That's what I'd become. Past shame or pride, I felt only the rush of possibility, of a chance at last.

It was a passing fantasy, but there wasn't much left to wager, which meant, by turns, there wasn't much left to lose. The man who offered me the tip refused to go himself; he was Jewish, and while the world might reap a toil, he wouldn't let it have his faith.

I had managed on my own and I would do so again. The journey added more grime to my dress, which was already half consumed by dirt. Mud clumped in my hair like that of a mangy dog. Thin and dirty, that's how I arrived at the Followers of St. Celestine, though the sign merely said, *ST. CELESTINE'S*. A fine-looking white-painted arch stood as a fenceless entrance, and each structure after was similarly white-painted, each raised a little so runoff from the nearby hill wouldn't wash them out.

Figures in gray, tan, and white went about their days. Some were thin, while others were rounded off, full figured, moving with purpose, carrying buckets, burlap food bags, or tools. They moved with the practiced understanding of routine. The sight of me didn't cause alarm. In fact, it produced a coterie of greeters. "Young woman, are you lost?" a man of fifty asked me. The small procession flanking him wore variations of whites, grays, and a few blacks; none were threadbare, and most of the apparel had flowers or dyed patterns. None wore rosaries, for despite the naming convention, none were Catholic.

The man, Jeremiah, as I'd learn, spoke eloquently. They all did. "I know it must look like a mirage, but this is no desert. Though I think you could speak to any of us and hear the word *oasis* frequently or such synonyms as that."

"I ain't…" My schooling from when I was sent to Maryland during the war came back. "I am not lost," I croaked.

"You've heard of us?" a matronly woman, Meave, asked. Although her pleated hair was as colorless as overcast light, her eyes were cheery.

"I heard work would bring food and shelter. I'm a hard worker. I've had to be all my life. What needs doing— whatever needs to be seen to—can do it, or learn it, with ease."

"Very good. Certainly, come, be welcome." Meave alighted. "We shall have you cleaned up, and then you can meet Mr. Montgomery—Patrick. He's the one who put this all together. You can meet him when he's finished teaching class."

St. Celestine's required no oaths or paperwork. By stepping through that arch, I became one of them. The woman who washed me asked if I was ever married or a widower; *divorcee* hung unspoken in the air. "Never," I told her truthfully. "Are you going to… Do you need to check?"

"No, no, no, we have faith in you. Your virtue is yours. Lying about it is between you and God."

When my hair was brushed, they put me in a white linen dress. It wasn't particularly modest, being sleeveless and low-cut. Tied with a belt at the waist, it hung without shape, which Meave reassured me would return once I had a full belly again.

They escorted me to a building adjoined to the main chapel and schoolhouse, the accommodations of Patrick Montgomery. The man wore a tweed suit and a silk tie. He was cleanly shaven, had short brown hair, and an average, if not offensive, face. In a holistic summary, he was indistinguishable from any businessman, save one: his eyes brimmed and overflowed with intrigue and intellect. This produced in him an abundance of charm and charisma.

His appraisal was as quick as it was pitiless. There was no mistaking the interest in his eyes, the man's wants, even if he attempted to conceal them. "What is your name?" Carefully he set the book he'd been reading on one stack among his litany, his eyes expectant.

"Ashley, but mostly I go by Ash."

* * *

*   *   *

Winter made the mountain barren, life hidden away, and only a damning silence persists. Three men patrolling the woods, firearms in hand, peered into the growing twilight. They argued back and forth. One of them sniffled, whining about losing track of time. His hand hesitated on his weapon, his fingerless gloves doing little to protect against the chill. The whistling frigid wind mocked them, the rustling naked trees laughing. The very forest itself was a threat, waiting, silent as the grave, anticipating that single beckoning noise.

The frostbitten ground cracked and ashy dirt was sent up in a cloud from atop the rise of a crevice. The men raised their rifles, but it as already too late. Chilled frigid skin was traded for warm blood. Talons, glistening, produced from a paw larger than any natural beast, limbs faster than their bulk should allow, a blur of matted dark fur, slick with ichor. The beast carved through flesh and bone. One hacked-apart corpse was thrown into another. The last man, fallen on his back, plead mercy, his final words cut off as his head was crushed in. Everything inside burst like a flower's pulp.

Only heavy panting and a stream of heated exhales remained. The quiet was interrupted as a furious vocalization split the black ice.

*   *   *

Spring arrived quicker than I'd expected. We were cooped up inside for most of the winter. The mountains were becoming dangerous. (As the elders continually reminded us.) Patrick was implored to put in a stricter curfew and restrict who was allowed to venture out. He refused, for he likened it to a breach of freedom. Faith and liberty were his cornerstones. While he wept for each who went missing, he refused to "punish all of you for those who will not listen."

St Celestine's was tucked into the slope of the mountain. The schoolhouse,

Patrick's home, the elders' building, and the storehouse were three stories tall. Then, an inner ring of two-story houses for the families. The outer ring was for the new or those without a family, each a single story. This was where I was placed. There was a living room and two bedrooms, split between the four of us. Annie and Jolene took one room, seeing as how they were twins. My roommate was a woman near my age with an unmistakable world-weary attitude.

"I'm Amberlyn." That moment stuck in my memory, her hand thrust forward, the light softly wrapping around the left side of her cheek. That side of her face bore a scar from the father she'd fled.

Her hair was a mane of deep black. "Raven," I concluded one night.

"Crow," she cooed in reply.

"Amberlyn" was a fitting name, for her eyes were indeed amber, her pupils like an insect caught in the jewel. The rest of her face was severe and gaunt by nature and nurture, her expression ever steadfast and observant.

She joined in the spring and was an excellent tutor. We would lay in our beds, and she'd keep me apace long into the night till we greeted the dawn.

Amber wasn't my only teacher. "Age matters not in the eyes of education," Patrick dictated. Therefore, everyone participated, arranged by peer group. I downplayed how much I knew; that made it easier. Higher learning was never a possibility for me, and that didn't change at the sanctuary. Not on account of funds or location more so the fact that I was a woman. This mattered a great deal to the followers of St. Celestine's. Instead I spent the time daydreaming and teasing Amber. "Ash," she'd hiss under her breath, which made it all the better.

Trouble followed me. The more comfortable I felt, the more I erred—a little rule-breaking for fun and the thrill of it. I fostered a reputation among those of the younger age bracket as the woman who could make mischief out of nothing. Everything was strict at St Celestine's, days made into a maddening routine as if each minute of every hour must be accounted for. The work was never done—the fields, the laundry, the learning—baneful, disheartening… I hated the nauseating mundanity and despised the way we were preached to without every uttering the name *of God*—lessons and learning. Fairly quickly I understood there were eyes everywhere. We were our own wardens. That was a mantra. Self-discipline. Easily interpreted to mean we must keep reciprocal responsibility over one another.

Everyone else was culled by it, the challenge of it, but it invigorated me. Even the smallest offenses carried plenty of risk. Something as simple as stealing laundry. Amber was against it. As we saddled up at the wash house, her eyes fretted over every possible sightline, even the mountain rising above us. But Mass was in session and school was soon to follow; we'd slipped away unnoticed. No one was about, no eyes except hers pleading with me to stop.

"Think of it this way: when they find it, we'll have to clean them up again, and you always say you like laundry better than the fields," I insisted.

She pouted and tapped her foot. "You like the fields better, though."

"Precisely. Noble and full of self-sacrifice." I placed a hand on my chest as if invoking an oath.

Amber sent an annoyed glance toward the heavens, likely wondering how she'd gotten so unlucky. We both knew, however, this was no indemnity but an active choice. My chest swirled with excitement, watching her ponder, waiting for my satisfaction. Every second made the result more appealing—the success harder earned. This connection deepened, hardening into something solid, something I could grasp. The thrill of misadventure was our bond, the foundation of our friendship.

"The lock will be easy," she said, at last, pulling a pin from her hair.

The house was small, stone floored, and ever and always stuffy from the humidity of boiling water. It didn't take us long to fill up our arms with bundles of fresh clothes, and it only took three seconds for me to decide where to stow them all.

It took half a day for anyone to discover the articles, smelling and wafting of every spice in the storehouse, and form there three hours to deduce the culprits…or culprit. When we were brought before Patrick, in all his simmering rage, he spoke nicely to us. "Fun and games can ease our monotony, but the clothes on our back are sacred, not because of a verse of the word of God but because of human necessity. We are not animals. We are flesh, and flesh requires warmth. Skin requires protection from the world's million abrasions. Please confess and we can move on from this."

My hands were bound tightly, my heart beating faster. Patrick singled me out in class most days, directing questions to me, many times; I answered with purposeful falsehoods so as not to draw attention to myself, yet the attention persisted. This favoritism and his present necessity were key. If I found a way to admit it without implicating Amber, he'd go easy on me. I knew he would.

"It was me," Amber said. My calculations were far too slow. "Ash did nothing but look out for others. I said I had work to do. She didn't know the plan I'd formulated."

"So you hauled all the clothes by yourself?"

"Yes, two trips. When she realized what I was doing, she told me to stop."

I stared at her, wide-eyed like a fool, and my stomach sank further when Patrick fixed me with an apathetic look. "Is this true?"

Amber inclined her head, urging me to say yes. I couldn't say no to her, deny her this self sacrifice. "Yes," I lied.

He sent me out into the hall, back to my chores. But I waited there, on the naked wood of the bench, hearing him shout and berate Amber for what felt like an eternity. All his cruelty and authority he'd spared us was unleashed the moment he believed I wasn't the one at fault.

I think he was far more onerous to her because of it. He thought she might be corrupting me, leading me astray. That made everything choke up, knowing she was being blamed for my sundering impulse, accused of what I was doing, what I'd done. When she was finally released, I stood and watched her, begging her with my expression, if not my words. Tearfully she stormed past me, not so much as meeting my eye.

I found her out at last, at the edge of the fields, near where the forest began. Her slender legs were curled up to her chest, her skirts forming a beige-gray tent, her shoulders hunched, eyes squinting as she stared at nothing in particular. I fell in beside her, the soft dirt shifting under my weight, which I felt in powdery droves.

Amber had a welt under her eye. The same purpling conflagration I'd received from my pa, just as she had from hers. The sort the elders reserved for adequate breaches of conduct, the kind they reveled in doling out when they finally got the opportunity.

Taking her hand in mine, I apologized to her again and again. Nothing worked, and my guilt grew and evolved, active and aflutter like a flame. She was still crying; her tears hadn't dried. She was hurt—I'd hurt her in my way. After unfurling one hand from hers, I reached into my pocket and pulled out my handkerchief, then gently dabbing where the moisture ran like rain down her slender cheeks. She offered only a pointed, stubborn scowl. I paid her no heed. "This was my sister's. She gave it to me when I left."

"I'm not your sister and I don't want to be," she said.

"I'm not asking you to be. I'm just asking if, when I act like a fucking moron, you'll still be here. That you might forgive me. Just as she always did, though, I doubt she'll ever forgive me for leaving her."

"Why did you then?"

"We hadn't the food to feed us both."

"Self-sacrifice."

I forced a wan smirk. "I'm not completely full of shit."

Her eyelids dropped, heavy with thick lashes, doe-like and delicate and beautiful, a contrasting, splendid counterpoint to her firm ferocity. Her chapped lips parted, and a gentle hum spilled from between her teeth, soon turning into a song. A lullaby—her mother's. From before the tuberculosis had found her.

Her voice made all that guilt and remorse melt away; the remaining remnants ran like lava, spilling into some fresh cauldron, steaming and solidifying into something altogether new and unknown. I couldn't name it and I couldn't run away from it. I just wanted to peek over the rim and see what it was she had stirred to life.

From that day forward, I was far more careful and observant and didn't waste time on silly rebellions. I pined for gold, for those breaks in the rock that might hold a diamond in the rough. My crowning achievement, in a way, was the matter of Norbert. He came to us as one of the boys in his suspenders and linen shirt. The boys tended to steer clear of the women's housing, propriety and all. But we found him returning something, an article of clothing; a dress had been put in with his laundry. Yet the way he held it between his hands, catching the thin light, I could tell something was amiss.

A surreptitious flight of impulse fluttered through me. "Why do you hold it so?" I asked. "It's just cloth."

He bowed his head and thrust the garment forward, and I pushed it away. A sly, ridiculous thought crossed my mind. "Why don't you put it on? What kind of man would be so craven to refuse a dare?"

My housemates protested, but a hand held aloft quieted them. "Go on," I urged. "You can use my room to change and you'll be vouchsafed. Those three know it is I who put you up to it."

Norbert obeyed, disappearing into the bedroom. "Have a little sense of adventure," I scolded my roommates as they glared. Amber gave up to pout in her chair. A moment later, the door opened again, revealing a flushing face, the stooping posture traded for a careful arc, hands unsure what to make of themselves, settling at last, clasped at the waist, timid, shy, and happy, laced together.

"Look at the ravishing visage," I announced before making a few adjustments to the dress to better suit the wearer. I stepped away, pleased and grinning.

Norbert's first visit lasted only forty minutes, growing each time till it was simply routine and he became a fifth member of our little cottage. My wit had won again, paired with another sly smile. "'Nora' sounds better than 'Norbert,' doesn't it? Rather a hideous thing to name a child."

"Nora…I would like that very much," Nora said, beaming in those subtle ways of joy.

She started borrowing dresses and shifts from us. She had some small privacy in her room. Spared the trouble of a roommate on account of the disappearances.

One day we worked the fields together, and no one noticed the extra set of hands. Only by nightfall, when they feared the wilderness had taken her, did she return to her normal guise. When we returned to the house, our mirth felt as if it had no end, the giggling noteworthy enough for Meave to comment, "What a high-pitched gaggle of hens you are."

On another day we were spared discovery only by the driving rain, which brought thick mist and low visibility. Still, as I looked across the throw of the spread-out housing, I could tell Jeremiah and a few others were looking our way.

The twins were rattled by this. Annie rounded on me, her generous eyes filled with impudent wrath. "Did you not see how close we were to discovery? Because you insist on this game of dress-up. We have had our fun and our laughs. Now none of us are laughing."

Nora sat huddled in the far corner, curled in on herself. She looked up at me through the strands of her hair, which she'd been growing out at my encouragement. Amber, meanwhile, sat at the desk and offered no relief. If anyone were to rise to the occasion, it would fall on my shoulders. Tempering my own rage, I chose the diplomatic option—the logical, kindly sort.

"This isn't any great offense. And I'd tell Patrick that myself. He's the one who preaches understanding and seeing to our own. 'Plant the seeds of friendship and they sprout in unexpected ways.' Well, here is a very unexpected one but no less lovely."

Jolene shook her head, agreeing with her sister. "Mother always told us to look out for ourselves first and foremost, as no one else will. Why should we risk punishment now? You know how many are going missing, how much stricter everything has gotten. They'll think he's here to protect himself. Coward and craven."

Nora, in the corner, buried her face between her knees, the shame penetrating deeply. I, however, would have none of it. "You are both wrong, not in your worry but in your lack of candor. We are here as a community. To sow compassion. Well, that starts here with h—" I stopped myself short; they didn't understand, and I didn't know how to explain it to them. The way Nora was *one of us*, not one of them. They couldn't see deeper than flesh and attributions.

"Go collect our clothes," I ordered.

"In this downpour?" one of them asked.

"You want clothes to wear tomorrow? Or should I send you out in your shifts?"

Scowling, they ran out into the rain, little bits of scrap wood held above their heads for protection—two bobbing blond ducklings.

"You shouldn't press them so hard," Amber chided from her table.

There was something entirely domestic about her matter-of-fact tone that left me smirking. "They're fearful of Patrick's authority. Reason will only get so far with them. Sometimes I have to be equally scary." I spoke and shrugged, falling to the couch nearest poor Nora, still hiding like a rabbit.

"It's okay," I whispered. "Amber, can you get her a glass of tea? Poor thing is shaking."

She shot me a look, a question loaded within. "Can *she* not ask after her own needs?"

"Just get it anyway. Please."

Nora watched her work for a moment—we both did before she opened up her body just that little bit required to let the truth out, limbs spread, heart bared. "You both should know I've been caught before. With clothes I've found or…stolen…makeup as well…powder blush…lipstick." She gulped after speaking that last word, the ghost of a pleasant memory on her delicate features soon poisoned by what came next. "They punished me for it and said if I ever relapsed as a heretic, it would be much worse—will be much worse…because that's what I am, relapsed."

Her voice rose, high and whistling just like the kettle, while her eyes bugled and her thin body quaked, a delicate leaf on the branch. I went to her and held her by the shoulders. My tone was firm as iron. "I shall not let that happen."

An easy egotism. The picture of brashness.

This continued into the boiling humidity of summer. Our labors were exhausting, and the house offered little reprieve. At night, when there was no sun to hide from, one could still feel the heat like an oppressive blanket. I'd had enough of it and stripped off the cloth that stuck to my sweating body, tossing it to the floor and lying on my bed. The moonlight pooled over me, and I felt… observed. In the dark were those eyes, amber and glowing. She had seen me plenty of times. This time, however, my breath left me, and a moment dragged out for an eon.

I slipped off the mattress and made a slender movement. After crossing to her bed, I crouched beside her, and the entire time we never left each other's eyes. The intensity mounted as I reached up, took her hand, and brought it to my bare skin…

That night we shared few words and little sleep. The dawn arose to kiss the sky, and I kissed Amber again, for the hundredth time, countless times, and innumerable times after.

*   *   *

Cloth clung to wet, sweat-slicked bodies, now running with blood, seven corpses this time, and more to be made. Those left prepared to fight, as running would be pointless. Courage was the only thing their bodies had left. What little good it did. A rake, a knife, a hatchet, a revolver. The final man seized the moment, sending a clout of buckshot at the raging muzzle. He bought himself two full seconds before the bleeding muzzle returned, breaching the smoky cloud of gunpowder. This time the fangs tore with a pained fervor, the shotgun ripped away and snapped in two. Its broken metal made for a fine spear to impale its previous wielder.

*   *   *

One day I set out to the forest, searching for a more private sanctuary. I discovered a small glen with a pair of boulders forming a natural diminutive cave. The nearby stream let me practice fishing via stolen rods, tackle, and bait. I brought Amber there once it was ready or as near as I could manage without her talents. It became our heaven, a little slice of the woods to ourselves. For our fun and those mature games we played.

We talked more than ever. Often lying atop the boulders, peering through the changing trees at the cloudy August sky, an adjective alone, as September and its changing leaves had set in.

"My mother called this a traveling day…when the clouds above move so fast you can see them dart across the sky. She said these were her favorite days

225

to do nothing. To lie back and appreciate what she had." Amber reminisced.

My head lolled to one side, my cheek now at her collarbone. I nuzzled into her, showing my appreciation instead of stating it outright.

She enjoyed this; red flooded her cheeks and her shoulders rose, her body squirming a little. I knew she felt a bit giddy because that's how I felt. Giddy and contented.

Then, like the clouds hurrying across the sea blue sky, Amber modulated, dipping toward a scar. "What if she were wrong? What if she were a hypocrite? It was a day like the one when she left me. When she journeyed to a place I could not follow. What if this were the exact sort of day to *want* things?" She shook her head as close to rueful as she could get. "What would you do, Ash? If you had money, if you had means? Beyond mischief, beyond games."

"I would dye my hair properly and crop it short, wear a dress without a back, and underneath that dress I would wear pants so my skirt could be cut to purposeful tatters. When I moved, it would shift about, little tendrils of silk."

"Silk? What about velvet?" she purred.

"That would be your domain, Amber."

"You have me there… What else? Not things, not stuff…a life, yours and mine, the freedom not to care."

I spoke into her skin. "Well, a day might be like this but without the need to return, without *those* worries we share. And if I had money, I could pay for something, a little piece of paper, one you have to earn."

"Not much of a riddle," she teased, maneuvering her head so it pressed into mine.

"It wasn't meant to be. I need to save my thinking for getting that diploma."

"Hmm, I'd love to be a nurse or a doctor…if I was smart enough."

"You are…and you have such *dexterity*, you could be a surgeon."

"Grisly," she said, screwing up her petite nose, the only thing not sharp about her features.

"Don't lie to me. You aren't squeamish."

"Guilty," she whispered, and then we were kissing again.

Two weeks later, I brought Nora to our unnamed retreat. It was well hidden and a tricky hike if one didn't know the path, but she learned quickly. I never told Annie and Jolene of our glen nor our relationship. I had become weary of them, and the punishments at St. Celestine's had grown worse; the elders doled out physical recompense far more often now. Their zealotry and fear, one thing or the other—I couldn't risk either.

One day I was called to Patrick's office. He never taught faith in the most direct ways. He attended the sermons, further instilling their mandatory nature. He preached his little sayings or favorite biblical quotes. He spent careful time on those who arrived at the sanctuary of a different faith or had abandoned their fate. He said that the way of Christ was one of charity, that alms would prove what "real benediction brings," and that given enough time, they would all find the light. He taught these in private, in small groups or sessions. The orderly activities, the pulpit, and the masses fell to Jeremiah or one of our other elders, and the longest ceremonies were held during the monthly bonfire nights. Patrick was only ever truly invested in those. The nights were reckless abandon, and impulses were more permissible. Every other time, and every other day, purity ruled the sanctuary.

I curtsied and entered his office, fighting to maintain my composure. I was certain the twins had ratted us out. Patrick didn't stay behind his desk. Instead he chose the seat beside me so we faced each other. I kept my hands in my lap, hiding my brackish mood and my alighted nerves.

"Ashley, do you know how I came to be here? Has anyone ever told you the tale in its entirety?" When I shook my head, he held up a palm, smiling, "This is not a test. It's a good thing, actually, for I tend to keep it close to the chest. But you've been with us nearly a year or thereabouts," he amended with a little raise of his chin. "Our little slice of heaven has a story behind it. The book of scripture I was given as a gift. That's what it felt like when I purchased it at auction." He reached to his desk and shifted a pile of books to produce a leather-bound thing, much the worse for wear, stained and cracked. The symbol on its front was a ghostly afterimage, perhaps a cross or anything one configured it to be.

"I wasn't much of a religious man until I read this. It showed me *truth* and made it tangible. But in my sin, I used this writing for greed, to play the stock market."

"It is no great sin to wish for money when, in our day, it is a synonym for simple subsistence," I said.

He nodded. "Spoken better than I ever could, Ashley. Though at the time, I had no view of that, for I felt as a king might while observing his fiefdom and wanting more, so much more. But even I was helpless when Black Tuesday arrived."

Patrick didn't speak mournfully; instead he gestured broadly with his free hand. "I was suitably *humbled.* My path forward wasn't money or being a titan of industry, of this ever-changing landscape of technology and war and politics. He shook his head vividly, passionately his words never graceless but so rapid they nearly slurred together. "I knew what I had to do: to share in my discoveries, to find likeminded folks or those not yet shown the truth. If I could be shown that truth, then anyone could be. I still possessed enough to found this bastion—a perfect paradise, free from the sectarian squabbles, built on the wisdom of the ages." He gestured to the book, cherishing it.

He fell still, waiting for a response I knew not how to formulate. "A good story," I stammered. Fear made me indecisive, but his gaze was too penetrating. This wasn't like in class, where I could fib my way through my answers; there was no hiding from him this time. "You're both great and humble in it. And you're wise, I suppose, to keep it so secretive, for if that book can answer so much, many a man or woman would kill for it."

His eyes narrowed, not with reprisal. This intrigue was deeply rooted, an old oak with fresh bloom upon the branches. "One could interpret that as cynical."

"And what do you interpret it as?"

"Clever. That is what you are. You have had prior education. There's no denying it."

"Others came to you already well-learned."

Patrick shifted forward, the book on his lap, both palms resting his weight upon it (an odd stance given the broadness of his shoulders when hunched over in this way). "Yes, indeed, Ashley, but none have hidden this fact. You did because being the smartest person in the room is only half as good as secreting that fact away. No one would ever suspect you. No one would jostle for your favor or expect action from you. It isn't a king's position—it's better. The man behind the crown, in the shadow of the throne. That's where the real power lies."

"Go on…" I said, unsure what else to say.

"Ashley, my deepest hope is to share these truths with you. To uncover the myriad of secrets held within these pages. I need someone smart. Someone tenacious. And if I might be selfish just once, I want more company in the darkness. Away from the world and its civilization, it's lonely. But there's never been anyone worthy of my attention"—he placed one firm hand on my thigh, solidifying what we'd both known since I'd arrived—"or my affections. Until you."

Gulping, I reached down, fighting my quivering fear, and removed his hand. I waited for when he'd fight back and stop me. I didn't know what I'd do when he did. Instead Patrick let me do so, saying, "It has only been a year and I am a patient man." He leaned back, returning the book to the desk. His causal air belied the truth: he saw it as an inevitability. After all, I had nowhere else to go.

"You may go, Ashley." He watched me the entire time, and I felt a hundred spiders crawl up my spine and burrow under my skin, each tiny leg an extension of him, of the territory he wanted to claim. And would sooner or later.

In the month that followed, Patrick made no further overtures beyond a lingering glance or stare. Otherwise I was left to my devices.

For all my cleverness, I knew no escape save for one: "Amber, do you know of Saint Cecilia?"

"Yes, she was a martyr and patron of saint of music." She pouted. "You know I like to pray to her."

"I know. I know you have a fear of losing your singing voice."

"Mm-hmm," she hummed with a perfect shift in pitch.

"She refused to give up her virginity. Even when she married," I explained. "So if Patrick tries to wed me, he'll be breaking an oath to Mary and God above, and Jesus his son and all the rest, the Holy Spirit. Every last one of them. I will swear it loudly enough that everyone here will know my vow."

Amber's brow furrowed. "But you're not...."

"It can be easily breached. I lost it a decade ago, trying to soften my cycle. I'll blame that."

"And us?"

"They won't want to acknowledge such a thing. And they'll never know of it."

"Fine. If you say so. I trust you... I love you... You know that, Ash, don't you?"

I nodded. "I love you too...like an instinct."

She smiled and fell back atop me, wreathing my neck in her long limbs.

Patrick sneered when I told him of my vow, his charm broken for the briefest of moments. "Very well then." His sneer disappeared as he cloaked himself anew. I mistook it for a man's irritation. The conquest and invasion were rebuffed, and I'd thought I'd won.

I was wrong as a person can be. Thinking one's self the smartest in a room is how one misses the knife flitting out in the darkness.

Amber and I kept going to our hidden, private glen, but one rainy night in the middle of October, I grew needy and impatient. I begged off from the bonfire, lying about my cycle to compel sympathy, Amber made an excuse of her own, which bought us our privacy. "Amber," I hissed, letting my desire form into sound, pulling her against me, pushing her onto my bed. She humored me, and the rush was sublime—we gave and gave to each other, our shifts still on, rifled up to give us access, but we never left each other's eyes. No, we laid side by side, our hands at play, our connection deepening. We'd made love before. We'd confessed our love so many times. This, however, struck a different chord as if we'd found someplace beyond love, a heat, and calm, a glowing splendor invented, discovered, just her and me. This sensation lingered, clinging to our bodies as we lay in each other's arms, kissing lightly, murmuring wordless devotions.

In the span between one calm breath and the next, the door crashed open, bulky figures filling the doorway, their eyes wide as the sin was confirmed, as my stomach lurched and my body went numb. The screaming was instant, the fighting and biting and clawing and kicking came next. Then a blow to my head, my world spinning out of control. The twins, our betrayers at last, watched as the men dragged us into the downpour outside. Despite this, bonfires were lit across the sanctuary. Their flames blazed across my delirium. Somewhere nearby, they were shouting at us, calling us sinners, the noise drawing an ever-growing crowd. Amber and I reached out desperately to each other, scraping and pulling at the arms that held us.

Once more I felt the time between ticks on the clock. An opportunity presented itself, the rain loosening grips so I got but a single hairsbreadth of freedom, time aplenty, to tackle one of the pair holding Amber. I hadn't thought how to contend with the second man, but I didn't have to. Nora was there socking him square in the jaw with a perfectly thrown punch.

"*Run!*" I shouted, and they didn't hesitate, disappearing into the night. To buy this tie, I had to pay the price. One might think a scrawny woman couldn't fend off five hardened laborers, yet I survived their beating for just as many seconds as it took to cover my fleeing loved ones.

As they at last presented me crouching in the mulch before their leader, I felt such pride flow through me. For I still thought I had everything figured out, that I could endure whatever pain they conjured up.

Patrick slapped me, which stung and seared. "You'll never see Amber again. You know that, don't you?" he murmured, so low only I could hear.

I struggled all the way across the yard and into the storehouse. They brought me to where it met the mountain, its thin wall peeling back like skin, revealing a system of warrens. Here along the wall were runes and symbols, and blood, so much blood, limbs cut to pieces, desiccated corpses, and murals and paintings, each to the last worshiping the inverse, the opposite, the image being womanly instead of that white-bearded patriarch.

Mounting horror stilled my vain attempts to escape. Noting this cessation, Patrick spoke to me as a doctor might, one poisoned by zealotry. "When we began, I thought it needed to be a man and that any old fool would do." He gestured to a few of the courses we passed. "The process brings madness—the mind cannot handle it and perishes. So I began to educate. That, as well, was enough to *ascend*. I realized if it is sin made manifest, one must find the origin of sin in order to purify it. A woman."

They'd taken me into a tiled chamber as resplendent as any cathedral might be. Really, it was a demented operating theater. Implements were laid out beside an obsidian table filled with glowering blades, powders, and things I didn't recognize.

"You are the answer. A woman, smart, and that final piece of the conundrum: a blasphemer. To become sin and be purged of it, you must already be a sinner. You are perfect."

"You're a monster," I shouted as they threw me inelegantly onto the stone, my back lighting up in pain. They tied me down quickly, my wounds bloodying the tethers.

"No, I'm an answer. One you will know…and it will probably be the only thing you know." He smiled, magnanimous and cruel, a hand swiping through his hair—that hand remaining raised, directed upward, pointing. "Rejoice, Ashley! You're being saved. Any final words or prayers before salvation arrives?"

"Fuck you," I snarled.

"A curse then. Just as well."

He knelt next to me and stroked my cheek as I grimaced. The women encircling us began cutting into me, peeling off my clothes. My handkerchief fell soaked through with red. The little piece of my life before, my last memory of my sister. I never should have left her. I never should have been so stupid as to risk Amber's safety. I should have been better…smarter; I was never clever at all.

"Shh," Patrick soothed. "Everyone, deep down, wants to be saved." He rose and recited orders, reading from his precious book as though it were a science.

My body became numbed to the pain as they sawed at my bones, then arrived from the deep a single sundering tremor. That's when everything started to *grow*. Blood coated my sight, and I screamed until the agony consumed me and I became something else. For the briefest of moments, I beheld the burning light of passion, rage, and fury incarnate. Everything collapsed; I was dying.

"It's happening again," a voice called out from a thousand miles away,

"Here I thought we might be close."

The darkness took me. A singing voice, a memory, was the last thing I heard.

*   *   *

I woke choking and spitting. The taste of dirt clogged my throat—it was all around me. I couldn't even scream, though my mind did, with terror and pain. This was a worse death, dying all over again in the darkness without anyone to hear, not even my own ears. Instinct is a miracle, a true one. With every ounce, every drop of willpower, I fought, clawed, and pulled, the weight like a mountain shifting around me, brutal, guttural euphoria filling me as I felt motion. The dirt fell away and I burst out of my forest grave. The moon was bright and high above. Water sat in trembling puddles, and I stretched toward one of them—my body in agony, every limb so heavy and strained. At last I reached a pool large enough to observe myself, what I'd become—a bony elongated muzzle, fur tattered and running in streams, *ash* colored by the moonlight, ash as dark as night and as shadow. My arms were huge, and my hands ended in talons deep below. The suffering was a kiln, a roaring flame stronger than a train engine, each heartbeat a mortar exploding, a great sundering inside my skull, my mind trying to understand what I'd become. The book, the speech, the knives, the alchemical fusion of blood, belief, and barbarity strung out along ligaments, sinew, and teeth. This is what they had made me. Their ritual had succeeded.

I ran. I was terrified, alighted, and alive.

When I came upon a group in my way, I ripped them apart. I felt the unbridled strength, and with each second I grew accustomed to my new form, I found delight. I couldn't smile, yet I felt such glee. There was no hunger, only their screams. The last skull burst beneath my heel. The forest was silent for only a moment; then it tore through it faster than before, the wind urging me on, the animals fleeing my path. I had but one thing to do: a final hope, a fear more fully fledged than any before.

I reached the glen and slowed, exhaling a burning plume in the cold night. My taloned hands dug into the soil as I crossed the small clearing, waiting, whimpering until she came forward. She was shuddering and scared, her movements stilted. As she stepped closer, her hand flew to her chest, something catching in the glowing amber of her eyes. She peered directly into mine, and then she knew. With a slender movement in the moonlight, she touched my wet cheek, stained by blood and a single ruddy teardrop.

"*Ambbberrrr...*" I groaned, discovering my new voice, lower, a warped epithalamium. "*I will kill them all.*"

*   *   *

It was October again. A myriad of splendid colors coated the forest floor, more than I could ever perceive before. The smells were just as full, my hearing matching. I reveled in each and what was to come. Those leaves would soon be a uniform red beneath the wash of moonlight.

I left venison for Amber and Nora to sup upon. I took my meat raw these days, but never a human's, for I wanted them found in all their disparate pieces, a warning to the others, the sign of their end.

After letting out a sound to shatter the stillness, I drank in the calm before the fury.

Tonight was a night for the hunt...

My hunt.

Acknowledgements

Art is a labor of love and a journey of a thousand incremental steps. From nightmares to a Lera Lynn song ("Black River"), the inception of each of these stories was unique and cherishable, and the process of writing them, revising them, and putting them together in this collection has been one of the most rewarding experiences of my life. Truly a dream come true. Even though this book has one name front and center (mine), there are so many people who helped make it possible.

First and foremost, I want to thank my family, who have been my biggest pillars of support since day zero (Pazu and Sheeta, my cats, provided cuddle support, which is crucial). Special shoutout to my father, Jerry. He was the one who told me (after reading a very odd sort of treatment for a screenplay), "Hey, at some point (no pressure) you need to write a book." well look dad, I did it! He also was the first reader on many of these stories, and provided wonderful feedback, and a surprising lack of awkwardness, when it came to some of the content, ha! Thank you to my sister Noelle for all the tips and tricks on how to start as an indie author; you bring honor to eldest siblings everywhere. Thanks mom [Norkika], for always being there to listen to my info dumping, and always being willing to experiment with new dishes! (She's like Dr. Frankenstein in the kitchen, but like in a good, inventive way.)

To my editor Angela Brown, I owe a massive debt of gratitude; she whipped this thing into shape and made my prose truly *sing*. A similarly big thank you to my beta readers, Eli and Anna. Your feedback was incisive, and you both gave me the necessary confidence to keep going. Addtionally I want to thank Kai Charles for doing a sensitivity read on *The Crossing*.

A cover is not the book, they say, and that you shouldn't judge a book by it but I truly hope that you did with this one! Onita did an absolutely phenomenal job bringing my pitch to life. Please check out some more of her work
(@Onita.K_ on socials). Her works are one-of-a-kind and brilliant!

To all the employees of *The Open Book*, thank you for your support of this project (and suffering through my endless yapping about it). Don't worry, I highly you'll be getting a unique "spiceless" copy of this book!

recommend *Lesbian Nuns Breaking Silence,* edited by Nancy Manahan & Rosemary Keefe, which was a major primary source for *Harrowing Habits,* along with *Immodest Acts: The Life of a Lesbian Nun in Renaissance Italy* by Judith C. Brown. I also want to give special thanks to the essayist and YouTuber Mars Nova. Her video essay "Rape Revenge and Recovery" was the spark that caught the kindling of my mind.

And last but certainly not least, I have to thank you. My work has been a rather solitary endeavour up until now, full of passion and joy and accomplishment, but it was missing that last *pixie dust,* and that is you. I have dreamed of the day my work would start getting into people's hands. The mere thought of sharing my stories with you makes me giddy. At a time when "A.I." is putting the publishing industry in a precarious position, and the current state of the world is making queer stories more and more difficult to get out there, it is more vital than ever to support indie authors and emerging talent (hey, that's me, I'm those things!). By reading this collection, you are contributing to the mesmerizing and eternal act of storytelling that is so innate in hummanity. From campfire stories to Sappho to this modern era, where queer writers like me can be out and proud. Being a part of this continuity is my life's work. I am grateful to each and every one of you who chose to spend some time with these characters and their stories. *Thank you.*

Full Warning Index:

The Dead Breathe Of Night: Strong sexual content/nudity/"open door" sex scene | age gap | blood kink | graphic imagery | implied homophobia | Non-accepting parents/family | references to implied mental illness | sexism | there is a moment where a character erronously thinks that someone might have taken their own life

Twilight In Tinsel Town: Disturbing images | strong sexual content | body horror | sexual acts involving using an egg-shaped object like a sex toy | cosmic horror | body horror | reference to cheating | vomiting | use of a since reclaimed derogatory term toward effeminate men | possession/manipulation by a supernatural entity | sexism

The Crossing: Racism | Separation from family | violence | reference to witch trials and executions | body horror (painful physical transformation) [consenting]

Repossed: Clausterphobia | suffocation | natural diasters | toxic relationship | gory violence | sexual content | toxic relationship

Dusk, Day, and Dawn: Violence/death

My Eyes, Those Eyes: Graphic, gory violence | ritualistic torture | occult experimentation | reference to parental abuse | body horror (non-consenting torturous body transformation) | homophobia | sexism | transphobia | being forcibly outed | separation from sibling | attempted sexual coercion (using a position of power)

Harrowing Habits: Discussion of rape | references to real-life sex crimes | reference to indigenous genocide and the residential school system in Canada | brief gory violence | reference to physical abuse | discussion of homophobic religious doctrine | homophobia | sexism

About The Author

C.C. Cope resides in sunny Los Angeles with her two cats, Pazu and Sheeta. Her background is in cinematography and photography. When not writing, she's a bookseller, urging people to read *Carmilla* and more Edith Wharton. *Harrowing Habits* is her debut collection.

You can find her @the_real_c.c.cope on social media